TWO

AA Milne

AA Milne is best known as the creator of Winnie-the-Pooh and that bear's escapades with his friends in the Hundred Acre Wood. He was also a successful playwright (*Toad of Toad Hall*) and admired novelist. Milne died in Sussex in 1956, aged 76.

Ann Thwaite has published five biographies among her many other books. Her *A.A. Milne: His Life* was the Whitbread Biography of the Year in 1990. She lives in Norfolk with her husband, the poet Anthony Thwaite.

Two People

Two People

———————————

AA Milne

FOREWORD BY ANN THWAITE

CAPUCHIN CLASSICS

CAPUCHIN CLASSICS
LONDON

Two People
First published in 1931

This edition published by Capuchin Classics 2009

© A A Milne 1931
2 4 6 8 0 9 7 5 3 1

Capuchin Classics
128 Kensington Church Street, London W8 4BH
Telephone: +44 (0)20 7221 7166
Fax: +44 (0)20 7792 9288
E-mail: info@capuchin-classics.co.uk
www.capuchin-classics.co.uk

Châtelaine of Capuchin Classics: Emma Howard

ISBN: 978-0-9559156-9-7

Foreword

The jacket of AA Milne's autobiography solemnly describes him as 'a writer of unusual diversity of achievement.' The children's books, which made him a celebrity and Winnie-the-Pooh the most famous bear in the world, occupy fewer than ten pages of his own three hundred pages about his life.

Some people remember – perhaps from reading my biography – that Milne started life as a humourist as a contributor to *Punch* and, later, an extremely successful playwright – the Alan Ayckbourn of his day. There was a point when five of his plays were running, 'three in America, one in London, one in Liverpool.' The names of some may linger in people's memories: *The Dover Road*, *Mr Pim Passes By* and, above all, *Toad of Toad Hall*, his adaptation of Kenneth Grahame's *The Wind in the Willows*. They were for many years staples of amateur dramatic societies across England.

Other people will perhaps recall that Milne was a pacifist and that after serving in the First World War and being invalided home from the Somme, he wrote a pacifist bestseller, *Peace with Honour* and then, years later, when he realised fascism must be fought, *War with Honour*.

What hardly anyone realises is that AA Milne was also a novelist. His first novel for adults was an adaptation in 1921 of one of his plays. He called it simply *Mr Pim* and insisted it was a 'real book' and 'not just the dialogue with "he said" and "she said" tacked on.' At that point he had already written what was to be his most lucrative novel, a detective story called *The Red House Mystery*, not published until 1922. This book was such a success that his publishers, on both sides of the Atlantic, wanted another in the same genre. But he refused to be typecast. It was always more interesting to write something new and different. *When We Were Very Young* followed the detective story.

If a writer, why not write
On whatever comes in sight?
So – children's books: a short
Intermezzo of a sort;
When I wrote them, little thinking
All my years of pen-and-inking
Would be almost lost among
Those four trifles for the young.

It gives me great pleasure, as the biographer of this complex, attractive, difficult man, that his novel *Two People* should not be lost, but reissued, three-quarters of a century after its first appearance, by an enterprising publisher.

Two People was dedicated to Milne's wife Daphne, and it is tempting to identify her closely with Sylvia, the wife in the novel. Christopher Milne, their son, certainly did. Sylvia has neither imagination nor intelligence but is altogether desirable and has entwined herself in her husband's heart. Daphne's own taste in books, Milne said, was for the 'delightfully twaddly'. His own taste was very different, but there are times when *Two People* appears to qualify for that description, or at least as an easy, light read. But the book has a serious undercurrent. As the *Boston Transcript* put it in October 1931: 'While his style is as mercurial as ever, and his touch as delicate as the down on the butterfly's wing, Mr Milne here achieves something no less impressive than a symposium on married life.'

The novel considers how two people can make a relationship work when the people concerned have little in common but that shared past when they fell in love with each other. Biographically it is of tremendous interest, written, as it was, at a time when Milne's own marriage was under strain, when Milne was recognising, as his character, the novelist Reginald Wellard does, that he wanted to be free, but 'I want her not to be.' 'I am less free than she is,' Wellard thinks, 'for I have this uneasy feeling of disloyalty to her when I am with another woman. Does she have that feeling? Of course not.' There is an extremely good scene when Reginald, having braced himself to tell Sylvia something he should have told her ages before (that he has had tea with an actress), finds she not only knows already, but doesn't attach any importance to it whatsoever.

Christopher Milne once wrote 'My father's heart remained buttoned up throughout his life.' But in *Two People* AA Milne reveals a great deal about himself. The reader should not be put off by the beginning. Read on, even if you have an aversion to novels about writers. If you have already bought the book, you will be able to feel smug, whether you live in the country or not, at the fun Milne has with the non-book-buying neighbours, including the one who once knew a fellow in India who wrote a book.

Two People is perhaps best characterised as a funny, cautionary tale for writers, with much period detail. (Have nothing to do with the theatre. Stay out of London. Live in the country and write what you want to write.) If it was easier for Milne, with the income from his children's books, then it is for most to follow this advice. It still makes a good story.

Ann Thwaite
Norfolk, August 2008

Chapter One

R eginald Wellard made a pretence of filling his pipe while he waited for his wife's comment. It came.

'Fancy!' she said.

Reginald, for some reason which he couldn't explain, felt suddenly on the defensive.

'After all,' he said, 'a man must do something.'

'Darling,' smiled Sylvia lovingly, 'I'm not *blaming* you.'

Reginald thought this over for a moment. It seemed to him that he now definitely had his back to the wall. Absurd!

'When a man tells his wife that he has written a novel,' he began, 'the entire absence of blame is in itself, no doubt, a sort of encouragement. At the same time, if anything more enthusiastic should be offered him——'

'But, darling,' said Sylvia, 'all I said was "Fancy!" '

'I know. That was all.'

'I was just taken by surprise. Because I think it's so wonderful of you. I'm sure *I* couldn't write a novel to save my life.'

Reginald Wellard opened his mouth to answer this, and then closed it again. What *was* the answer? There was none. The conversation had to die there. A pity. When Shakespeare told Ann Hathaway that he had written *Othello*, did she say 'Fancy! I'm sure *I* couldn't'? Probably not. Well, as it happened, he had left her before he wrote it, so—— But when Milton told his wife that he had written *Paradise Lost*, do you suppose she—no, that wouldn't do either. Milton dictated *Paradise Lost* to his wife, didn't he, so naturally she told him *she'd* written it. Well, when Keats—no, he wasn't married. Dash these fellows. Well, anyhow, Sylvia had said the wrong thing again. A pity to be as sweet and pretty and lovable as she, and yet to say the wrong thing almost instinctively. A pity also that he had registered this wrongness instinctively of late. He loved her just as much. In its way a tribute to their love for each other.

He began the conversation again.

'Well, would you like to read it now, or wait until it's really in print?' He laughed at his own hopefulness. 'I mean, if it ever is.'

'But of *course* it will be, darling.'

That should have encouraged him, but somehow it didn't.

'I mean,' she went on, 'if you've written a book, of course any publisher would be only too *glad* to publish it.'

Reginald now had no hope at all of his book being published.

'Well?' he said. 'Which?'

'I think when it's a real book, don't you? Think how exciting to find it on my plate one morning, and curl up on the sofa with it.'

Wellard told himself that this was the answer he had hoped she would give . . . and wondered why it wasn't.

'Besides,' she went on, 'ordinary writing is always so difficult to read.'

'This is typed,' he explained.

'You *have* been secret about it all, haven't you?' she laughed. And he laughed too. And she caught at his hand as he went past her, and kissed it lightly and suddenly, and looked suddenly more sweet and pretty and lovable than ever, and he had to stop and tell her so. To which she said 'Am I?' and waited for him to tell her so again. But she said no more of the book. Nor did he.

Certainly he had been secret about it. He was forty. He had been married six years. Even now she was only twenty-five. They lived in the country, with occasional visits to Town, and he weeded the garden and took an interest in twelve bee-hives. They don't pay you as much for this as they should; but as he had what is called 'money of his own', by which is meant money which is left to you when the owner has no further use for it, not money which you have earned your own self, he did not bother about the economics either of hives or weeds. In fact, he spent his time very happily, proving to the drones in their twelve establishments that they had chosen the better part of it, after all.

However, when you have made quite sure that your wife is happy too, and have weeded the garden, and have walked past twelve bee-hives, you are, on this or that day, left with a certain amount of time in which to wonder whether it is time to weed the garden again. Now it has been said that every one of us has within him the material for at least one book—this in addition to the knowledge necessary for taking an interest in twelve bee-hives, or whatever it may be; and on a day when Reginald was contemplating a ceanothus (*Gloire de Versailles*) which was climbing up a convolvulus, or being climbed up by it, it was difficult to say which, he suddenly began to laugh. . . . And five minutes later, the convolvulus still being there, he said to himself, 'You know, that would make rather a good story.'

At first it seemed to him the sort of joke which you tell to Baxter (of Seven Streams), whose nephew writes for *Punch* (or, anyhow, to it); and then it seemed rather better than that. Good enough, next week, to tell Hildersham (of Mallows) who had once met W. W. Jacobs. Jacobs might like to work it up into a short story. Then, a week later, it seemed good enough to tell Coleby (of Redding Farm) who knew a man who had played golf with P. G. Wodehouse. Wodehouse could almost make a novel of it. . . . But as the days went on, and he watched a sow-thistle which had got into his sidalceas change into a sidalcea which had got into his sow-thistles, he began to see the story grow without this precarious aid; grow under his own sudden leadership, grow to his own eager following, into a story, a novel, which he (why not?) would write himself.

He began. He had a room, known to Sylvia as his office, in which, from time to time, he multiplied the number of hives by something small, subtracted something rather more, and wrote a cheque for the remainder. Sylvia liked him to be busy in here. She was not actually absorbed in bees; but her manner of looking into the office, saying, 'Busy, darling? I won't disturb you,' and, with an exaggerated noiselessness, closing the door again, seemed to put her on full partnership terms in this exhausting business of bee-farming. In his office he could write in secret. After all, there is nothing to prevent a man tearing up anything which he has written. He would just write (for the fun of it) and see what happened. He could always tear it up.

He did not tear it up. The weeks went on. The novel went on. Summer changed to autumn, autumn to winter. Nor were the changes in Reginald Wellard's novel less complete. The story still showed what the *New Statesman* subsequently called, without over-stating the case, 'this vein of humour'; there were passages in it which *The Times* itself could describe as 'not unamusing'; but Reginald had fallen too much in love with his characters, even before the frost had killed his dahlias, to leave them with no deeper roots than this. They had become living, emotional people to him; so much so, indeed, that at times the inter-play of emotion between them would land him into scenes rightly adjudged by the *Saturday Review* as 'not without pathos', and by the *Morning Post* as 'not lacking in a certain pleasing sentiment'. But, of course, Reginald did not know about this until later. Through the autumn and winter he was merely telling himself that it was 'not bad'. It is curious how easily a book comes to be described in terms of the things which it isn't.

II

'*Dear Sir,*' wrote Mr Albert Pump, '*I am very interested in your story "Bindweed", and if you can make it convenient to call upon me at 3 o'clock any afternoon I shall be glad to discuss it with you.'*

So Reginald Wellard made it convenient on Thursday. He put his tall, lean figure, with the permanent wave in it, into his other pair of trousers, he brushed, more carefully than usual, his unruly hair, he kissed Sylvia goodbye and then came back to kiss her again, he climbed into a car two sizes too small for him, tried to start it without turning on the petrol, and (subsequently) without switching on the engine, and (subsequently again) without taking off the brake, and then, having caught the 11.30 (which runs on Sundays only) by a triumphant thirty seconds, sat down in Little Malling station to wait, with an automatic machine to keep him company, until the 12.50 should be ready for him. Was this the man to do business on equal terms with a publisher like Mr Pump? No.

Mr Pump received him graciously. Mr Pump talked to him on general topics for five minutes. At the end of that time Mr Pump had summed him up as the sort of man who might know every weed, and even every bee, in his garden by name, but who would certainly catch a Sundays-only train on a Thursday morning. Whereupon Mr Pump produced what he called 'the usual agreement between author and publisher'. By this he meant that he usually tried it on an inexperienced author and generally got away with it.

'Ah!' said Reginald, frowning at it. The agreement gave a 10 per cent. royalty to Reginald, and, among other things, a half-share in translation rights, play-rights, film-rights, broadcasting-rights, gramophone-rights and all other possible rights to Mr Pump. If you ask why these things should be given to Mr Pump, the only answer is that he wanted the money.

Reginald Wellard did not ask why. He was trying to work out a 10 per cent. royalty on 150,000 copies at 7s. 6d. each. It was an impossible sum to do in the head; in fact, really a case for the office. Perhaps tomorrow morning—— Meanwhile, all that the words in front of him were saying, nay, shouting aloud, was that *the* book, *his* book, was going to be published! He signed the agreement eagerly. Mr Pump watched him with a sort of wistful remorse, thinking that he might have got off his other agreement after all: 'the customary agreement between author and publisher', by which Mr Wellard gives Mr Pump the copyright of the book and £150, and Mr Pump gives Mr Wellard six free copies. Even now it might not be too late. But something made him hesitate; not so much conscience as the set of Reginald's jaw as he wrote, and the length of him. A fool for the plucking, but even fools get angry after they are plucked.

And now Reginald is coming home again. He is coming by the 4.20 from Victoria, which doesn't stop at Little Malling on Thursdays. His car, however, does not know about this, and is still waiting for him at Little Malling under the friendly eye of the station-master. Does it matter whether he walks from Burdon (six miles) or waits two hours for a train back? It does not matter. He gets home again.

He sees Sylvia again.

When they have kissed, Sylvia says:

'But you haven't, darling!'

'Haven't what?'

'Got it cut.'

Reginald remembers that he was going to London to get his hair cut.

'Oh? Oh, that. Sorry, Sylvia, but the fact is I had some business in London.'

Sylvia purses up her lips and nods with complete understanding. The farm, prices, outgoings, exports, imports— big business. She understands exactly how it is. A woman less used to bee-farming would have said 'What?' stupidly.

The 'What?' not coming, Reginald has to explain. Nonchalantly.

'I've been arranging with a publisher about my book.'

'Oh,' says Sylvia, really quite interested, 'when's it coming out?'

Reginald sighs to himself. All his cleverness in finding Mr Pump, all his firmness in doing business with Mr Pump, gone for nothing. Sylvia has skipped that part of the conversation. Oh, well.

'In the spring. About April.'

'Darling! You *are* clever!'

Sylvia is really looking ridiculously beautiful this evening, but she *will* be so general in her praise. 'Clever' means nothing, said like that.

And then suddenly Reginald felt ashamed of himself.

'Sweetheart,' he says, 'now that I've got this book off my mind, is there anywhere you'd like to go to specially?'

'How do you mean, darling?'

'Holiday — Jaunt — Expedition. Riviera — Switzerland — South Sea Islands. London. Anything.'

With a wrinkle in her pretty forehead Sylvia pays all these places the briefest possible visit.

'I'm perfectly happy here, darling,' she announces, 'if you are.'

'I shouldn't mind a change.'

'Sure you wouldn't rather go away by yourself? Or play golf?'

'Quite.'

She gives a little sigh of happiness.

'I should simply love it,' she says like an eager child. 'Let's go to Switzerland.'

Well, dash it, what can you do with a wife like that but kiss her?

III

Reginald was talking to Edwards about half-hardy annuals when the first batch of proofs came down the steps of the kitchen garden and, seeing Mr Wellard, saved themselves a journey to the back door. He put them in his pocket.

There were two gardeners at Westaways: Challinor who attended to the bees and looked after the garden in his spare time, and Edwards who attended to the garden and looked after the bees in his spare time. Each grudgingly took orders from the other when off his own ground, and it was difficult to say which was head-man of the estate. Edwards had the higher wage. Challinor had the cottage. Reginald had had Challinor longer, but was more afraid of Edwards.

Challinor was a quick, black little man with quick, black eyes and a black waterfall moustache. He was really neither a bee-man nor a gardener by trade, he was just the handiest man of the neighbourhood, and he had become, anyhow to Reginald, a specialist in bees, not because he knew more about them than about flowers, tools or cows, but because other people, Reginald anyhow, knew less. Challinor wore black trousers, a black waistcoat with a brass watch-chain from which depended the badge of some secret society, and a grey shirt, rolled up to the elbows so that the bees could sting him better.

'But of course,' said Reginald to Sylvia, 'the idea really is to establish a mutual confidence with the bees. They go about saying to each other, "We can't sting a man like this, it wouldn't be fair. He trusts us. Let's sting the man Wellard instead." '

'I suppose so, darling,' said Sylvia, and then, as Reginald still seemed to be waiting for something, gave her charming little laugh. 'Darling, you are absurd. They haven't really stung you again, have they?'

'No, Sylvia, no.' He looked at her almost unbelievable white arms, and added, 'If a single bee ever dares to sting *you* , I'll brain him.'

Edwards was a slow, heavy-footed, thick-fingered man. He would take a dozen young birches, which had been lying out for a week as they had come from the nurseryman's, with their roots exposed, dig a dozen holes in the places which Mr Wellard had carefully rejected for them, stamp them in with his heavy boots, and go back to the work which Mr Wellard had thus interrupted . . . and the young birches would love it, and grow as birches never grew before.

'And look at me,' said Reginald to Sylvia, who was looking at the goldfish. 'Endowed by Nature with delicate hands'—he held one up and admired it—'and delightful feet, can I prick out or plant a single blessed thing as Edwards can? How he ever separates one snap-dragon from another, working entirely with two bunches of sausages, is a mystery to me. Yet nothing ever dies on Edwards. Remarkable.'

'I'm sure you could do it as well if you tried, darling,' said Sylvia. 'Besides, he's used to it.'

Reginald watched her silently, as silently she watched the goldfish in their pool. 'Isn't that a pretty one?' she said suddenly, pointing a foot at it.

'Yes,' said Reginald, 'yes. And why I talk about my own delightful feet, I don't know. Yours are a song.'

Sylvia's cheeks went a little pinker.

'Well,' said Reginald, 'I suppose I must get busy.'

'Of course, darling. I won't disturb you.'

'I meant these.' He took them from his pocket. 'Proofs.'

Surely Sylvia will want to know what proofs are.

She doesn't.

Or she knows, and is thinking of something else.

'I won't disturb you, darling,' she says again.

So Reginald goes in with his proofs. There are two sets, each going up to page 64. Why two sets? Has he got to correct both? There is a note begging him not to make more corrections than are absolutely necessary. He promises not to.

He begins to read. As he reads, he notices one or two little mistakes; not many, for Mr Pump, or whoever does the actual printing, however one actually does the printing, has done his work well. Just one or two. He will go through it again afterwards and correct them. For the moment it is interesting to read the story straight off—well, up to page 64—and see how it strikes him. Funny how much better it seems in print. Sylvia was right to wait . . .

'*It was not too much to say that if . . .* ' Bother! Now we shall have to wait for page 65.

He turned to page 1 again. He read the sixty-four pages again. He is imagining himself Sylvia, curled up on the sofa. Does she smile here? Does a tear come for a moment there to her throat? How strange is it to her that he, her husband, should have written this? He reads, wondering.

'*It was not too much to say that if . . .* ' Bother! Now Sylvia will have to wait for page 65.

He is reading it a third time. Now he, imagining himself a reviewer. On *The Times* or somewhere. *Bindweed,* by Reginald Wellard. Never heard of him. Well, let's see what it's like . . . H'm . . . Ha . . .

'*It was not too much to say . . .* ' Oh, well, let's get it corrected. There were one or two little mistakes. One right at the beginning, wasn't it, and one about page 30, and one ———

He looks. He reads it again . . . and again. The mistakes have vanished. Yet it is certain that they were there.

Now, once more, very carefully.

IV

The success of *Bindweed* is now a matter of history in every publishing office. Two years ago no publisher had supposed that 100,000 words arranged in the order in which Reginald Wellard had arranged them could sell nearly a quarter of a million copies. Today every publisher, and every young author, is convinced that any similar arrangement of 100,000 words can sell nearly a quarter of a million copies. Hopefully they seek such an arrangement. You never know. It may be 'another *Bindweed*' on their tables.

Theatrical managers also (for the play was equally successful) tell each other over their cigars. 'My boy, I've got another *Bindweed*,' or encourage young dramatists by saying that this is the sort of play for which they are looking. Men who have made money in pork, cotton, ships, wool and hardware regret daily that they do not see their way clear to financing Shakespeare, Strindberg, opera, expressionism and the Russians, but add kindly that if you came to them with another *Bindweed* they might risk a small gamble. Fortunes were made over *Bindweed,* but fortunes also were lost—if money is ever lost in the theatrical world which is merely transferred from one theatrical pocket to another.

But all this did not happen at once. Reginald Wellard did not wake to find himself famous. He woke to find himself the owner of six copies of *Bindweed* and one review of it. This was in *The Times Literary Supplement,* and drew attention in a kindly way to the superficial area of the book. 7½ by 5½. This was news to Reginald, who had never measured it. He measured it now, and found that *The Times,* as usual, was right. He wondered idly if there was a man in the office who did this, and nothing but this. An interesting job which brought one into contact with good literature, yet made no unfair demand on the intellect. Vaguely he sketched out in his mind an application for the post.

As the weeks went by, longer reviews came in. Favourable, encouraging. The writers did not, as they put it, seem to have heard of Mr Reginald Wellard before. As it happened, Mr Reginald Wellard had never heard of *them* before, so there was nothing in that. They opined that he wrote intelligently and not without understanding. Mr Wellard, reading this, opined that they also wrote intelligently and not without understanding, so there was still nothing between them. They cordially hoped that Mr Wellard would go on writing novels . . . and Mr Wellard cordially hoped that they would go on writing reviews. Things couldn't have been more friendly. But it is probable that, if they had known that *Bindweed* was going to sell a quarter of a million copies, they would not have had such a high opinion of Mr Wellard's work. Nor he, in that case, of theirs.

Mr Pump quoted the best parts of these reviews, indicating by dots that much other equally favourable matter was being left out, owing to the exigencies of space.

Now although the great *Bindweed* boom had not yet begun, there was enough movement underground to convince Sylvia that she was already a famous author's wife. She had read the book, curled up on the sofa as she had promised, and she had loved it. What she had loved best was the Dedication. 'To Sylvia, who has entwined herself in my heart.' Pretty, of course, with its slight play on the convolvulus idea, but not really difficult to write. Not to be compared with Chapter V. Wellard had hoped for some special comment on Chapter V, not only from the reviewers, most of whom had been unable, owing to the exigencies of time, to get as far, but more particularly from Sylvia, who had once had, though she might have lost it, the key to that chapter. At Ventimiglia . . . on their honeymoon . . . that day, that sun-kist day . . . However she loved the Dedication best; and since she loved it all, presumably she loved also Chapter V. One mustn't become exacting, just because one has written a book.

Sylvia, then, loved the book, and she was the wife (think of it!) of the author Reginald Wellard. As Mrs Wellard, if she happened to meet a maid-servant on the way, she was conducted into, or through, the houses of Seven Streams, Mallows and Redding Farm in search of their owners. Possibly she did not establish contact with a maid-servant, and then was hailed from the herbaceous border or the raspberry canes or the stables as, 'Hallo, Sylvia,' and made no further pretence of formality. Yet she was soon Mrs Wellard again. Wife of Reginald Wellard—the author, not the bee-farmer. Round mouth, pursed mouth, large eyes, closed eyes, little shrugs, little faces, airs of adorable mystery, all her enchanting repertoire of expression, expressing no more than that her husband had written a book, and—well, dear, you know how it is. But, of course, they didn't. And Sylvia, for all her pretty airs, could not tell them.

'I saw Betty Baxter,' she says, on returning to Westaways.

'Oh?' says Reginald.

He doesn't like the Baxter woman. Besides annoying him in almost every other way, she talks to flowers as most women talk to puppies and kittens. Conceivably a kitten may respond intelligibly to an inquiry phrased in the words 'Didums wantums 'ickle dinkums milkums then?'—not, it may be, recognizing the actual words, but convinced by the tone that food is near. It is inconceivable, at least by Reginald, that a bed of zinnias should make any coherent reply at all to the Baxter woman, when asked in the same sort of voice if it wishes to be watered. Most gardeners, again, will tell you that flowers respond to one hand rather than to another; Reginald did not, from his own experience, doubt it; but he refused to believe that the Shirley poppies raised their heads and went quite pink when Mrs Baxter came into the garden. 'They know me, they do really, Mr Wellard.' The woman was a fool.

'I know you don't like her, darling, but she's ever so fond of *you*.'

How easily and recklessly Sylvia would say this of her friends!

'Well, I'm a very nice man, Sylvia.'

'You are, darling!' She throws him a kiss. 'And she's heard such a lot of your book, and is *so* interested.'

'Has she read it?' asks the author as carelessly as he can.

'No, darling, you see, they've given up their library subscription, it lapsed or something, she did explain to me, and so—— But she's going to, as soon as ever she can get hold of a copy.'

'She can buy it,' said Reginald, annoyed with the woman.

'I must tell her. I don't think she thought of that. She wants us to play tennis on Saturday. Of course I told her that you were very busy and I couldn't say.'

'I *shall* be rather busy on Saturday,' says Reginald Wellard.

Grace Hildersham is also going to read it, as soon as she can get hold of a copy. Grace is a large fair woman, with a perpetually pink face over which the fair hair perpetually strays. She isn't always under the raspberry net, picking raspberries for her famous jams, but if it happens to be there that you first meet her, you always expect to meet her there afterwards, or, meeting her elsewhere, conclude that she has just come from there. Only so could she be so flushed and untidy. A dear, obviously. She must always have had a lot of children, or a lot of raspberries, or a lot of something, to keep her busy. Reginald feels that the chances of Grace Hildersham's reading *Bindweed* are not so good. Not only has she to get hold of the book (always a difficult matter for the inexperienced) but she has also to get hold of the time.

'You do like her, don't you?' says Sylvia, on her return from her visit.

'Tremendously,' says Reginald.

'I'm so glad. She likes you tremendously too.'

The adverb seems to have been chosen by Reginald rather than by Grace Hildersham. However, no doubt she likes him.

'She's *longing* to read it.'

'Good.'

'She wants us to go over to tea one day this week. What day would suit you, darling? I know how it is, of course.'

'Saturday,' says Reginald.

Lena Coleby is also longing to read it. When you meet her she pulls off a big pair of brown gauntlets, and, to your surprise, is still gloved when she shakes hands with you. Don't talk to her about food. She feeds a husband, three children, a horse, a pony, four cows, two pigs, a goat, half a dozen pigeons, and ducks and chickens numerable, but, by Reginald, uncounted. She is always considering food, mixing food, carrying food, adding up accounts about food, ordering food and making food. This is wearing work, but she has kept her hands. No other woman could have done it. Big, slow, romantic Coleby loved her hands when he wooed her, and almost articulated some pretty thought about them; she knew what she was in for when she married a farmer, but she swore to herself that she would keep her hands. She has. And save for the half-lemon in the bathroom, if you should be invited to wash there, and the two pairs of gloves, you will never guess how much time and thought and pride those hands have commanded.

'You do like her, don't you?' says Sylvia, on her return from her visit.

'I admire her terrifically,' says Reginald.

'I'm so glad. She admires you terrifically too.'

Reginald knew she was going to.

'She wants to order it from the library at Burdon when they go in next week for the market. I don't think they belong, but you pay half a crown deposit, and then tuppence a time. It's quite easy.'

Reginald knew the circulating library at Burdon. It moved with the times, but had started thirty years behind them and had never got any nearer. Unless one of the Kingsleys had written a book called *Bindweed*, Lena Coleby would have to ask for something else.

'Oh, and can we come over to supper one evening?'

'If you like, sweetheart, of course.'

Whatever future was awaiting *Bindweed* in London, the country for the moment gave no signs of it.

Chapter Two

Reginald was going to London again to get his hair cut. This hair business was a nuisance. As if shave, shave, shave every morning wasn't enough. Apart from the wasted day, consider the expense. *Five miles to the station:* say sixpence for petrol and tyres. *Turning round and backing at the station:* say half a crown for the fence, unless one hit the same place as last time. *Return ticket* (and, coming back with your hair newly cut, you must go first-class) 13s. 8d. *Lunch at the club:* say 6s. 6d. *Hair cut and tip:* 1s. 6d. *Station-master at Little Malling for not stealing the car:* 1s. Total, £1 5s. 8d. You could get a permanent wave for that.

However, Sylvia liked him with his hair cut. If she were reading, or needling, or arranging flowers, or looking at the goldfish, whatever she were doing, if he came up behind her, she would know without looking whether he had had his hair cut, or were wearing the blue tie, which she liked, or the open flannel shirt, which she liked better; whether he had used the new shaving-soap yet, or smoked a cigarette that morning. She had a sixth sense for all of her husband that was apprehensible by the senses. Nothing of the physical Reginald Wellard escaped her.

Reginald backed the Morris slowly out of the barn. From time to time (each time beginning about six weeks after he had last tried) he thought that it would be more workmanlike to back the car into the barn when he put her away, and then drive her straight out in the morning . . . and then, from time to time he changed his mind about this. It was more workmanlike to drive in forwards, and leave the backwards for the coming out. . . .

Not so good this morning. That was because Sylvia was watching him. He felt her there suddenly. It was his custom to get the car well out of the barn first, and headed for the open road, before he went back to kiss Sylvia goodbye. In this way, if she saw him, she saw him at his best. At least, she had more chance of doing so. He might absently turn off the petrol on dismounting, and forget to turn it on again; he might—oh, well, there were a lot of things one might do. But there would be none of this backing business.

He struggled out.

'Darling, I was coming down to say goodbye.'

'I'll drive you there if you like,' said Sylvia dreamily.

'I say, will you really? But look here, that means you'll have to meet me too, you know. Won't that be rather a bore for you?'

Sylvia was already at the wheel.

'It's such a lovely day,' she explained.

There was a mile of road, private but for a right of way, up to the main road, and Mrs Edwards (mother, not wife, of Edwards) lived at a cottage, two-thirds of a mile along, where you got into second. Mrs Edwards was bedridden, but she would say to Edwards when he came home that night, 'So *she* took the car out today.' It was curious, that. Reginald, whenever he went into second, made enormous preparations against waking the baby, with the result that he achieved grinding, tearing noises of such malignity that he almost went back into third as a protest. Sylvia dreamily stroked herself into this or that gear, her thoughts far away, her eyes on the road in front of her—no, not on the road in front, thought Reginald watching her; on the distant end of the road where it reached the stars, or some world of her own where none could follow her.

They caught a train (was it the 11.30) which would certainly have run on Sundays only if Reginald had been driving, but felt that it could not disappoint Sylvia who had come specially to see it. 'Here we are, Sylvia. We heard you five miles away not making the noise Reginald makes, and oiled ourselves and got steam up as quickly as we could.'

Rather a sell for the train, thinks Reginald. Sylvia isn't going.

'Goodbye, sweetheart. Thank you so much for driving me.'

'Goodbye, darling.'

'And it's the 3.10 back; 4.45 this end.'

It is pretty certain now that the 3.10 will stop at Little Malling. Otherwise, as likely as not, it would have run straight through to Burdon. Perhaps, thinks Reginald, it would be safer to mention casually, but loudly, at Victoria also, that Sylvia is meeting him. Then there can be no mistake.

He kisses her again. The train moves out of the station—disappointed, of course, at not having Sylvia on board, but resigned. Reginald waves, then goes across to the other window, from which you can see Sylvia crossing the line by the bridge . . . and sees Sylvia crossing the bridge; serene, remote, ridiculously lovely.

II

Reginald had a secret from his wife this morning. He often had secrets from her; almost it might be said that he always had secrets, for even if he told them, they remained secrets, since he could not share them with her. Some times he thought that she was just a child, intellectually not grown up, with whom he could never be in communion . . . and then sometimes he wondered if he were not really the child, and she the ineffably wise mother who could never be in communion with him.

His secret today was this. He was going to get his hair cut, he really *was* going to get his hair cut, but he was going gladly, even excitedly, because he wanted to see what London was doing about *Bindweed.* For Mr Pump had just announced that a Third Large Impression was printing. Now you can't, so it seemed to Reginald, announce to London that a Third Large Impression of Reginald Wellard's *Bindweed* is printing without there being left on London some faint awareness of the man Wellard's existence. He did not expect to be welcomed at Victoria, pointed to in Piccadilly, but he did have some small hope that in his club a man might be lunching who had heard of the book, even if he had not read it. 'Any relation of yours,' he might be asked, 'this man Wellard who has just written that book?' In London, exciting London, questions could take this form. In the country they merely said, 'Any relation to Milton of Hammerponds?' when you quoted *Lycidas*.

It was May 6th, a good day for walking; Reginald would walk across St James's Park to Pall Mall. He gave up his ticket, and started to walk by way of the bookstall, just in case; but of course it was absurd, because it was notorious that they only had Edgar Wallace. However . . . and suddenly embarrassment overwhelmed him, and his scalp pricked and tingled, as the whole station, passengers, porters, enginedrivers, bookstall-clerks, and policemen raised their voices in one loud cry of 'Wellard! It's Wellard!'

'Wellard, sir,' shouted the Chairman of the Company to the Prince of Wales as, hat in hand, he conducted his Royal Highness past the bookstall. 'There, sir; turning over the pages of his book *Bindweed*.'

'*Wellard!*' roared a porter to the deaf old lady whose parrot he was carrying. 'Author of *Bindweed!* That's 'im there. 'Aving a read of it.'

'So *that's* what he looks like!' shrieked one surprised schoolgirl to another. 'So *that's* Wellard!'

And, suddenly again, the whole station shouted 'Wellard!' together, and every finger pointed at him. . . .

Or didn't it?

Nervously, eyes on ground, Reginald switched round his head. Nervously he took his eyes up his neighbour from her feet to her knees (ugly knees), from her knees to her waist, from her waist to her neck, to her eyes . . . The eyes took no notice of him. They were reading a copy of the *Sketch,* suspended above him. Other eyes were equally indifferent. Nobody was looking at him. Nobody was talking about him. Nobody had heard of him. He was on a desert island, with his book *Bindweed* which nobody but himself had read, nor would read ever.

But that was equally absurd. Mr Pump had announced a Third Large Impression. Was Mr Pump a liar? Impossible.

The bookstall clerk spared him a moment.

'Reading very well, that book, sir,' he says, slapping down elevenpence at somebody on his right.

'Really?' says Reginald, trying to hide his excitement. 'Selling well, eh?'

'Quite a demand for it . . . And four's six,' he adds, slapping down fourpence on his left.

'Ah!' says Reginald.

Now then, he says to himself, if I turn it down after this, what will the clerk think? Hopeless to try and get a Wellard off. They take one look at him, and then buy an umbrella-ring. Much better stick to Wallace. But if I buy it . . . I *must* buy it. The whole future of *Bindweed* hangs on this moment.

'Ah, well, I must try it,' says Reginald, handing over three half-crowns. 'It looks pretty good.'

'Thank you, sir. Wrap it up for you?'

'No, thanks.'

Now he is in a hurry to be gone.

'And five's six, and six is a shilling,' says the clerk to a new acquaintance, and Reginald, realizing reluctantly that there is to be no more talk about *Bindweed,* goes.

But what on earth is he going to do with the dashed thing? Well, one thing is certain. He can't walk through St James's Park now. Authors don't promenade the parks of London with copies of their latest works held conspicuously in their hands. Or perhaps they do. If so, he wasn't an author. He was just up from the country for the day, and had written a book by accident, and had had a copy of the dashed thing forced on him, and objected strongly to carrying it about in London. He would have a taxi. He waved his stick, got into a taxi and gave the address of his club. At his club he would hide the dashed thing under his hat.

III

Reginald's club was political. In order to belong to it, you had first to belong to one of the great political parties. It didn't seem to matter which one. Perhaps, though, that is to do the club an injustice; it might be more true to say that it didn't matter what your political opinions were, so long as in your own mind you associated your opinions with the one particular party. It is obvious that, if you write to *The Times* (as most of the club did) and sign your letter DISGUSTED LIBERAL, you may find yourself saying the same sort of things about Mr Lloyd George or Free Trade or Land Policy, as is the man in the club over the way who is signing his letter TRUE CONSERVATIVE, but the fact remains that you are as widely removed from him in politics as is DISGUSTED CONSERVATIVE from TRUE LIBERAL. In other words, Liberals are Liberals and Conservatives are Conservatives, and to turn a man out of his club because he remains constant to the opinions which his Party has basely forsworn is no way to treat a fellow-voter, always supposing that he is still good for the twentyguinea subscription.

Reginald had no politics. There are at least a million voters who have no politics. This makes them entirely unprejudiced when they vote Conservative. They can quote themselves in an unprejudiced way as an example to waverers. Here am I. I don't belong to any party. Never have. But if you ask me how I'm going to vote, I tell you frankly . . . Very effective it sounds. Some overdo it and add that they are really Liberals, but that the time has come when all honest men . . .

Reginald, however, was not one of these. A belief in the comfort of the club was all the politics he had. He never voted. Hildersham, who did everything which a man should do, asked him once what he thought would happen if nobody voted.

'I don't know,' said Reginald frankly. 'What do *you* think?'

Hildersham, who had never thought, replied indignantly that civilization, as such, would come to an end.

'So it would', said Reginald, 'if nobody made roads. But I'm dashed', he added, 'if I'm going to be a road-mender.'

Hildersham wavered between saying that that was different and pointing out once more that Wellard really ought to do something about his own road, even if it didn't actually belong to him. The local problem seeming the more pressing, he settled down to it. A couple of cart-loads of rubble——

Sylvia was also going to be a voter, so it was said. She had asked Reginald what she ought to do with her vote when she had it. Reginald said, 'Pair with me,' and Sylvia, who had seen many pretty things pair in the spring-time, and thought that Reginald was just being loving, gave him her eyes for a moment and nodded. So the question of the vote stood over, or was settled, whichever you please.

Reginald went into his club, looking as much like a man who was not carrying a copy of *BindWeed* as was possible to a man who undoubtedly was. Once in the cloak-room, he balanced it on a peg and put his hat over it. Then he went in to lunch. He was doing tricks with spaghetti when his solitude was disturbed.

'Hallo, Wellard. Mind if we join you? Rather crowded today.'

Not very well put, thought Reginald. But with a neck that thick, what could you do? He nodded.

'D'you know Raglan?'

By name, of course ; who didn't? Not otherwise. Introductions were made. . . .

Any hope?

None. They began talking about Raglan.

'I'm a countryman', said Reginald, 'and know nothing of these things. What's the difference between an edition and an impression, and how many copies are there in each?'

Raglan explained that in the slovenly mind of the average publisher there was no difference, but that technically a new edition should contain new matter, or anyhow be a new setting-up of type, but that a new impression was just a re-printing of the old type.

'I see. Then if a book was, say, in its third impression, how many copies would have been sold? Roughly.'

Lord Ormsby laughed in his thick-necked way. Damn him. Raglan, who liked explaining things in his slow cultured voice, explained that it depended on the author, my dear fellow.

'I see,' said Reginald again, feeling that this was hardly worth coming to London for.

'What did they give Holland this time?' asked Ormsby, with an air of saying to Wellard, 'Now *you* listen to this.'

'Twenty thousand,' said Raglan, trying to say it modestly but knowing that it was hopeless, since it was he who had made Holland.

'First edition?' asked Reginald.

'Yes. But then, you see, he happens to be the fashion just for the moment. With an unknown writer it would only be a thousand, possibly five hundred. Clearly it's safer to keep well below what you think you're going to sell. You can always print more afterwards.'

'I see.'

'In itself it all means nothing. A swindler and a bloodsucker like Pump, for instance'—(Reginald bent down to his spaghetti again)— 'he advertises "Sixth Large Impression". Probably what's happened is that he started printing a thousand which he called First and Second Impression—five hundred each. He unloaded that on the booksellers, and has since had one or two inquiries from the trade. So he prints another thousand, two more impressions, and binds half of them. That takes him to the fourth impression. As for the other fifth and sixth he may have asked the printers to stand by in case he wanted another thousand or he may just be lying. And as for the "large", well, it's a matter of opinion, isn't it? In fact "Sixth Large Impression" may mean that he has sold just over a thousand to the booksellers— and perhaps that the booksellers have sold no more than a hundred to the public.'

'I see,' said Reginald. 'Well, I must be getting on.' He added a careless goodbye, and went to the desk to pay.

What a detestable man Raglan was! Was there ever a more loathsome fellow than Ormsby? Why had he ever come to London? Oh, of course, to get his hair cut. He'd a good mind now not to get it cut. Just to annoy Raglan. Only Raglan wouldn't know. Well, anyhow he wouldn't read Raglan's next book. He paid his bill, he clapped his hat on his head, *Bindweed* fell into the place reserved for umbrellas, and he left it there. Damn all books. Let's have our hair cut and get back to Sylvia.

It was very restful at Alderson's. Either this Alderson, or an earlier one, had cut either Dr.Johnson's hair or the Duke of Wellington's, as you guessed at once when you saw the bowfronted window. If anybody else—Kipling or Mr Baldwin— was having his hair cut when you arrived, you did not see him. You saw nobody but Mr Alderson, who seemed surprised that you wanted your hair cut, but thought he could manage it. He had a room somewhere upstairs if he could find it. Perhaps you wouldn't mind coming with him and helping him to look? Somewhere this way, he thought. Ah, here's a room, but there doesn't seem to be a chair. Wait a bit, we shall find another room directly *with* a chair. Here we are.

Reginald sat down, happily, sleepily. Damn all books. Let's have our hair cut.

Wait a moment, says Mr Alderson. Scissors. I knew there was something. Now where did I see a pair of scissors? Ah! Now then,

Mr Wellard, you like it short at the back, but not too short in front. Precisely.

He clips. Snip, snip, snip. Very peaceful. Reginald wonders what will happen when the first man says that he *does* want his hair too short in front. Snip, snip, snip. Very quiet and cool and peaceful. And Sylvia meeting the 3.10. Westaways and Sylvia. Between them what a ridiculous place they made London seem, what a ridiculous business writing. Sylvia, still and lovely, waiting for him on the platform.

IV

Reginald had ten minutes to himself at Victoria; time enough to buy all the women's papers for Sylvia. How to be Beautiful— How to look Beautiful—How to keep Beautiful. How to get thinner—How to get plumper. How to remove hair—How to make it grow. What nonsense was talked about woman's craving for beauty! What but the craving for beauty distinguished us from the animals? Why, if not to seek beauty, were we alive? Leonardo painted Mona Lisa, and the world bowed down to him in homage. Yet was not Sylvia's achievement greater? She was Beauty itself, not a copy of it. And if you said, as the clergyman on his right, who was trying to read a leading article in the *Spectator* without paying for it, would certainly say, 'God gave your wife her beauty, and it is no cause of pride to her, whereas da Vinci devoted years of labour——' why, damn it, sir, you aren't a clergyman at all if you deny that Leonardo's genius came also from God. And as for 'years of labour', isn't that just what I'm saying? Years of labour women spend on trying to be as beautiful as Sylvia, and who's to blame them? Not I, to whom Sylvia has given her beauty.

At this point in his reflections, the bookstall clerk slapped a book in front of him with the words, 'Seen that, sir? Reading very well just now,' and left Reginald face to face with a copy of *Bindweed*. Damn! He'd forgotten about the beastly thing.

'Going well, is it?' he asked automatically.

'Won't be the first copy I've sold today,' said the clerk truthfully, and feeling that a little romance was excusable on this delightful May day, added, 'Not by a long chalk.'

It looked like another seven-and-six. No, not seven-and-six, because ten per cent of it would come back to him. Ninepence. That settles it. You can't throw away ninepence like that.

'Well, I'll try it,' said Reginald, handing over a note. 'And these.'

'Thank you, sir, and six is thirteen, and seven's twenty.'

Surely, thought Reginald, as he started his search for the 3.10, that fellow's faith in Wellards is now a living thing, and it is I who have made it so.

The 3.10, knowing that Sylvia was to meet it, and feeling friendly to everybody in consequence, had arranged to start close to the bookstall, and to have an empty first-class smoker waiting for Reginald just where he wanted it. He stacked his *Perfect Ladies* and *Complete Gentlewomen* on the seat beside him, and opened *Bindweed*. He was a stockbroker going down to his beastly mansion in Surrey, all gables and white balconies and glass, and the bookstall clerk had pushed a copy of *Bindweed* into his hand, and he was taking it home to the missus. Might as well have a look at it on the way. . . .

Ha! Damn clever that. Who's the fellow? Reginald Wellard. Never heard of him. . . .

Reginald read on, forgetting that he was a stockbroker; absorbed in his own work. How on earth had he done it?

But at Chapter V he put the book down, and went back into his thoughts again. Can we separate the physical from the spiritual so completely? If Sylvia were less imperceptive, would she not be less beautiful? If he could share all his jokes with her, knowing that this May day would be lived twice, once as he had lived it in London, once again in the telling of it to her —no, doubly in the sharing of it with her—would she be Sylvia, the lovely, the unfathomable, the aloof? And who could say that there was nothing to fathom? Even if her mind was shallow, he had not fathomed the shallowness of it. Of one thing he was certain. In marriage, anyhow, you could not disentangle the physical from the spiritual. They were inextricably wound together. The loveliness of Sylvia was a perpetual comfort to him. They had different roots, but they had met and twined. He was the bindweed —well, call it convolvulus, it would sound better —and he lived on her beauty . . .

There seemed to be a lot of bindweed about. This fellow Pump, what did Raglan say about him? Bloodsucker! All right, let him try. Oh, but damn the book, he had decided not to think about that any more. Here, *you* have it!

He picked it up and tossed it on to the rack. Then he lit his pipe, let down the window and waited for Little Malling.

V

Sylvia was on the platform. He had watched her, his head out of the window, from the moment when they came through the bridge. She had her back to him, her little head held up to one side, as if she were thinking; her thoughts (how trivial? how profound?) undisturbed by the rattle of the train.

But as soon as he was out of the carriage she was up to him, and had given him her cool hand. She blushed a little, as if even this touch of him after his long absence were an intimacy for themselves alone. He wanted to kiss her, but her eyes said, 'Wait. The whole world is getting out at this station. Wait till we are together.'

'So it did stop here,' said Reginald. 'I knew it would.'

'You never remember about the trains, do you, darling? The 3.10 stops here altogether.'

'Altogether? I didn't know we were so important.'

'It isn't importance, darling. It always does.'

(You are right, Sylvia, it isn't importance, it always does. But I don't care what you say, I adore you.)

He gave up his ticket to the handy-man of the station, and told him it was a lovely day.

'Bit warm in London, too, sir, I dare say?'

'Well, depends what you're doing,' said Reginald.

'That's so, sir.'

Good Heavens, could anything be more futile than that? And yet he despised Sylvia. No, he didn't. He was going home to tea with her.

They came to the car.

'Will you drive, or shall I?' said Sylvia.

'I'll drive, and you shall give me a lesson.'

'Darling, don't be silly. You drive just as well as I do.'

'Sylvia, how *can* you say that?'

'Well, I mean it's only because you can't give your mind to it. Naturally you're thinking of something else all the time.'

'That's just what I'm not doing. My mind is glued on the gears from the moment that I see a hill in the distance. I have an absolute picture in my mind of steel teeth snapping and growling at each other and refusing to get interlocked. My mind is utterly convinced that I shall stampede the cattle, and it's always right.'

'Well, that's what I mean,' said Sylvia. 'You think about it too much.'

But just now she said—oh, well, never mind.

'Very well then,' said Reginald. 'You shall hold my hand, and I shan't be able to think about it at all.'

But before he got out of neutral, he turned to her, and she to him, and they looked at each other, happily, almost shyly again, and smiled , and kissed.

Down a hill out of the station and up a hill which you rushed . . . no, not quite . . . very well, then, noiselessly into second. . . .

'I'm terribly sorry, Sylvia.'

'It's all right, darling.'

'A 5.9 exploding in the Lesser Cat House at the Zoo would give just that effect, but more expensively. What shall we do about it?'

'You'll be better next time.'

'Well, you must tell me.'

Across the main road, down a long winding hill—carefully now, because of the narrow bridge over the stream at the bottom, through the village —then all out so as to get a flying start for the long climb up on to the common. . . .

'Now,' said Sylvia, 'clutch out.'

'It is.'

'Into neutral.'

'But I always—oh, all right.'

'Just touch the accelerator.'

'Done.'

'Now *right* down with the clutch, and *feel* your way back into second.'

'Gosh, this is—Sylvia, you're a ——'

'Accelerate, quick. There! It's quite easy, isn't it?'

'If you're here.'

'Of course you could do it if you tried, darling.'

They sailed up on to the common, over the common, along the top of the world, where wild cherry, wild plum and blackthorn hung daintily white against the blue beyond, through a beechwood so delicately green, so fresh and young and fragrant and unattainable that one thought in whispers as one went past; out and to the left, through the broken gate, past the cottage, and so easily down through long rolling sheepcropped fields to where the little walled island of Westaways raised three stiff chimneys above a ruffle of orchard.

Reginald stopped the car, and took a deep breath. How he loved Westaways! How he loved it! Oh God, thank you for thinking of Westaways, and thank you for letting me have it.

'I expect you want your tea,' said Sylvia. 'I'll put the car away if you like.'

'Sorry. What did you say, sweetheart? Oh!' Reginald woke up. 'I'll let you put it away if you'll do it backwards and let me watch you.'

'You *are* silly, darling.'

'No, I'm not, I want to learn.'

'Well, it's quite easy.'

It was as she did it.

Now why on earth, said Reginald, watching her, do I think I'm cleverer than she is? She can do a hundred things that I can't do, and why should my things be the test of cleverness and not hers? And why do I tell myself like a prig that she isn't as responsive to beauty as I am? Why should she be? She *is* Beauty. Is God as interested in the Theory of Relativity as some tuppenny-ha' Professor of Physics? How can He be? He *is* the Theory of Relativity. Anyway, I want my tea.

'Well done, Sylvia.'

They walk down the steps and through the old stone court-yard into the house.

'I do love you with your hair cut,' says Sylvia. 'Except for the slight brushiness. I wish you could take your own brushes with you.'

'Well, that's not for another month, thank Heaven. I hate leaving the country at this time of year. I hate London. Hooray for Westaways and Sylvia.'

He was disappointed in London. Whatever future was awaiting *Bindweed* in the country, London for the moment gave no signs of it.

Chapter Three

I

Reginald often wondered, dumbly, why he was not allowed to brain Betty Baxter; why it should be wrong, uncivic, immoral, to do the natural thing; but he never felt more resentful of the inhibitions of modern life than when she talked about Westaways. She called it 'amusing'.

She called many things amusing which did not noticeably amuse. Her lips were so much ruddier than the cherry that Baxter, easy-going man, was moved one morning to an 'Oh, really, Betty! Oh, well, if *you* like it'; after which he resumed his breakfast.

'What?' said Betty innocently.

'Why women *want* to stick paint on themselves—who's supposed to admire it? Who are you supposed to deceive? Even the blindest lunatic—oh, well, if *you* like it.'

'It happens to be the fashion.'

Baxter grunted.

'I think it's rather amusing,' said Betty.

The Baxters were not really country, because they had a house in London. In London, of course, everybody is amusing, so there was more excuse for Betty, and less for her husband. You can't spend five days of the week being really funny, and then relapse into dullness over the week-end. Naturally she brought her lip-stick with her.

Westaways was strange and charming and beautiful. Any of those adjectives Reginald would allow you. Even, if you liked the word, you might call it quaint. It was the wrong word, but perhaps you were one of those people who liked using the wrong word. Quaint was not actually offensive. But 'amusing' with its hint of superiority was forbidden. The Baxter woman was no longer invited to Westaways. . . . However, she continued to come.

Westaways was a little oasis in the rolling fields, walled in to preserve its flavour. Like most cottages in this part of England it had been a farm; like most cottages it had made iron and bricks. Let other, statelier mansions claim that it was they (as undoubtedly it was) who boarded Elizabeth, hid Charles and introduced Henry to Anne. We are humbler. We merely say that we forged the last iron gates of the country-side, we baked the first bricks. And if we are told that a good many last gates seemed to have been forged in this part of the world, a good many first bricks baked, we answer that this is not more surprising than that Elizabeth was always sleeping round about here, Charles always hiding and Henry always being introduced. In short, that there are plenty of impostors about, but that we are the genuine thing.

Westaways was within rectangular stone walls, built centuries ago as if to say to the world, 'I don't care who has the rest of you, but this bit's mine.' Naturally, as soon as the wall was built, the owner found that he had spoken too quickly, and that the boundaries of the outside world might very well withdraw a hundred yards or so. The wall was now his inner fortress, a strip of land round it his moat. The barn in which Sylvia has just put the car was outside the castle walls. When the original Westaways had pulled up his drawbridge and let down the portcullis, the Morris (if he had had one) was abandoned to the enemy. In case there were still enemies about, Reginald locked up the barn, and put the key in the gutter, a place where nobody but himself and Sylvia, and anybody else who wanted temporary shelter for a car, would think of looking. The car parked, the iron gates ('the last iron gates of the country-side', or not, we can't be sure) were now waiting for the visitors' entrance. Perhaps if her ladyship were making a formal call she went through them, a footman or two having first unfastened them. Ordinary people just stepped over the stile which adjoined them, and found themselves within the high stone walls and in an apple-orchard. Slowly the orchard became more formal as they followed the little path; they were among marigolds suddenly and fingering their ties or powdering their noses; the path became steps down a rock-garden; now they were in a stone-paved courtyard, with a pool in the middle; and there opposite was the house, L-shaped, filling up two of the sides. Most amusing.

The other side of the house was not so funny. There were lawns and flowers and brick paths, almost as they might have been in anybody else's garden; there was a door in the wall for tradesmen, which was fairly amusing; there were the bee-hives, more flowers, and what had once been a duck-pond, but was now a pond in which wild duck nested; and beneath the lower wall a little river went peacefully on its way.

'And how is that delightful Westaways?' Betty Baxter would ask, meeting Reginald at her house or another's.

What's the answer. What *is* the answer? Forbidden a battle-axe Reginald can think of none. He achieves a smile.

'Mr Wellard has the most amusing house you ever saw,' she says to the strange woman in a pink jumper, standing by.

'Oh?' says the strange woman, with the reserved interest of one who has now nearly, but not quite, been introduced to Mr Wellard.

'You really ought to see it. It's too quaint. Really *most* amusing.'

The pink jumper now has half an invitation to add to her half-introduction. A note of still deeper reserve creeps into her voice.

'I'm sure it must be delightful,' she says.

'Do you live round about?' asks Reginald, feeling that he must say something.

'Oh, no, I'm just down for the week-end.'

Good, then he needn't see *her* again.

II

Even without the woman in the pink jumper there was plenty of life within the four stone walls of Westaways.

Bees.

Bees everywhere. Bees in the erigeron; well, you would expect them there. Bees in the eryngium—deceived by the name, perhaps. Was there ever more unpromising material? Bees going into the snap-dragons, and coming out backwards, a little annoyed. Bees on the zinnias, unaware of so much beauty, aware, only, of so much honey. A bee's-eye view of a garden, how strange, how different! Food, food, no food, more food, less food. What a life! Bees in the lavender, looking for food.

Futile things, bees, thought Reginald. What are we in the world for? The creation of beauty, the discovery of beauty, the realization of beauty. What else? Well, knowledge, says that gargoyle Professor Pumpernickel. Very well; write 'truth' for 'beauty', if you will, and you have summed up the whole business of man. Are the bees for beauty, for truth? No. Just for existence. Existence, propagation, death, birth, existence, propagation, death, birth, existence, propagation, death . . . on and on through the centuries. Why this passion to reproduce oneself rather than to fulfil oneself? Not bees only; men and women. The birth-rate is going down! We are lost! What shall we do without children, more children, still more children, bungalows, more bungalows, still more bungalows? Here is a lovely corner of England, but there are no ugly little houses in it! Why aren't we spreading? Why aren't we having more and more families, so that we can keep on and on and on . . . reproducing?

I suppose, thought Reginald, we are afraid of ourselves. Like in that game we play at the Hildershams' at Christmas——Up Jenkins. All our hands busy under the table passing the sixpence to each other, all of us trying to get the sixpence into somebody else's hand, so that when the command 'Up Jenkins!' comes from across the table, it shall not be we who are responsible, not our hands which shall give away the secret. We have had the sixpence for a moment, we have passed it on successfully to little Tony Hildersham, we have done our part. If he is caught with it, that is his affair, if he has passed it on to the Coleby girl, that is her affair; our hands are clean.

So when we are asked 'What did you do with life?' we can answer quickly, 'Passed it on, Lord.'

Was that to be Reginald's answer? Well, he had not passed it on yet. He was not sure that he wanted to. He wanted Sylvia a wife, not a mother. But whether he did or not, it would not be his answer to the question, 'What did you do with life?' His answer would be, 'Loved it terribly and was bewildered by it.'

Futile things bees, the worker bees. The drones had the best of it. At least they died for love. . . .

Butterflies.

Butterflies everywhere. Whites, orange tips, brimstones, tortoiseshells, red admirals, peacocks, painted ladies, walls, blues, heaths, small coppers, every sort of butterfly. Shadows of butterflies in the early sunshine swimming over the flowers. Peacocks on the buddleia . . . ten . . . twelve . . . and there a painted lady; peacocks folding their wings into blackness, opening them into beauty; red admirals on the buddleia, red and black velvet on lilac; brimstones delicately yellow, folding into a delicate green, with just a beauty-spot of orange put on with artistry by the mirror of the pool. Useless, beautiful butterflies—how much prouder God must be of you than of bees! How much more worth while to have made you!

Birds.

First the pigeons in the dovecot. Black Nuns. Black-and-White Nuns. Two of them, to begin with; nuns; undisturbed by men. They laid eggs, hopefully, but nothing happened. Perhaps, they told each other, it was the dovecot which was wrong; the aspect, the ventilation. They went to the roof and laid them hopefully there—facing north, facing south, on tiles, on stone. Still no babies. Pathetic. Then Reginald went to London to have his hair cut, and bought a Black Monk (and had his hair cut), and now it didn't matter where the eggs were laid, dishevelled and surprised babies came out of them and grew to serenity. There were six; sitting lazily on the roof, making a lazy toilet by the pool, love-making lazily; happy, lazy, beautiful Nuns.

Then the mallards on the pond. To make them feel that they were no longer visitors, but part of the establishment, Reginald had given them an old dog-kennel to sleep in, nest in, meditate in. The duck retired within; meditated, slept on it, and decided to nest. Only two eggs were hatched. The drake, feeling, perhaps, that life was getting altogether too domestic, returned to his marsh in the woods; the dog-kennel was sent back to the barn; and three ducks settled down to a happy life on the pond, lived sometimes horizontally, sometimes vertically. 'Look at that green on the back of the neck,' thought Reginald reverently. 'How does He do it?'

The kingfisher who flashed past them on his rare visits—ah, there was beauty! The white owl who came over in the dusk on some deep and secret business, as if holding his breath as he passed you, and then letting it out in one gentle expiration, more noiseless than silence. The call of the rooks in the elms on spring mornings, blackbirds in February, thrushes in April, the cuckoo who re-awakens in you the memory of every summer; the song of birds in early summer and then the strange silence of birds in late summer—could you ever forget that you shared the world with birds?

Goldfish in the pool, gold, black and gold, black and red, silver and gold. A strange, remote, sexless life they led. Breathing, thinking, breathing, thinking. Ascetics, living on nothing. Thinking, north and south; a turn of the tail, and they are thinking east and west. Waiting for something, some revelation, perhaps. Or was it ants' eggs? Why ants' eggs for goldfish? As well expect rabbits to like rooks' eggs. Perhaps they do, thought

Reginald, and wait hopefully at the bottom of trees. Sylvia looked beautiful, feeding the goldfish. Standing over the pool, another, more shadowy, Sylvia watching her, dropping in the food for them, or perhaps dropping in her silent thoughts, she also thinking, breathing, thinking, she, too, waiting for some-thing, some revelation.

Cats. Three of them. Grandmamma, John Wesley and Marmalade. Poor Grandmamma was small and anxious, and would have been more anxious still if she had been a better arithmetician. 'I thought I had seven children,' she would say anxiously, 'and I can only find one. Do you know where the other one is?' Poor Grandmamma. There is no limit to the number of babies wanted, only to the number of kittens. John Wesley and Marmalade are the two Westaways survivors of twelve families in six years, but nobody can quite remember now whether they are brothers, half-brothers or uncle and nephew. John Wesley is long and black, and follows Reginald to heel, waiting for him to bend down to a weed. Then with a spring he is on his master's shoulder, round his neck, content. Marmalade, Orange Marmalade, is more distant. Reginald can get very little out of him.

'Hallo, Marmalade, where are you off to?'

'A little private business, Mr Wellard. An engagement in the fields, Mr Wellard. Not unconnected with a mole, Mr Wellard.'

'Well, don't bring the bag in here. I won't have dead things left about the lawns. Do you understand?'

'No, Mr Wellard. I don't know what you're talking about, Mr Wellard. See you again some time, if you're still here.' He steps on his way, dignified, unhurried.

'Marmalade!'

Shall I look back? No. Not worth it.

'Marmalade!' This time in Sylvia's voice. That's another matter.

'Yes, Mrs Wellard?'

'Mr Wellard is talking to you.'

'No birds, Marmalade. Remember. No birds allowed,' says Reginald.

'What *is* the man talking about?' says Marmalade to Sylvia.

Sylvia laughs and says something to Reginald.

'Goodbye, Marmalade,' he calls out.

'Goodbye, *Mrs* Wellard,' says Marmalade, and leaves them.

III

The weeks went by (nearly time for another hair-cut) and still Mrs Baxter, Mrs Hildersham and Mrs Coleby were hopeful that some day, somehow, they would find themselves in possession of *Bindweed*.

Betty Baxter had been, it may be supposed, the most hopeful. She was in London now, save at week-ends, and there are undoubtedly shops in London. Possibly she had tried at the Court florist's, the Court hairdresser's and that delightful little place off the Brompton Road, unpatronized as yet by Royalty, where almost everything is hand-painted and amusing. Failing to get the book at any of these establishments, she may have lost heart. There were other shops, of course, but one simply couldn't drive all over London until one came to the right one. And then the question may have come into her mind, 'Does one buy books?' Had any of her friends ever mentioned in her hearing as a fact of interest, or, in the case of one or two of them, of no possible interest whatever, that she had bought a book? 'I picked up such a charming old decanter': 'I simply had to go in for a bead necklace': these were commonplaces of conversation; but who had ever said, 'I bought such a delightful book in that shop in Wigmore Street'? Nobody. And then there was another point. Since this was the only book one was likely to buy (if one did) one would have to pay cash for it. Would one not? And whoever heard of paying cash for anything?

Betty Baxter began to feel less hopeful. She was still, she told Sylvia, thrilled at the thought of reading it, but hadn't managed to get hold of it just for the moment.

Grace Hildersham was also a little less hopeful than she had been, though not yet despairing. She had neither raspberries nor children on her hands at the moment, and was just in the mood for a lazy day with a nice novel. Finding herself in the village, she had wondered at the post office, which anyhow sold diaries, envelopes and china dogs, if they knew of a book called *Woodbine*. She was offered a packet of cigarettes which she accepted absently without prejudice to her original suggestion. A book. It was a book. Called *Woodbine*. However, it appeared that there was nothing in the shop more literary than a picture-postcard of Venus rising from the Brighton waves, and saying, with an economy of words and costume, 'I am in the pink. How are you?' Mrs Hildersham rejected this with a large, pleasantly embarrassed smile, and went home again. Half-way up the hill she remembered that the book was called *Bindweed*, but it was evidently no use to go back. She must try again when next she was in Burdon.

Mrs Coleby was the warmest of the three. She had joined the library at Burdon, had paid her tuppence (as Sylvia and she had assured each other, it was quite easy) and had taken out a book called *By Order of the Czar*. Tom Coleby was reading it now. Slowly.

So much for Sylvia's friends. So much, it seemed, for Burdon and Little Malling. But no. There was one who had read it. Of all surprising people, old Mrs Edwards.

Reginald and Edwards were looking at the snap-dragons in the nursery bed. Six hundred of them. Sown in boxes. Pricked out into other boxes. Transplanted to the nursery. Now to be transplanted into the real grown-up world in place of the tulips whose short day was done. Reginald glanced sideways at the enormous right hand of Edwards which was responsible for all this, and marvelled.

'Make a fine show,' said Edwards grudgingly.

'If they're the right colours.'

'They're all right. Look at 'em.'

'They all look healthy enough, if that's what you mean. But I don't want any of those pale yellow ones again. We said we'd stick to Fire King and Guardsman and ——'

'That's what I said, look at 'em.'

Now then, thought Reginald, am I going to sack Edwards, or is he going to sack me?

'Look at the stalk. See that? Red. There's your Fire King. See that? Dark green. That means crimson. Now then, see that? Pale green, isn't it? That means yellow. Only just those few of 'em. Thought you'd like just a few. That's why I said, look at 'em.'

'Well!' said Reginald. 'I never knew that!'

'Lots of things people don't know. I didn't know you'd written a book.'

'Oh?' said Reginald pinkly. 'Well, I— er——'

'Mother's been reading it.'

Reginald was too surprised, too pleased, too flattered to say anything. This was authorship. Only now had he realized what it meant. Mr Pump's 'third large impression'—well, we all know what *that* means. We aren't taken in by that. A hundred copies or so bought by the circulating libraries and never circulated. But here, in his own territory, a bedridden old woman had actually—— Three pounds a week he gave Edwards. Edwards had probably heard about it from the kitchen—Mrs Hosken or Alice—and had bought it for his mother. Seven-and-six-pence out of three pounds! It was monstrous! He ought to have given her a copy. But then who would have guessed that she would want to read it?

'Tell you how it was,' said Edwards. 'Young Mitchell, up at the station, comes down to us of an evening, like. See, he gets papers left behind in the trains or handed to him by gentlemen coming out. Mother likes a read—nothing else to do. So young Mitchell brings his papers and all when he comes, like. Other day sure enough there's a book in the carriage so he brings it along. "Here, Charlie," he says, "this by your gentleman?" "Well, it might be," I said, but I didn't know like as you wrote books. Well it was, you see—long of Mother reading out bits to me, and you'd got the garden and all. That's how it was.'

'I see,' said Reginald. 'Well——' and he went off.

He always had to say that 'Well' when he left Edwards or Challinor. There seemed to be no other way of going. 'Well——' meant 'Well, I'm a very busy man and can't stop talking to *you* all day,' or it meant, 'Well, you're a very busy man, at least you ought to be, and you can't stop talking to *me* all day.' Reginald hated saying it, it seemed so stupid and unnecessary, and yet, dash it, you couldn't just leave the man.

So that's how it was. His own copy which he had bought at Victoria and thrown away in the train! Forced on Mrs Edwards who had nothing else to do but read. No doubt if you're bedridden, even a Wellard is better than nothing.

Yes, and that reminded him—curse that fellow Edwards. Did Reginald say in plain understandable English, 'No pale yellow snap-dragons this year'? He did. And what does Edwards say? 'Thought you'd like just a few.' It was always the way. Tell your cook you don't like onions, and she thinks you mean you don't like a lot of onions. Tell your gardener you don't like yellow snap-dragons, and he thinks you'd like just a few of them. We all hedge so much, we are all so afraid of committing ourselves, that when we hear a definite statement we suspect that there is some reservation attached to it.

Anyhow, she had read the book. What on earth can she have made of it?

He must find Sylvia and tell her . . .

Or not?

Well, what did it matter what she said, when she looked so lovely saying it?

He told Sylvia. 'I say who do you think's read *Bindweed?* Old Mrs Edwards.'

'Fancy!' said Sylvia. 'I expect Mrs Hosken told Edwards, and he bought it for her. He's a tremendous admirer of yours, *really*.'

Reginald looked at her fondly.

'I wish you'd always wear that dress,' he said.

'Do you like it, darling?'

'I love it. You look so utterly and adorably feminine.'

Sylvia looked at him, and dropped her eyes.

'Do you remember what you said in your dedication?' she said softly.

'Yes.'

'It was true, wasn't it?'

'Yes.'

She put up a hand and ruffled his hair.

'Almost time to get it cut again,' she said. 'I think I'll come up with you, darling.'

'Oh do! What fun!'

'Friday?'

'Rather. Think of a good place for lunch.' And then after a pause, 'Well——' and he moved away.

No, damn it, not 'Well——' to Sylvia. Horrible. He came back quickly, kissed her, laughed and went off.

Chapter Four

I

To write a book, thought Reginald; what an achievement! The labour of it. The physical labour of the hundred thousand words, any words, put down on paper. Then the anguish, the despair, the exhilaration of finding the right words. A hundred thousand words to be chosen, each one of which could be bettered by a better man. How had he dared to do it? How had he contrived to do it? And then when he had done it—all those pages, those hundreds of pages, written by him—out it goes into the world, and nobody minds. Splash it goes . . . and then not a ripple. Not a ripple in London, not a ripple in the country. It is as if he had never written it.

Well, not quite. Sylvia loved it . . . did she? . . . and it had helped Mrs Edwards to get through a few long hours on her way to the churchyard.

So thought Reginald; but then he did not know what Raglan and Lord Ormsby were doing.

They were a curious couple. Raglan liked being near Ormsby, because he liked being next to money, and Ormsby liked being near Raglan, because he liked being close to culture. Raglan was not merely cultured, he was Culture, just as Ormsby was not merely rich, he was Money. So they went about together, and one was master and one servant, but nobody knew which.

Raglan had never written a novel; nor a play; nor a poem; nor a short story. He had hardly written an essay whose subject he had invented for himself. He lived on other writers, as the fruit-farmer lives on fruit-trees. The apple-tree grows the apple, but the farmer is the authority; for how little the apple-tree knows (or cares) of the processes it went through to produce the apple; how little it knows of the apple after it is grown. Raglan introduced other writers to the world; apologized for them, classified them, analysed them, collated them, cross-indexed them, rinsed them, put them through the mangle, and hung them up to dry. When he wrote of Thomas Dekker or Nicholas Breton or George Colman the younger, you felt that three more celebrities, Dekker, Breton and Colman, had now written about Raglan; that he was by that the more famous. The announcement of his edition of *Hudibras* as 'probably Ambrose Raglan's masterpiece' left open the possibility that Butler might have written it after all, but summed up the position very fairly. You felt that if Butler were alive, he would say, 'After you, my dear fellow,' as they joined the ladies. Nobody had heard of Butler but had heard of Raglan; thousands had heard of Raglan who had never heard of Butler. Whether it would be so in three hundred years' time was not yet known.

Ormsby owned newspapers and racehorses. By virtue of the former he was 'Robert, first Baron Ormsby', by virtue of the latter he was 'good old Bob'. He had a nose like a small button, stiff upstanding hair, a thick neck and a cleft in his chin. There was no vulgarity, no indecency, no treachery too low for his papers, but since business is business, and he had won the Derby, and smoked habitually a cigar so long that the indication of it in a cartoon was enough to identify the owner, he was a national figure, and therefore, in himself, a model of English respectability. But on one point, poor fellow, he was queer. He had this odd fancy for books.

He had asked Raglan to come and see him. Raglan came. Doubtless Ormsby was starting a new literary monthly and wished him to edit it. Given a free hand he might consent. But he would stand no interference from a vulgar fellow like Ormsby.

'How do you do, Mr Raglan. Pleased to meet you. Smoke?'

Raglan flinched at the cigar offered, and with a murmur, Oxford and polite, took out his cigarette-case.

'Light? Now then, let's get down to it. Don't know if you read my papers, don't suppose you do. Go racing at all?'

Mr Raglan's gentle smile made it clear that he didn't.

'Right. But if you did, you'd know that my Racing Correspondent is the greatest living expert in England today. Cricket? Football? You don't? Well, ask any of your friends. Any cricketer or footballer would tell you. Married? Well, any of your lady friends. They'd tell you. Fashions, Flying, Cricket, Motoring, whatever it is, there's just one question I ask myself. Who is the greatest living expert in England today? Mr Blasted Brown? Then I want Mr Blasted Brown for my paper. *And* I get 'im.'

'A very sound policy, I should say,' said Raglan kindly, watching his cigarette smoke up to the ceiling.

'I'm going to develop the literary side. Always meant to, but had to get the other sides working first. So I look round for the greatest living expert on Literature in England today. Everybody tells me the same. Ambrose Raglan.'

Raglan gave his high little laugh and fingered his little beard. How right everybody was.

'I'm going to have book talk daily, just as I have racing talk. I want you to edit that. At least I want your name. We'll get somebody else to do it, but you can keep an eye on him. What I really want from you is a weekly article on books, syndicated to all my papers. How does it strike you?'

'Well,' said Raglan with a little smile, 'I hardly think———'

'I'll give you £5,000 a year,' said Ormsby, and then, before Raglan could recover, added, carelessly, 'Same as I give my Racing Correspondent.'

Five thousand a year! Who could refuse? (Even if the Racing Correspondent got it too.) *Jonson and the Poetasters* might deserve all which other critics had so carefully said about it, but one did not make five thousand a year with books like this. Five *thousand!* Who *could* refuse?

'You allow me a free hand?' he asked as negligently as he could, but the hand was trembling.

'We shan't quarrel about that,' said Ormsby, getting up. 'Come along and I'll show you the shop.'

They didn't quarrel. But a month later Ormsby sent for the greatest living expert on Literature and opened his heart to him.

'Look here, Raglan. You've got the wrong idea.' He flicked at the papers on his desk. 'This literary page, why d'you think I do it?'

Raglan smiled in his faintly amused way.

'Really, I have been wondering. It can hardly be profitable. A feeling for the complete newspaper, perhaps.'

'Complete nothing. There are only two reasons why anything goes into my paper. One, because the public wants it. And if the public doesn't want it, Two, because *I* want it. Now then, is the public interested in the sexual apparatus of the sponge? No. Well, do I look as if I were? No. Well, that's why sponges go on making love to each other and having small sponges however they damn well please, and we say nothing about it in our papers. Well, now, is the public interested in books? No. Not yet. Am I? *Yes!* And it's my ambition, Raglan,' and he thumped his desk, 'to bring books into every home, to make every man want a book on his Saturday night, as much as he wants a—well, anything else.'

'A very praiseworthy ambition.'

'Right.' He pulled a paper in front of him and flicked over the pages. 'I want people to read books. Now then, November the 17th, that's last Friday. *Fireside Friends.* Edited by Ambrose Raglan. Book of the Week. Reviewed by Ambrose Raglan. Here it is. *Seventeenth Century Ceramics,* by Pierre Dupleix, however you pronounce it, translated by—Hell matters who. Three guineas. Right.' He flicked over another page. 'Now here's my Racing Expert's tip for the Woodbury Stakes—Elysium. Right.

Now how many people d'you think got up from their breakfast-tables on Friday and said, "I must put five bob on Elysium"? Thousands. Beaten a short head, but that's not the point. And how many people got up from their breakfast-tables on Friday and said, "I must put three guineas on *Seventeenth Century Ceramics* by this hell-be-jiggered Frenchman"? Not one blasted soul. Well, that's not bringing literature into the home, old man. Honest-to-God it's not.'

Raglan had never been called 'old man' before, at least not since he was a young boy. Coming from a peer and a millionaire, it warmed him.

'Surely it's the publisher's business to sell his books, not ours?' he suggested.

At the 'ours' Ormsby also felt warmed suddenly. Raglan, with that word, had taken the paper under his cultured wing. It was *his* child now, not a stranger to whom he was giving a correspondence course.

'Look here, Raglan—sorry, have a cigar? No? I'm not doing this for money. You can't go on doing things for money all the time. Why did I spent the week-end—well, never mind that. Any damn way I didn't do it for money. On the contrary—and then a pearl necklace on the top of that. Well, I'm doing this because I'm grateful to books. When I was fourteen I had bought and read every book that Dickens ever wrote.' He repeated it again slowly, and Raglan shivered. 'I was earning ten shillings a week, and took seven home to my mother.' He murmured to himself again. 'Every Hell-be-jiggered book, on three shillings a week,' and added aloud, 'But of course that's nothing to you, because you're a real book lover.'

Raglan, who hadn't bought a book for twenty years, wondered uncomfortably if he was. But why buy books when publishers and editors and authors give them to you?

Ormsby was flicking open more of his papers, and murmuring to himself.

'*The Life of Thomas Heywood,* thirty bob—*Pastoral Poets of the Renaissance,* Limited edition, five guineas—*The Aesthetic of Vorticism,* five bob—you had a cheap one there, but hardly catchy—and now this *Seventeenth Century God-save-us.* See what I mean, old man?' He was silent for a moment, and then said, almost shyly, 'Don't mind my asking you, but these books— well, these four, just as an example—do you really *enjoy* them? I just wondered. Get as much blood-and-bones from 'em as I got from *Pickwick?*'

'It's a different sort of enjoyment, perhaps.'

'Oh, quite, quite,' said Ormsby quickly. 'A damn fool question to ask. Well now, what it comes to is this. I want people to get up from their breakfast-tables, or get out of their trains, whenever they read the paper, and say "Dammit, I can't miss that book. If Ambrose Raglan recommends it, that's good enough for me." Well but, dear old man, they aren't going to say that of the— what's its blasted name?—*The Aesthetic of Vorticism.* Now, are they?'

Raglan laughed; the most genuine laugh he had achieved in that office.

'Not offended?' said Ormsby quickly.

'Not a bit. Go on.'

'Well, this is how it is. I should like to feel that every one of my readers was going to read every one of Dickens's books, same as I did. Too late. You can't make 'em now. They say, Stands to reason modern authors write better than Dickens, with all these years more progress. Look at trains—and flying. Very well, then, I say, let 'em think so. And the long and short of it is that you've got to find a book for 'em every week— better than Dickens.'

'Great novels aren't written every week. Or are they?'

'I dare say not. But *some* book is the book of the week, and I say that whatever book you choose has got to be a book that ordinary people can read. People who put their five shillings on a horse and write letters to the Press signed Ratepayer. Well, that's how it is. Think it over, old man.'

Old man Raglan thought it over. Money was dear to him, but his reputation was also dear. It was his business to lead the literary fashion of the moment, not to follow it. Yet since literary fashions went round in circles, who was to tell whether one was a leader or a follower? Let him imagine himself starting a crusade in favour of the old-fashioned English novel. Gradually, of course; making it clear from which point in the circle he started. Ahead of the newest fashion; so far ahead that he had now got round to Dickens again. . . .

And now eighteen months later Raglan was enjoying it. He had power and popularity (and, at last, money), where before he had only had a jealous admiration. A new novel, recommended by him, added by that fifteen thousand to its sale. To be able to put, once a week, a thousand pounds into an author's pocket, and Heaven knows how much more into a publisher's, gave him a new complacence. And when he also put, on his own head, a grey top-hat of the latest fashion, and went racing with his friend Lord Ormsby, he felt that he was almost a figure in the old-fashioned English novel himself. Unique. The cultured sportsman.

You may imagine him then, one day in May, looking at the pile of books on his table, and wondering which was to be 'The Book of the Week' this time . . . No . . . No . . . Oh, *no!* . . . A first novel, if possible . . . And certainly not a Pump. But Wellard, though. He'd heard that name somewhere. Last week at lunch, of course. Would that be the man? Looked as if he might write . . . Said he was a countryman, though, didn't he, and knew nothing about . . .

He read, standing, for five minutes. . . .

Then he read, sitting down, for five minutes. . . .

Then he got up, put on his hat (not the Ascot one) and went home with *Bindweed* under the arm.

He had found the book of the week.

II

For business purposes Mr Pump wore a long beard, an old-fashioned frock-coat and a black silk hat with a curly brim. It established confidence in young authors. The frock-coat and the beard spoke of the days when his firm, had it been in existence, would undoubtedly have published for Thackeray and Trollope; the curliness of the hat's brim reminded you that even a firm with history behind it must adopt up-to-date methods. Since Mr Pump took his beard and his frock-coat round with the plate on the one day of the week when he was not publishing, he may be said to have lived in an atmosphere of respectability; and since he was publishing on the six days of the week when he was not taking round the plate, he may also be said to have lived with an air of sidelong calculation in his eye.

But Mr Pump was not a hypocrite. He was a religious man, whose religion was too sacred a thing to be carried into his business. The top-hat which he hung up in his office was not the top-hat which he prayed into before placing it, thus hallowed, between his feet, even if the frock-coat and the aspect of benevolence were the same. He had two top-hats, and one hat-box for them. On the Monday morning he put God reverently away for the week and took out Mammon. On the Sunday morning he came back—gratefully or hopefully, according to business done—to God. No man can serve two masters simultaneously.

Mr Pump would tell you that he didn't go in for best sellers—possibly because they didn't go in very much for him. He published as many books as he could get hold of, and looked to make a small profit on each. With the 'customary agreement between author and publisher' in his safe, the small profit was certain; with the 'usual agreement' it was at least a pleasant probability. For he specialized in novels with 'a strong sex interest'; and though they only took you to the moment when the bedside lamp went out, they left you with a row of stars to

light up your imagination, and a strong hope that some day
. . . But Mr Pump was not taking that sort of risk. He preferred
to keep you hoping.

The appearance of *Bindweed*, then, as the Book of the Week
was to him astonishing. Editors and reviewers had, notoriously,
a prejudice against him. The space they gave him in return for his
advertisements was sinful. Even though *Bindweed* was not—
well—'that sort of book'—it was surprising that Ambrose
Raglan—— Now which agreement had he made? Wellard . . .
Wellard . . .

He went to his safe, found the agreement and brought it back
to his desk.

H'm. Still, he had the next six books . . . and half all the rights . . .
and accounts paid once yearly. . . . Not so bad. Yes, there was money
in this. He must get to work . . .

Mr Pump picked up his telephone and got to work.

Chapter Five

I

If you had flipped through the pages of a dictionary in front of Reginald, the word 'bindweed' would now have leaped out at him; if you had fluttered a telephone directory before him, a Wellard, not himself, would have caught his eye. So it is to be an author and write your first book.

Sylvia and he and the three cats were breakfasting together; Sylvia on grape-fruit, the cats on milk out of her saucer, Reginald on scrambled eggs. There was, to Reginald, a sort of dewiness on Sylvia in the early morning, an untouched fragrance that he feared of dispelling by a touch, a breath, a word; an air almost of holiness about her; a look of virginal wonder in her eyes, as if she were trying to remember some beautiful and innocent dream. To have her sitting there opposite to him, smiling shyly, a secret smile between them, when she felt his look on her, to know that this was Westaways, and this was Sylvia, both his, to see the lawns and flowers of Westaways wandering through the open door to him, calling to him to come out to them, gave him a happiness which could not bear thought or expression, a happiness at which he dared not look lest it leave him. So he would read yesterday's evening paper, which had come by post, and tell himself that, if he didn't go into the matter too carefully, the absurd dream that he was married to Sylvia and they were living at Westaways together would go on.

At nineteen Reginald was dreaming about Cambridge. The death of his father, and of his father's pension with him, ended the dream. His qualifications for life were sixth-form classics and moderate skill at games. There is only one profession in the world which wants these qualities, and wants them only to pass them on. Reginald grew a moustache as quickly as he could, and became an assistant-master at a second-rate grammar school. He existed there for four miserable years. Then, having added a little mathematics to his classics, he shaved his moustache and served an equal sentence in a bank. The war broke out, he grew his moustache and served another four years. The war ended. He shaved again. . . .

This was life as lived by men. Twelve years of ugliness.

Selby Grammar School. The ink-smudged form-room, the ink-smudged desks, the ink-smudged boys. The ink-smudged minds of the older boys, the dulled minds of the masters. The futile noise of the place. Noise and ugliness. The clatter of ugly boots in ugly passages, the clatter of ugly voices in ugly rooms. The sordidness, the futility of it all. For ever and for ever . . .

The bank. The clatter of London. The noisy, horrible lodgings. The city at luncheontime. The struggle, the clatter, the unendurable smell of the underground tea-shops. The futility of the work; round and round and round. The conversation of his fellow-clerks; their sordid loves. The unloveliness of it all. For ever and for ever . . .

The army. The war. The uttermost depths of futility and noise and ugliness. Man's final expression of his soul in one insane orgy of clatter and cruelty and filth. Now that we have found ourselves at last, now let us go on and on. For ever and for ever . . .

The war is over. Why? Why not go on? We have only noise and ugliness and futility to go back to. We have judged ourselves, found our standards, proclaimed our religion to God. Surely it is easier to go on. Why stop, and then have to begin all over again?

But the war was ended. Well, what is there to do? Shave one's moustache again, and then what?

Then he met Sylvia. He was thirty-two; tall, lean, hard, resentful, futile himself now in his impotent anger with life, hopeless, possessionless. She was seventeen, remote and lovely, the supreme expression of all the beauty and the quietness which he had missed. Well, if he could just look at her sometimes, he would be content. . . .

He was not content. The year which followed was a year of pain and turmoil and confusion beside which the years of war seemed now to have been peace. Heaven and Hell, Heaven and Hell, first one, then the other. She loved him, she loved him not—how could she? He had no money. What the Hell did money matter? But if he were poor, how in Heaven's name could he take her? He was rich— absurd, how could *he* be rich?—somebody had died—who was it? Well, now he was rich. Now he could ask her. How could he ask her now, as if it were only his money which he was offering her? Oh, what the Hell did money matter? Of course it mattered. Or was it age that mattered? He was an old man, she was a child; no, it was she who had lived for ever, and he who knew nothing. Oh Sylvia, Sylvia, the unattainable, if I could just be near you, if I could just look at you for ever, I should be content!

He tried to imagine himself married to her. No good. It brought her down to earth. She was Mrs Wellard in a flat; Mrs Wellard at Biarritz; Mrs Wellard at home in her drawingroom. Wherever he put her, it was wrong. Wherever he put her, he was taking something from the fragrant untouched Sylvia of his dream.

And then he found Westaways. Westaways —the complement of Sylvia. Sylvia and Westaways. Westaways and Sylvia. The two most lovely things in the world. That was her home. That was where she should be. It had been waiting for Sylvia. She had been waiting for Westaways. Now he would offer it to her, and, humbly, himself with it.

So Sylvia came to Westaways . . . as she would have come anywhere to Reginald, had he but known it.

II

So it was that Reginald sat opposite to Sylvia at Westaways, and read the evening paper in the intervals of breakfast. So it was that the name Wellard leapt out at him from an advertisement.

THE BOOK OF THE WEEK

> *BINDWEED* by Reginald Wellard.

THE NOVEL OF THE YEAR

> *BINDWEED* by Reginald Wellard.

THE ACHIEVEMENT OF THE CENTURY

> *BINDWEED* by Reginald Wellard.

'Hallo!' said Reginald, and went suddenly red at this indecent exposure of himself.

'What is it, darling?'

. 'Nothing.'

What had happened? Why had Pump burst out like this?

He turned over again his unopened letters. All ha'pennies. Nothing from Pump. Nothing from anybody. Bills, receipts, advertisements. The National Press-cutting Agency—that wasn't his. One of the many others who wanted his custom. He opened it idly, and found a sample cutting inside.

THE BOOK OF THE WEEK

REVIEWED BY AMBROSE RAGLAN

BINDWEED, by REGINALD WELLARD

(Pumps Limited, 7s. 6d.)

Raglan!

He glanced across at Sylvia to make sure that he was alone. She was miles away, a cat on her lap, her eyes out of the window, her thoughts—where? He had Raglan to himself. He was alone with Raglan, listening to his praise. . . . He read, slowly . . .

Ah! He gave a long sigh of relief. So his book was as good as that. After breakfast he would read *Bindweed* again—as Raglan must have read it.

A pity they had put that stupid photograph of him in the middle. 'A recent study of Mr Reginald Wellard, whose book is reviewed by Mr Ambrose Raglan'—taken on leave, ten years ago! Where did they get it from? How did they get it? People in London talking about him, asking where they could get his photograph, ringing up photographers. 'Willard—no, *Wellard.*'

He looked across at Sylvia, guiltily. Oh, Sylvia, darling, do say the right thing! Do understand how I feel! But how can you? Oh, well, I love you anyhow. I wouldn't have you different. You'll have to see it. Here goes.

'Look here, Sylvia,' he said with a little laugh. 'Here's fame!' He passed the cutting across to her.

Sylvia took it, wrinkled her adorable nose at it, frowned.

'But, darling, this isn't *you!*'

'What? Oh, the photograph.' Of course she would notice that, think only of that. . . . Well, what wife wouldn't? It was the natural thing for anybody to say who knew him. He kept the disappointment out of his voice.

'Oh, *that*! I suppose I looked like that once.'

'But you never had a moustache!'

'Well, of course I had one in the Army. That was taken in 1917, when I was on leave.'

'Oh, before I knew you,' said Sylvia, dismissing the moustache, as she had always dismissed the ante-Sylvia Reginald. To her, life began for both of them on the day that they met. All that had gone to the making of him was nothing. He sprang, complete, into her arms.

'Ambrose Raglan is supposed to be rather a fellow,' said Reginald, as carelessly as he could manage.

'Who?' she asked, still looking from the photograph to the original. 'Darling, you are much better-looking now. Ought they to use an old photograph like this without your permission?'

'Well, I suppose they were in a hurry, and it was all they could get.'

'But they could easily have waited a week and written to you. That one you had taken last year—with your chin in your hand—I loved that.'

Waited a week! Oh, Sylvia, Sylvia! I have been waiting all these weeks for some real notice of my book, and now, when at last it comes, you carelessly suggest waiting another week, just because of a silly photograph. Sweetheart, don't you understand?

'I hate to think of thousands of people seeing it, and thinking that you really look like that.'

'Oh, what does it matter?' he thinks.

Aloud he says, 'What seems more important to me is that thousands of people should read it, and think that I really wrote a book like that.' Had he made that sound unkind? No. But to take the unkindness, if there were any, away, he added with a laugh, 'Nobody buys books because of an author's face. They say that a notice like that, by Raglan, always sells thousands of copies.'

Now she is reading it. Noiselessly he helps himself to marmalade. Noiselessly he goes on with his breakfast. Not a sound. . . .

She looks up at him.

'He likes it, doesn't he?' she says.

He begins to breathe naturally again.

'Yes, he seems pretty keen.' He gives a little deprecatory laugh. 'Particularly about Chapter Five.'

'I wonder why he liked that so particularly.'

Reginald knows. Raglan knows. It seems that Sylvia will never know.

'I rather liked it myself,' he says.

'I loved it all,' said Sylvia seriously. 'But then, of course, I'm prejudiced.'

Funny darling Sylvia. But they are over the worst of it now, and can exchange banalities in a friendly way.

'You see,' said Reginald, 'that's what makes it so jolly getting a notice like this from a man like Raglan. You know that he *isn't* prejudiced.'

She nods with interest and understanding.

'And just because he isn't prejudiced, people take his advice about books. They know it really is his opinion.'

'Yes, I see,' she says with her adorable little frown.

He goes on to explain what a great man Ambrose Raglan is. 'I expect that notice'— he indicates it with a careless knife—'will make thousands of people order the book at once.'

'Fancy! Thousands! Darling, it *is* clever of you. I *am* proud.'

'Are you?' he asked, with a loving smile.

She nodded.

'I like to think of them all talking about you, and knowing you're mine.' She looked at him for a long moment, and dropped her eyes.

He loved her. He held out his hand to her across the table. She misunderstood him, and passed the cutting back, her thoughts far away. But the photograph caught her eye again, and she said:

'Do you know Mr Raglan, I mean personally?'

Now it was his turn to misunderstand, and he said hastily, to reassure himself as much as her, that, though they *had* just met once, for five minutes, there was no reason whatever why Raglan should——

'That's all right,' said Sylvia, nodding contentedly. 'Then he *does* know what you look like.'

III

Reginald took *Bindweed* and Raglan into his office, meaning to have a good morning with them. Sylvia had disappeared kitchenwards. He opened *Bindweed*, and read this:

'To Sylvia, who has entwined herself in my heart'

She was talking to Mrs Hosken. Through his open window he could hear the murmur of voices coming across the court-yard.

He picked up a pencil and wrote idly on a piece of paper.

Things Sylvia can do better than me.

Remembering Raglan, and his own position now in the world of letters, he put a line through 'me' and wrote 'I'.

1. She is supremely lovely. I am not. [NOTE.—If God gave her beauty and withheld it from me, He also gave me imagination, intelligence and all the other qualities on which I pride myself, and withheld them from Sylvia. If He did. And if I pride myself on having cultivated whatever qualities He gave me, has not Sylvia cultivated her beauty?]

2. She can drive a car, and play lawn-tennis and golf with a careless and beautiful efficiency. I do these things with a painstaking incompetence which she bears unflinchingly.

3. She does incredible things with a needle.

4. Animals adore her. [NOTE.—John Wesley likes *me*. Anyway there's not much in this, because if it's a question which of us is the more lovable, I retire altogether.]

5. She runs the house surpassingly well. I can't run anything. Both Challinor and Edwards have me in their pocket, and know it.

He read this through, added '6. I am a cad', put his pencil through the whole thing from north-east to south-west, and again from north-west to south-east, put a thick line across every line separately, tore the paper into sixty-four pieces, and dropped them into the waste-paper-basket. The murmur of voices still came through the open window.

How did she do it—run the house so well? It was an outrage that she should have to go into a hot kitchen just after breakfast, and talk about steak-and-kidney pudding. Did she? Perhaps she didn't. Perhaps she just looked steak-and-kidney pudding, and Mrs Hosken knew. Perhaps she just thought it, and the thought passed into Mrs Hosken's mind. Perhaps she didn't even think it—for he didn't like to think of her thinking anything so unbeautiful, particularly just after breakfast—perhaps she only thought 'violets', and Mrs Hosken, admirable woman, decoded the thought into kidneys. Was it so that the house was run, beautifully, efficiently, quietly?

Reginald had a childish love for the competence of his house. He turned on a tap in the bathroom and hot water came out. He watched it, and, metaphorically, threw out a hand and said, 'There you are!' No doubt hot water came out of other hot-water taps in other houses, but, looking at the mistress of the house, you were not surprised. Looking at Sylvia, you asked yourself how she did it? Coal, coke, anthracite, firewood, a stove to be lit, a stove to be lit by somebody at some definite time, a man to be called in if anything went wrong—all this was in Sylvia's lovely hands. She thought 'lavender', and another half-ton of coke hurried into the shed.

He walked into the sitting-room, and there on a shelf were four pipes and an unopened tin of tobacco. There was always an unopened tin of tobacco there. He opened the tin, and filled his pouch. Now you watch. In half an hour there will be a new tin there. Sylvia? Of course. Where does the tobacco come from? They don't sell this tobacco in the village. Where does the coke come from? Heaven knows.

He went upstairs for a handkerchief. He went through Sylvia's room, with so much of Sylvia in it, into his dressing-room. Handkerchiefs. Yesterday he had been looking for that blue tie and had found it (after a five-minutes' convulsion had passed over the chest of drawers) in his trouser pocket. Now all was peace again. He withdrew a handkerchief from its neat pile beneath a sprig of lavender, and went downstairs. On his way he opened the linen-cupboard. Clean clothes airing. Sylvia's pretty things. More coke.

What on earth did he want from Sylvia which she didn't give him? Intellectual companionship? Help!

Can any one give a man intellectual companionship? Can any other man take his thoughts down your road, hand in hand, his mind ready to diverge with yours, hither or thither, without warning, without question, two minds that think as one? Impossible, surely. Wasn't the whole joy of thinking, and, as he had just discovered, of writing, that you were quite, quite alone? Wasn't talk, intellectual talk as differing from chatter, really just a form of vanity? You wanted a listener, not a talker. Well, if you wrote a book, you had your listeners.

It was this confounded book which had made him suddenly critical of Sylvia. From the day, he thought, when I began to write it, and she must have wondered what I was doing, and she seemed to take no interest. From the day when I told her I had written it, and she said 'Fancy!' I suppose I'm touchy. Is a mother touchy about her child? Or, whatever it looks like, whatever its nature, does she feel an absolute assurance in her heart that it is perfect? One is touchy because one is uncertain, because one wants reassurance. Surely Shakespeare must have felt pretty certain about *A Midsummer Night's Dream*? Surely Keats wanted nobody to tell him that the *Nightingale* was good? Or is one always—well, I'm not really a writer, so I don't know.

But, Sylvia, you do understand, don't you, that this is my child? It is growing up suddenly. I don't know what will happen, except that I shall never have another. It is my only child. Oh, Sylvia, be tender to it. . . .

And now let's read Raglan again. Anyhow, Raglan likes it.

Chapter Six

I

The Baxters were giving a party at Seven Streams. No, that is to make too much of it. At Mallows it would undoubtedly have been a party. There would have been talk, preparations, more talk, decisions made, decisions revoked; more talk, and a sudden dash into Burdon by Hildersham, with additional instructions shouted to him as he turned out of the gate; a last-minute wonder whether a new net could be got down from London in time, a last-minute attempt to mend some of the gaps in the old net. But at Seven Streams one didn't behave like this. One just asked a few friends up to tennis, and hoped that Sylvia would manage to bring that delightful husband of hers.

Seven Streams was so called that the postman might know where to deliver the letters. It stood on a small hill, and Betty had persuaded herself, and apparently some of her friends, that seven underground streams flowed from the depths of the hill into seven different counties. Wasn't it odd, dear—she had not known about these streams when Bertie had bought the site and started to build. Seven Streams was just her idea of rather an amusing name for a house, so rural. And then when she began to make inquiries, it really seemed that the place was quite historical! The Romans, you know; all *that* time. And these underground streams having been there for *centuries*! Really *much* older than Westaways. . . .

However, the house was newer. It was half-tiled, the tiles being of that penetrating and indestructible red for which builders have been looking for so long. It had large white balconies outside the upstairs windows. It had large plateglass windows in the principal ground-floor rooms. It had glass-houses visibly disposed over the garden so that the peaches were always in sight. It had innumerable white-fronted gables. It had gutters and rain-pipes of a rich chocolate colour. In short (thought Reginald) the whole thing had escaped from Surrey when some stockbroker's back was turned, and was perfectly foul. Luckily it was ten miles away.

'I told Betty I couldn't be certain about you, naturally,' said Sylvia, 'but you will come, won't you, darling?'

'I hate Seven Goldfish Bowls,' said Reginald. 'I never know what to say to Baxter between 'How are you?' and 'Goodbye'. Betty maddens me and I want to brain her, and I play tennis abominably. For all of which reasons, and not because I love you, I will come with you on Saturday.'

'Darling! It won't be so bad when we're there.'

'It will be much much worse. At least let me feel that I am a martyr.'

'Betty always brings one or two interesting people down with her for the week-end. I expect they'll want to talk to you about your book.'

Reginald thought: 'I wish you wouldn't say *your* book. It's got a name. Bindweed. And if you don't like the name, sweetheart, say "the book"'. Aloud he said, 'There are no interesting people in London. The half-dozen portentous asses from whom she has delivered their friends for three short days will talk about themselves. I last saw my racquet in the apple-loft. That day I was killing wasps with it. Is it still there, do you think?'

'I'll find it, darling.'

So on Saturday he put on a pair of white flannel trousers, which he had forgotten about, and a pair of tennis shoes, which had mysteriously become white; and he came downstairs again, and found Sylvia in the hall with two racquets.

'That's yours,' she said, putting one in his hand.

Reginald gave it the merest glance and handed it back to her.

'This is a real racquet, darling. Mine was a cross between a harp and a landing-net.'

'Well, it's got your name on,' said Sylvia.

He looked. It had.

'A little present for you,' she said, going pink.

Reginald contemplated her with his head on one side.

'I suppose', he said, 'if I took you in my arms and kissed you violently six times, I should disarrange something?'

'Yes,' said Sylvia, 'but I shouldn't mind. I can go upstairs again.'

'Swear you'll look as perfect as you do now?'

She nodded seriously.

'You *are* a darling,' he cried, and took her in his arms.

So far the party was a success.

They came to Seven Streams. They abandoned the car, and followed a butler through the house to the lawns at the back. Betty, surrounded by a green tennis-court, a red tennis-court and several friends, was waiting for them.

'So you dragged him from his beloved Westaways,' she said to Sylvia. 'Such an amusing place,' she added to one of the friends. 'You must get Mr Wellard to tell you all about it. Darling, you *are* looking lovely. Doesn't she look sweet, Bertie? Colonel Rudge, do you know Mr Reginald Wellard? He's just written such a delightful book. Every one's talking about it.'

The Colonel, who had been hoping, as soon as he saw Sylvia, to get her into a corner and tell her all about India, said 'How do' unenthusiastically to Reginald.

'Well,' said Baxter, 'what about getting a game started? You'll play, Colonel?'

The Colonel thought that some of the younger ones had better show their paces first.

One of the younger ones, on being suddenly accosted, said modestly that he was ready to play if wanted, but on the other hand, quite ready to sit out if he was not wanted. And he was afraid that he wasn't much good.

Everybody else said at once that he (or she) was absolutely hopeless.

There are, of course, degrees of hopelessness. Nobody knew whether the other man's hopelessness was more or less hopeless than his own.

'I expect you're very good *really*,' said Betty to a tall young man in glasses, who had been particularly despairing of himself.

'I'm not really, Mrs Baxter,' he protested. 'At Eastbourne last year——'

Nobody waited to hear what had happened at Eastbourne last year. Anybody who could talk about Eastbourne at all like that was using a different language from theirs when he said he was hopeless. 'Hopeless to expect to take a set off Tilden' was what he meant.

'Sylvia, darling,' said Betty, feeling that the time for action had come, 'suppose *you* play with Mr Palliser—Mrs Wellard'—a stoutish young man bowed to Sylvia—'and Margery—Mr Cobb, do you know Mrs Arkwright?'—the tall young man from Eastbourne said No, he didn't, How do you do?—'you play with Mr Cobb. There! We'll get up another set directly. Now let's sit down comfortably and enjoy ourselves. I expect Mr Cobb is very good.'

Mr Cobb was very good. Mrs Arkwright said 'Yours' and 'Sorry' at intervals, but did not otherwise take much part in the game. Mr Palliser said 'Mine' and 'Sorry' at intervals, until the score was four-love against them, and thereafter 'Yours' and 'Oh, well *played,* partner' until it was four-all. Reginald, his hat over his eyes, lay back and watched Sylvia happily.

'Fella in the Sixtieth out in India with me wrote a book,' said Colonel Rudge suddenly.

'Oh?' said Reginald.

'Fact,' said the Colonel. 'Fella in the Sixtieth.'

Reginald waited for the rest of the story, but it seemed that that was all. The Colonel was simply noting the coincidence of somebody over here writing a book and somebody in India also writing a book.

How easily Sylvia moved! How unhurried she always seemed! She was not really in the Eastbourne class, perhaps, but she had this natural gift of effortless physical expression. Timing, he supposed.

'Tranter, that was the fella,' came from his right. 'Expect you know him.'

Reginald woke and said that he was afraid he didn't. (Why 'afraid', he wondered. Afraid of what?)

'Well, he wrote a book,' said the Colonel stubbornly. 'Forget what it was called.'

Four-all. Sylvia was serving. 'Sorry,' said Mrs Arkwright. (*Fifteen-love.*) 'Sorry,' said Mr Palliser. (*Fifteen-all.*) 'Sorry,' said Mrs Arkwright. (*Thirty-fifteen*) 'Sorry,' said Mr Palliser. (*Thirty-all.*) 'Sorry,' said Mrs Arkwright. (*Forty-thirty.*) '*Yours!*' shouted Mr Palliser. 'Oh, well *played!*' 'Very sorry,' said Mrs Arkwright. (*Game.*)

'What d'you say *your* book was called?' said the Colonel, evidently hoping that this would give a clue to the title of Tranter's book.

'Bindweed,' grunted Reginald, feeling suddenly ashamed of it.

'What?'

'*Bindweed!*' (What the devil does it matter, he thought angrily.)

'Ah! . . . No, that wasn't it.'

Five-all. Mr Cobb has been doing wonderful Eastbourne things at the net.

'Bindweed,' said Colonel Rudge, pulling at his moustache. 'That's that stuff that climbs up things, what? Gets all over the garden.'

'Yes.'

'Thought so.'

Mr Palliser had found a service at last. . . . Oh, well played, darling. . . . The wretched Palliser will dream about you tonight, and, realizing that he may never see you again, blow his brains out in the morning. Think of all the men in the world not married to Sylvia. Poor devils.

'Sort of gardening book, what?' said Colonel Rudge.

'What? . . . Oh . . . No.'

'It is the stuff I mean, isn't it?'

'What is?'

'The what-d'you-call-it.'

'Is what?'

'What I said. Climbs up things. Gets all over the garden?'

'Oh yes, yes. Always!'

'What d'you say it was called? This stuff?'

'Bindweed.'

'Yes. And what d'you say your book was called?'

'Bindweed.'

'That's right,' said the Colonel fretfully. 'That's what I said.'

This, thought Reginald, is one of the interesting people brought down from London who want to talk to me about my book.

'This fella', thought the Colonel, 'doesn't seem to know what his own book's called. What's the matter with him?'

Six-all. Sylvia's service again. You do look lovely serving, darling. That poor devil Palliser will have to shoot himself tonight.

'This fella Tranter was always a bit queer. Not sure it wasn't poetry he wrote. I know it wasn't gardens. Expect you know a good deal about 'em, don't you?'

Seven-six. Well done, Sylvia.

'About what?'

'Gardens.' (Dammit, the fella's a fool.)

'I'm very keen on my own. I don't know much about it really.'

'Ah! Then it isn't what you'd call a textbook?'

'No.'

Double-fault from Mrs Arkwright. Unplayable return from Sylvia. *Love-thirty.* Now you've got them, darling.

'I know the fella who is really the fella who wrote *Field Service Regulations.* At least I used to know him. S'pose you never came across him?'

'No.'

'That wasn't Tranter, of course,' explained the Colonel carefully. 'Tranter wrote this book I was telling you about, and then left the service. That was in 'eighty-five. I did hear he got married, but I never heard whether it was true or not.'

'Really?' said Reginald.

'Funny you never ran into him.'

Palliser has gone berserk suddenly. He is at the net, everywhere. Sylvia, at the back of the court, is leaning on her racquet, laughing. Palliser smashing, Cobb returning smashes, Palliser tying himself into knots, but getting the ball over somehow, Cobb brushing his partner out of the way and trying to kill Palliser, Mrs Arkwright scuttling out of the way and bleating 'Yours', Sylvia still leaning on her racquet and laughing, a last smash from Palliser, a last heroic return from Eastbourne, a lob, 'Too good' from Eastbourne, game, set, apologies, congratulations, modesty, mock-modesty, thanks, retirement of the gladiators.

'Well done,' said Betty. 'Aren't you all very hot? Mr Cobb, there are drinks just over there, if you—or would you rather wait for tea, dear?'

Mrs Arkwright decided to wait. Mr Palliser insisted on giving Mrs Wellard a drink. They went off together. For ever, Palliser hoped. When another set had been arranged, Reginald found himself between Mrs Arkwright and his hostess.

'Well,' said Betty proudly, 'I've got your book.'

'Oh?' (The first copy known to have been sold, other than to himself. Or perhaps only borrowed?)

She leant across to Mrs Arkwright.

'Mr Wellard has written such a delightful book, all about all of us down here.'

Reginald opened his mouth to protest indignantly, but they had forgotten him.

'Oh?' said Mrs Arkwright. 'How amusing!'

'He was a little naughty about Bertie, I thought, but I've forgiven him because it was *so* clever. *And* true.'

'Oh, is Bertie in it?'

'Oh, my dear, we're all in it. You remember Grace Hildersham, don't you? That large fair woman who came to dinner when you were down in the spring.'

'Is *she* in it?'

'*Is* she! Mr Wellard was *very* naughty about *her*. But *so* amusing!'

'I must get it.'

'Oh, you must. Of course, not knowing all the people will spoil it for you a little——'

'Oh, but I know you and Bertie and Grace Hildersham and ——!'

'Let me think. Anybody else? Oh, yes, the last time you were down, do you remember coming into Burdon with me to try and get some liqueur chocolates——'

'Yes, yes, of course.'

'And on the way we passed a farm and I said, "That's Redding Farm, where the Colebys live" ——'

'Y-yes, I think I do.'

'And I told you about Lena Coleby, and what people were saying ——'

'I don't think so, darling.'

'No, perhaps it was—well, anyhow, *she's* in it.'

'I *must* get it,' said Mrs Arkwright. She looked curiously at the man across whom they had been talking. 'What a gift it must be!' she said. 'How *do* you do it?'

Books oughtn't to be published, thought Reginald. They ought to be written, and then one copy ought to be beautifully printed—no, two—one for the author and one for the author's wife, if he loved her, and the two copies should be kept in a very secret place, and only discovered there a hundred years after they were dead. And, meanwhile, any woman called Baxter and any women called Arkwright should be made to walk from the Mansion House to Hyde Park Corner, (stands having been erected along the route) wearing only a red chest-protector and a pair of football boots. Probably they wouldn't mind, damn them, but if they did, they would then have some faint idea of what indecent exposure meant to a sensitive person. . . .

A butler inclined his portliness towards Madam. Tea was served.

'Shall we go in?' said Betty. 'The tennis players can come when they're ready. Where is your lovely wife, Mr Wellard?'

The only bearable thing about Betty Baxter, thought Reginald, is that she knows Sylvia is beautiful.

He followed her in to tea. The party was now definitely a failure.

II

After tea Reginald had his heart's desire. He played one set with Sylvia as his partner. The casual intimacy of the lawn-tennis-court, such as is shared by any two players, became the more casual, the more delightful because of that much greater intimacy, shared in secret, which was always in their thoughts. Here am I, Reginald Wellard, just introduced to this lovely young woman. For the moment our hearts are set on the same thing; we have but one life which we live together; our hopes, our fears, our aspirations the same; she and I together against the world. But alas! for so short a time. In half an hour we are separated, and I shall never see her again. . . . And then for a moment their eyes meet. They smile at each other shyly. He will see her again.

Does she love playing with him as much as he loves it? He will never know. How can he possibly know? Perhaps, when she has prepared the way for the winning stroke, and he hits the ball feebly into the net, she feels as he feels, when he has prepared the way for a joke, and she smiles it innocently away. How fair, but how horrible, if she did! Well, he won't give her the chance, he will play brilliantly today. . . . He played brilliantly.

'I just loved that,' he said to her, when they had won.

'So did I, darling,' said Sylvia.

Later he was watching her again, Lena Coleby, an unexpected arrival, by his side.

'I couldn't come before, you know how it is, but I felt I must just look in,' she had explained to her hostess.

'Of course, dear. You know Mr Wellard. Talk to him, won't you? He looks so lonely.'

If Betty Baxter were introducing the latest murderer to the Archbishop of Canterbury, she would assume that they knew each other already, and if she were introducing the Archbishop to his wife, she would feel it necessary to record the assumption.

'Hallo!' said Reginald, as she dropped into a deck-chair by his side.

'I do just know you, don't I?' said Lena, 'and you aren't really lonely, are you?'

'Yes. No,' said Reginald.

They talked idly for a little, and then were silent, watching Sylvia.

'Yes,' said Lena with a sigh, 'she is, isn't she?'

'What?'

'The most beautiful woman in the world.'

Reginald looked round at her with a selfconscious smile.

'Did you know I was thinking that?'

'Of course.'

'I wasn't. Not beautiful. That isn't the word. That means something terrific, don't you think? Like Cleopatra.'

'Sorry. I don't know why I said beautiful. It was stupid of me. Utterly lovely.'

'Yes.'

They were silent again. Then Lena said:

'Isn't love funny?'

'Very,' said Reginald, for that was just what he was thinking.

'Could you have a marriage of intellects? A happy marriage?'

'It's generally supposed to be the only happy marriage, isn't it? The only lasting one.'

'Is it? It isn't true.'

'No. It couldn't be.'

'Why couldn't it be?'

'I've been wondering. I think, to be perfectly happy, you've got to be reaching out to something above you. Well, that's a truism, of course.'

'Why not to an intellect above you?'

'Exactly. But then the other one in the partnership is not reaching out. He, or she, is condescending.'

'You mean,' said Lena, preferring to have this in a less abstract form, 'a man could only be intellectually happy with a woman cleverer than himself, and she could only be happy with a man cleverer than herself, so they could never both be happy together.'

'That's the idea. Like all my ideas probably wrong. It's a tremendous business, married life, and I don't see how it can be done on a purely intellectual basis.'

'Two minds that beat as one,' murmured Lena.

'Rubbish. How could they?'

'What on, then? A purely physical basis?'

Reginald laughed.

'Of course that sounds hopeless, put like that.'

'Put it less hopelessly.'

'All right.' He thought for a moment. 'A happy marriage is best founded on a spiritual appreciation of physical qualities.'

'Yes, that certainly sounds better,' smiled Lena.

'The point is that physically men and women don't compete. Each can look up to the other. Admire the other.'

'We haven't all got Sylvias to admire.'

'You've got Tom,' said Reginald.

'In the same class—sex for sex?'

Reginald wasn't going to admit that.

'Ah, but that's the beauty of it,' he said quickly. 'There are no classes in physical attraction. It's subjective, not objective. The attraction may be no more than a lisp, which the rest of the world thinks affected, a dimple, a turn of the head, a pair of hands——'

Now, inevitably, they were both looking at hers, her left hand holding the fingers of her right as it drooped out of her lap.

'That can go on attracting for ever?' she said, colouring faintly.

'Well, that's love. Being attracted for ever.'

Lena was silent, twisting her wedding-ring round and round her finger.

'Tom is awfully good-looking, don't you think?' she said aloud, following up her thoughts.

'Oh, rather! But then I'm attracted by his mental qualities too.'

'Oh?' said Lena, raising her eyebrows. She thought for a moment and then said, 'Oh, well, I'm generally too tired in the evening to notice them.'

Reginald laughed.

'Try noticing them at breakfast.'

'My dear man, do you know *when* we have breakfast?'

'Sorry. Don't tell me. I couldn't bear it.'

'Gosh!' cried Lena suddenly and startlingly, 'it is a relief to talk to *you.*'

'How tired you'd get of it!'

'I wonder.' She gave him a sideways glance, and then looked back at Sylvia; hesitated, and said, 'Speaking as a cad, do *you* ever feel——' But stopped in time.

'What?' said Reginald stolidly.

'Oh, my dear Mr—— Do I call you Reginald? I forget.'

'You might try.'

'Then, my dear Reginald, don't say "What?" when you know perfectly well what I shied at saying.'

'That I like talking to you? Yes, I do.'

'It wasn't that.'

'That I have enjoyed my afternoon more than I thought I was going to? Yes. Much more.'

'It wasn't that, either.'

'I know it wasn't.'

'Of course you do. That's why I like talking to you.'

But still he hadn't answered her question. And now he seemed to be changing the subject.

'Do you like Westaways?' he asked, putting another match to his pipe.

'Who doesn't? You know how I feel. I'm utterly in love with it.'

'So am I,' said Reginald. He blew out his match, and pushed it into the ground by the side of his chair. 'Utterly.'

Lena gave him another sideways glance. She could see that he was conscious of her, though his eyes were on Sylvia. 'Do you ever feel that it is a relief to talk to somebody intelligent like me?' had been her question. His answer seemed to be, 'I adore Westaways, and Westaways doesn't talk at all.' Not quite an answer really.

'Well, I adore Tom,' said Lena firmly.

'That's good,' said Reginald.

III

The party had now definitely been a success. As they drove home Sylvia said:

'Did Lena tell you how much she liked your book?'

'No,' said Reginald, sitting up with a jerk, and then pulling the Morris back into safety. 'I didn't know she'd read it.'

'Oh, yes, she simply loves it, she told me.'

Funny, that. Why had she said nothing about it to him?

He tried to imagine her reading it. How much had she understood, guessed, imagined? He began to go through the book in his mind, putting himself into Lena's mind. . . .

'Tired, darling?'

Sylvia always thought he was tired when he was silent.

'Good Heavens, no. I've done nothing. You must be.'

'Not a bit really. All right after a bath, anyway.'

'I loved playing with you.'

'Did you, darling? So did I.'

'I wasn't so bad, was I?' he asked humbly.

'Of course you weren't, darling. You never are.'

His thoughts went back to his book. After dinner he would just glance through it again. He had never thought of it as being read by Lena. . . .

Chapter Seven

I

It was now time to get one's hair cut again. 'Anything you want in London?' asked Reginald at breakfast.

'I ought to have my hair done too,' said Sylvia, looking across at his. 'Darling, you must *not*.' This was to Grandmamma on her lap, stretching her claws a little forgetfully.

'Come with me,' said Reginald eagerly, and immediately repented of the eagerness . . . and immediately felt ashamed of the repentance. But today, surely, there would be news in London. All London, according to Mr Pump, was talking of his book; talking in a language which Sylvia would not understand. Let him have London to himself, just for today.

'I should have to make an appointment,' she said, 'and I promised to lunch with Margaret next time I came. I'll go by myself one day next week, and you can meet me.'

'I should love to,' said Reginald gladly. 'What about the car today? Will you want it? Say Yes, and then you'll have to take me to the train.'

She shook her head with a smile.

'If you come by the 3.10, I'll walk to the station.'

'Sweetheart, it's much too far, and much too hot for you.'

'I don't say I'll come all the way. You'll have to look out for me.' She blushed a little and said, 'I love meeting you.'

'So do I,' he agreed. 'I think more than anything else in the world.'

So it was arranged; and so, later in the morning, he found

himself for a moment at the Victoria bookstall again, a bookstall draped now in *Bindweed*.

'Read this, sir?' said the clerk, pushing a copy at him.

'Yes.'

They ought to have had a long conversation about the book, but they didn't. The clerk didn't seem to want to.

'Read *this*?' he asked, pushing forward an inferior work by an inferior writer.

'Well, as a matter of fact,' said Reginald, drifting away, 'I— er——' He lingered out of sight of the clock, watching the next victim. This was a stout young woman, who hesitated for a long time between *Bindweed* and *Weldon's Home Dressmaker*, and finally decided to make dresses at home.

He would have his hair cut first. Mr Alderson was as glad as ever to see him, as surprised as ever to hear that he wanted his hair cut, as doubtful as ever if the thing could be managed in his shop. These usual preliminaries over, Reginald settled down comfortably to the lullaby of Mr Alderson's scissors.

'And how is the country looking, sir?' asked Mr Alderson, in case Reginald felt talkative. It was his usual opening with country clients, and gave them illimitable opportunities of speech or silence, as they wished. Reginald's grunt left him uncertain how the country was looking, but assured of Reginald's feelings. He snipped on quietly. . . .

Reginald wondered suddenly if he had read *Bindweed*, smiled at the thought, and decided to ask him.

'Ever heard of a book called *Bindweed*?'

'No, sir,' said Mr Alderson. 'I am not what you would call much of a reader. But Mrs Alderson indulges in the habit frequently, and is always glad to hear of a book. What did you say was its name, sir?'

'*Bindweed*.'

'Ah! And suitable, you would say, for——Mrs Alderson does not care about anything racy.'

'No, it isn't racy,' said Reginald, smiling down at his inverted surplice.

'I will recommend it to her. Who is the author, if I might ask, sir? That sometimes helps in obtaining a book.'

Reginald hadn't expected this, and began to feel uncomfortable. With a carefully careless laugh he confessed that as a matter of fact—er —he was.

'Really, sir?' The scissors snipped thoughtfully. 'I shall give myself the pleasure of recommending it to Mrs Alderson.' (Snip, snip.) 'Did you ever hear of a Mr Walter Besant who was a writer? Afterwards he was knighted for his books, and became Sir Walter Besant'

'Oh, rather!'

'*He* used to come here a good deal.'

'Really?'

'Oh yes, sir. Many a time we have trimmed Sir Walter's hair for him. He used to write books with a Mr Rice. Now that strikes me as a funny thing, sir. Two men writing a book together. You wouldn't have thought it was possible. I did venture to inquire of him once how he did it. His reply, humorously given, of course, was that he used a thick nib and Mr Rice used a fine one. A gentleman told me once that Sir Walter had worked this little piece of humour into one of his books afterwards, but I never came across it myself.'

'That must have been a very long time ago. I mean, I shouldn't have thought——'

'Ah well, sir, it was of course my father who attended to Sir Walter mostly. I was a very young man at the time.'

'Oh, I see.'

'We have some curious gentlemen in here,' he went on in his quiet voice. 'There was a young gentleman came in once, an old customer, very smartly dressed he was, this time, with a pink carnation in his buttonhole, and he asked me for a shave, and when I had shaved him, he wanted his hair trimmed, and then a shampoo, and when I had dried his hair and left him for a moment, I saw him holding his hands up and looking at them, so I looked at them, and said, "Well, you don't want a manicure, Mr Tallow," —that was his name, a curious name—and he said, "I was wondering"—beautiful kept hands they were—"I was wondering," he said. "No, I think they'll do." Well, when I'd finished with him, he got up and went to the basin, I can see him now, standing there, his mind on something else, and he'd turned on the tap, and he was standing there letting the water run over his fingers, and he had this carnation in his left hand, and he was flicking the water on to it from his fingers to freshen it up. And then he put it back in his buttonhole, and fixed himself up in the glass, and said "Well, goodbye, Alderson, pray for me," and I said "Good luck, sir," not knowing of course what he was after, and he went out. That was in the morning, and in the evening paper that night I saw that they'd found his body. Shot through the head.'

'Good God!' burst out from Reginald.

'Yes, sir. I never knew which way it was. Sometimes I've thought he was getting himself up that way to meet his lady, and she'd refused him, and then sometimes I've thought that he'd dressed himself up, if you'll excuse me, sir, to meet his God. Poor young gentleman.'

'Didn't anything come out at the inquest?'

'No, sir. If there was a lady, she didn't come forward. Mrs Alderson and I were very unhappy for a time, thinking of him; and then the war came, and now I say, "Well, even if he had lived, he would have been killed in the war," and it doesn't seem so bad. There, sir, how's that?'

Reginald walked the short distance to his club, thinking to himself, I suppose there are a million people in London who could tell you a story like that; the one supremely tragic or beautiful or funny thing which has happened to them. How silly to write a made-up book!

II

How silly not to write a book!

'Morning, Wellard. Congratulations.'

'Oh, thanks.' . . .

'Morning, Wellard. I say, I suppose it *is* you, isn't it? I didn't know you went in for that sort of thing.'

'Must do something.'

'Well, you seem to have done it all right.' . . .

'Morning, Wellard. Congratulations.'

'Oh, thanks.'

'Matter of fact I'd read it long before old Raglan got hold of it. I meant to have written to you about it.'

'That's very kind of you,' said Reginald. To himself he thought, It isn't a bit kind. Anybody can mean to do a thing and not do it. It would have been kind if you *had* written. I should never have forgotten it.

'Morning, Wellard. How's it going?'

'Oh, pretty well.'

'That's good. I thought you'd be fairly safe, once Raglan fell for it. I've been telling him about it for weeks.'

'Oh, really? How nice of you.' . . .

'Hallo, how's the millionaire?'

Reginald laughed. All there was to do.

'I haven't read it yet, but I've got it.'

A pat on the shoulder and a quiet voice, 'Well done. Terribly good.' Reginald turned round quickly, and saw the back of—— Now who was that? Nobody he knew.

'Morning, Wellard. That's an awfully good book of yours.'

'Oh, have you read it?'

'My dear fellow, I should think I was about your first reader. As a matter of fact it was something I said in here which put Raglan on to it.'

'Really. Well, I'm very much obliged to you.'

And so on. He loved it and he hated it. If Reginald Wellard were his son, how proud he would be, standing here invisible, listening to them. There is no praise too extravagant or too insincere for the father or the mother of an adored one. I suppose, he thought, it is because *Bindweed* is my child that I yearn to hear it praised, and because it is really I who am being praised that I feel so uncomfortable. A real father knows how little he is responsible for the child which has come to him.

As he came into the dining-room, there was an imperative snap of the fingers from a table in the window. Wellard looked across.

'Here!' A finger summoned him.

I loathe Ormsby, thought Reginald. I think he's everything that's pernicious. Damned fools talk about eugenics and sterilization and God knows what, and leave Ormsby alive. Anybody feeling as I do about Ormsby would stop for a moment at his table to empty the salad-dressing on his head, and then pass on without a word to the most distant corner of the room. Being what I am, I shall fawn on him and thank him humbly for noticing me.

'Here, Wellard, come and sit here. You know Ambrose Raglan, don't you?'

Reginald and Raglan murmured polite things to each other.

'Well, my boy, feeling grateful to us? No need to. Duty of any one who can influence public opinion to put 'em on to a good thing. Go racing at all? Well, you can trust "The Flag Lieutenant". If he likes a horse, he'll tell you. And if Raglan likes a book, he'll tell you. Eh, old man?'

'Ever written anything before?' asked Raglan.

'No. My first and my last.'

Ormsby, who was making loud salad noises, intercepted them for a moment to say, 'That be damned.'

'Why do you say your last?' asked Raglan.

He looks like a well-bred fox, thought Reginald. What a pair of swindlers they would make.

'I only know a certain amount', he explained, 'and I seem to have used it all. And I don't suppose I shall ever get another idea. That one came by accident.'

'Ever read Dickens?' said Ormsby, waving a fork-full of green-stuff at him.

'Of course.'

Ormsby emptied the fork and munched, 'Like him?'

'Well, of course. Next to Shakespeare, he's——'

'You think that?' said Ormsby eagerly, putting down his knife and fork.

'I do.'

'Runs second to Shakespeare?'

'Yes.'

'What did I tell you?' he said to Raglan. He turned to Reginald. 'Your book reminded me of Dickens.'

'Oh no, Bob,' said Raglan gently.

'It did,' said Ormsby stubbornly, 'and I know what I'm talking about. You can't tell me anything about form, you can't tell me anything about newspaper production, and you can't tell me. anything about Dickens. I'd read every blasted book of Dickens when I was thirteen, Wellard. Bought 'em myself out of three shillings a week.'

'Did you like them?' asked Reginald.

'Well, what the hell do you think I bought 'em for?'

'What I meant was——'

'I've got a colt out of Lovely Lady that's going to beat the world. You wait. And what d'you think I'm going to call him?'

Lovely Lady! That was Sylvia.

'Mr Whiffers. There, that shows you what I think of Dickens.'

Reginald's laugh of assent was not quite good enough.

'Remember Mr Whiffers in *Pickwick*?' demanded Ormsby.

'Well, not for the moment,' confessed Reginald.

'No good asking *you*, Ambrose.'

'I'm afraid not. Who *was* Mr Whiffers?'

'He was employed to look out of the hallwindow as much as possible, in company with another gentleman. That convey anything to you?'

'The swarry?' hazarded Reginald, and received a nod and a friendly smile.

'O' course. You and I are educated men, not like Raglan here.'

'When did you last read *Pickwick*?' asked Raglan.

'Same as I told you, when I was thirteen.'

'Good Heavens, and I thought you took him to bed with you every night.'

'I don't take a book to bed with me,' chuckled Ormsby.

Vulgar beast. Detestable beast. But somehow, likeable beast, thought Reginald.

'And you remember Mr—— What was his name?'

'Whiffers. He'd once had to eat salt butter. Remember that, Wellard? Funny thing, I like salt butter.'

'You remember Mr Whiffers forty years afterwards?'

Ormsby produced another laugh from the salad, and leant confidentially over to Reginald.

'He doesn't understand, poor old Ambrose doesn't. He's the Greatest Living Expert on Literature, and he can tell you exactly when George Colman the Younger invented mustard, but he doesn't know why Dickens is a great man.' He turned back to Raglan. 'That's why, old boy. Because I remember Mr Whiffers. Forty years afterwards.'

'Rubbish. You remember him because he didn't like salt butter, and you do. If there'd been a man in Wellard's book that didn't like salad, you'd be talking about him when you were ninety-three.'

'Well, damn it, that's what I'm telling you. He's like Dickens.'

Absurd to blush when I'm forty-one, but I'm doing it, thought Reginald. To blush at praise from Ormsby!

'Well now, let's get to business. How many copies have you sold?'

Reginald laughed and said that he hadn't the faintest idea.

'You'd better keep an eye on Pump,' said Raglan.

'Now how on earth do I keep an eye on Pump? I live in the country, and come to London about once in three weeks.'

'Pump's a churchwarden,' said Ormsby, 'which means that if there's a legal way of swindling you, he won't ask Mother if he may.'

'Does that only apply to churchwardens?'

'It's a good general rule to apply to any man, but churchwardens bring a holy zeal to the business which leaves nothing on the plate. "Whoever thy hand findeth to do, do him with all thy might" is their motto.'

'Cheer up, Wellard,' smiled Raglan. 'You do get a royalty, I suppose?'

'Oh, yes. Ten per cent.'

'That all? Right through?'

'I think so.'

'Oh, well, you'll get that. Pump isn't going to prison for ten per cent.'

'We'll keep an eye on him for you,' said Ormsby, getting to work with his tooth-pick. 'People are going to buy your book— Raglan and I are seeing to that—and you may as well get the boodle as any blasted unhygienic Pump. Want it?'

Raglan shivered a little. Even after eighteen months. Reginald smiled, and said that he supposed every man wanted money, more or less.

'He does, my boy. Money and women. And one means the other. Give him those two, and let him sock some other man in the eye now and then, and he's perfectly happy.'

Raglan was watching Reginald, and saw him stiffen.

'Whom does Mr Wellard want to—how did you phrase it?— sock in the eye?' he asked gently. 'Our friend Pump?'

'No,' said Reginald slowly. 'Not our friend Pump. Not just at the moment.'

'I thought not,' murmured Raglan, smiling to himself.

Ormsby wasn't listening, being busy with his tooth-pick.

III

Mr Pump was in. Mr Pump would see Mr Wellard. Ah, good afternoon, Mr Wellard. Sit down, won't you? What can I do for you?

Well, what?

Now that he was here, Reginald wondered why he was here. To receive Mr Pump's congratulations was, he supposed, the real reason why he had come. To be flattered, praised, made much of. You could hardly say so to the Other man, if he didn't feel it for himself. Or was it to keep an eye on Mr Pump, as advised by Raglan? All right, he was keeping an eye on Mr Pump. Unfortunately at the moment Mr Pump wasn't faking accounts, forging cheques or taking money from the till. He wasn't even, as far as Reginald could see, counting thirteen as twelve. Just how did one keep an eye on Mr Pump? 'The fact is I came to keep an eye on you.' You see, one couldn't say that.

However, we must say something.

'I happened to be in London today—I don't often come—so I thought I'd just look in.' He gave a self-conscious little laugh and added, 'Just to see how the book was getting on.'

'Ah, yes, the book. Let me see. That would be—er——' He turned over papers on his table as if to refresh his memory.

'*Bindweed*,' explained Reginald.

'*Bindweed*; of course.'

Is there any one more *naïf* than a business man? Never will he lose his ingenuous belief in patter and tricks which would not deceive a child. I suppose, thought Reginald, business men are so stupid that, even when they are successful, they do not know what has brought them success, and dare not give up any of their stale properties lest, so doing, they discard the magic talisman.

For how many years has Mr Pump waited thus to be prompted by the author? *Bindweed*; of course!

'Well, Mr Wellard, you will be glad to hear that *Bindweed* has been doing very nicely, very nicely indeed.' He caressed his benevolent beard. 'It has been a bad season, of course, for publishers, but we have been fortunate. Not a wholly undeserved fortune, Mr Wellard, if I may say so. We have been building up for many years, and now we are reaping the harvest.' He referred, or pretended to refer, to a slip of paper at his elbow. '*Bindweed, A Maid though Married* and *The Surprising Honeymoon* have been our most notable successes, although *The Life Class* has run them close. In fact, really our only disappointment has been *An Island Bride.* It has done well, of course, but not quite what I expected.'

'Oh, yes.' No good leaving it at that. 'Er —just how many copies of *Bindweed* have you sold?'

'*Bindweed?* I haven't got the actual figures here. You will have a full statement, of course, when the time comes, and I think you will be surprised to find how many we have sold. It isn't always easy to get a new book before the public. I could get you the figures, of course, if you care to wait, but——'

Reginald, or, at least, a voice from his chair, hastened to say that it didn't really matter.

'Well, you will see when we send you your cheque along. I think you will find the figures on the cheque more interesting than any I could give you now.' He laughed automatically, and automatically Reginald responded.

'I'm glad it's doing well,' said Reginald. 'Of course Raglan's notice must have helped enormously. It was very lucky to get that.'

'Lucky if you like to put it so,' said Mr Pump, holding his beard firmly in his left hand. 'As it happened, I had called his particular attention to it when sending the book out. It struck me as the sort of book which would appeal to Raglan. One has to consider the class of book, and the appeal it makes.'

'So that's how it was. I wondered.'

'And when are we to have your new book?'

'New book?' said Reginald, startled by the idea. 'I'm not writing another.'

'Oh come, Mr Wellard,' said Mr Pump, shaking the end of his beard at him waggishly, 'you can't let your public down like that. You can't let *us* down. You—— What is it?'

Reginald was staring at the mantelpiece with his mouth open. 'Is that the time?'

'Approximately,' said Mr Pump, turning round. 'As I was saying——'

'Good Heavens!' Reginald jumped up. 'I'm terribly sorry. I shall miss my train. Good afternoon. I *say!*——' He hurried to the door, called over his shoulder, 'I'll write,' as if he had anything to write about, and dashed down the stairs into the street. *Taxi!* Hi! Here you are! Victoria—like hell. . . .

Victoria in five minutes? Impossible. What an idiot ever to have gone to Pump's. And there was Sylvia walking five miles to meet him at the station!

Just a chance. If we can get through here without being held up . . . Damn, that settles it. Now then, what? No good worrying now. We've missed it. Let's think. May as well think in the taxi as anywhere.

Sylvia darling, I'm terribly sorry. You said you loved meeting me. I can't bear to think of your walking all that way and expecting to meet me every moment, and not meeting me. And I love meeting *you*. We *must* meet. Darling, I *am* a beast. Telegraph and say the next train? But she would start at about half-past three. How long would a telegram take? No, that's no good.

Darling, I am terribly sorry. Now let's see. You'll walk to the common, anyway. That's where I should have expected you. Sitting on the common, your hat in your lap, in that lovely careless way you have, that way of dropping to the ground and being at rest there instantly, as if a painter with a flick or two of the brush had put you into an empty landscape. Yes, that is where you would have been. Well, now what will happen? You won't have a watch; you'll get tired of waiting, you will walk slowly on. You will get to the station, you will see the car there—well, that won't be so bad—you will guess what has happened. Then what will you do? Wait for the next train. . . . But if you have got a watch, then what? You will be waiting on the common, looking at your watch, wondering if I have had an accident. You will keep looking at your watch, and working it out again, and saying, 'Perhaps the train is late,' and then not believing it, and feeling frightened suddenly, and——

No, dash it, I can't.

He put his head out of the window. 'Never mind Victoria. Drive me to some place where I can hire a car.' He dropped back on to the seat and thought, 'That's what people call throwing away five pounds. Idiots! What's the use of money? None unless you can buy happiness with it, or prevent unhappiness. I threw away a hundred pounds' worth of happiness by fooling about at Pump's, and now I'm buying it back for five pounds. The best value for the money I shall ever get.'

He looked at his watch again. If he could get a fast car at once and a good driver, he could just do it. . . .

IV

For the twentieth time he looked at his watch. Fifteen miles to the station, half an hour before the train was due, open country. Only fifteen miles now. He was safe. Thank God. . . .

How like Milburn to say that he had recommended my book to Raglan. One of those fat white men who spread all over an arm-chair, and when you tell them that Lloyd George has gone over to Rome, wheeze, 'Yes, I know. As a matter of fact it was something I said in here——' Gone over to Rome: extraordinary expression. Could a Roman Catholic 'go over' to London? Probably he wouldn't want to. The whole point of being a Roman Catholic was that you were safe. Didn't have to bother any more. When strange people in railwaycarriages asked you suddenly if you were saved, what they really meant was, 'Are you safe?' Have you stopped bothering? Like getting into the Four Hundred in New York. You are a lady, and no more questions asked.

It would be nice to be certain of a God; not for myself, but for other people. 'God bless my darling Sylvia, and keep her safe'— well, I say it now, and oh! God, I mean it with all my heart, and it's the only prayer I ever want You to consider. No, it isn't, here's another one. 'May she always go on loving me.' Oh Lord, that doesn't end it: 'May I always go on loving her'—that's the important one. We can put those two into one if You like: May we always go on loving each other. There! And if You like, Pump can swindle me. I don't mind. . . .

Now, what about Ormsby? He was a difficult problem. What was going to happen to *him* in the next world? I believe Hell is an entire invention of Man's for the storing of people he doesn't like. Must put 'em somewhere, but can't have 'em with *Us*. Now take Betty Baxter. If we meet in the next world, it's Hell. If we don't, it's Heaven. Well, I mean, that makes it difficult. It doesn't seem to depend on me as it ought to. Or take it the other way round. If I went to Hell, then there would be no Heaven available for Sylvia at all. She would have to be with me—in which case it would be heavenly for me, but jolly bad luck on her. Of course that's equally true in this world. No good woman can be happy if she loves a bad man. But the whole idea of the next world is that it makes up for the inequalities and unfairnesses of this one. How can it? . . .

Also, the more you feel certain that the next world makes up for the unfairness of this, the less you trouble to remedy that unfairness. Isn't that so? I mean, if you were plumb certain that this was the only world, you would have to put all you knew into making it better. As it is, all the really good men are concentrating on the next world. A pity.

Anyway, what's the matter with this one? It has been in existence a million years, and we have just discovered wireless. Which means that wireless has been waiting a million years for us to discover. Which means that even if we go on another million years before we discover anything else, it will have been waiting for us all that time. Two million years. Really it does seem as if we had everything in this world, if only we looked for it properly.

We! I haven't discovered much. . . . Except the combination of Sylvia and Westaways. . . .

Those sheep we've put in that field so as to keep the grass short for mashie-shots. Splendid idea, but what do the sheep think about it? Well, of course they think they are there because I take an interest in them. But I don't. Only in the field. Supposing God only takes an interest in the world; not in us. Awful thought. But it might be. After all, the interest must end somewhere. We have a million bacteria alive in us. So they say. Terrible liars, scientists. Well, naturally these bacteria think that they are It. And if one little bacterium, living happily in the world of Ormsby, and bowling along a country vein going to meet his Sylvia, suddenly began to wonder whether God only took an interest in Ormsby and not in himself, well, he might be right, mightn't he? In spite of the bacterium-theologian. And the bacterium-scientist, with a laboratory in the left-hand corner of Ormsby's liver, would be quite wrong in saying dogmatically that Ormsby was the only inhabited world. Just as we may be wrong about all the other worlds. Just as, to God, the world may be the individual, with a soul to which each of us makes his infinitesimal contribution.

Odd people, scientists. Almost as odd as fundamentalists, or whatever you call them. Of course geologians have entirely proved the absurdity of the book of Genesis . . . and yet an omnipotent God who couldn't make a world, and shove fossil remains, and strata, and anything else He liked, into it, for His own purposes, is hardly an omnipotent God. So what's the truth about anything? God knows—and that's the only answer. . . .

Reginald took out his watch for the twentyfirst time. Another mile and one more minute to do it in. Well, the train might have been a minute or two late. Sylvia wouldn't worry about that. Bless her. I'm going to meet you, Sylvia! Hooray! You utterly lovely, unfathomable wonder. There must be a God.

Chapter Eight

I

Reginald was contemplating his three ducks. It was getting difficult now to say which was the mother and which were the babies. Sylvia knew, or said she did—'There, that one, darling.' But when he was alone again, the difficulty remained. However, that didn't matter. What mattered was that nobody knew whether the babies were ducks or drakes, because nobody does know until the end of September. It's very odd, thought Reginald, that a drake should look his own magnificent self in the winter, and be content to masquerade as a duck all the summer. It was also very exciting watching the three ducks at the end of July, and trying to detect the first faint signs of change. Surely Ellen's chest is lighter this evening? No? Oh, well! What do *you* think, Marmalade?

Marmalade sat a little way off, as indifferent as only a cat can be. Ducks and pigeons no longer disturbed him. There was a time, in his youth, when he had supposed them to be birds, but Mr Wellard had smacked his head in a way which looked as if some people thought that they were really vegetables. Well, if the man Wellard thought that they were really vegetables, one must humour him. All this head-smacking didn't do a cat any good. Vegetables, are they? All right, what about it? Who wants to bother about three up-ended vegetables in a pond?

No answer from Marmalade. Difficult to talk to the fur-collar round your neck, but what do *you* think, John Wesley? John Wesley, purring happily to himself, accelerated loudly for a moment at sound of the loved voice, and went to sleep again, leaving his engine running.

Then Reginald too heard the voice which he loved.

'Hallo, darling.'

'Hallo, Sylvia Wellard. You're just what I wanted. Stand about somewhere, will you? Everything looks so gorgeous this evening.'

'Doesn't it? Don't forget that the Hildershams are coming to dinner.'

'Oh lord, not so gorgeous. I *had* forgotten.'

'I'm just going to dress. I thought I'd better remind you.'

'Oh, bother and blow. Oh, curse and dash.'

'Darling,' said Sylvia anxiously, 'you do like the Hildershams, don't you? I know you said you liked Grace. That's why I asked them.'

'I love them deeply, but nobody ought to dress for dinner in the country. It means throwing away the best half-hour of the day.'

'Oh, but, darling, you couldn't just go in to dinner as you are, when people are coming.'

'I could, easily. I might squander a minute in washing my hands, but that's all.'

'Darling, you will dress, won't you, because of course *they* will.'

'On one condition,' said Reginald solemnly.

'What?'

'That you wear the lowest and most utterly improper frock you have, so that I can gaze upon you madly all the evening.'

Sylvia blushed her lovely wild-rose colour—he knew she would, and wanted her to—and murmured, 'Dresses aren't low now.'

'Then the highest—starting from the ground.'

The wild-rose deepened. 'You *are* silly,' she said, looking at him bravely, and no sooner had the words registered themselves in his mind as ugly and commonplace, than in the magic which her eyes were weaving over him, the words had never been said.

'I'll wear a very pretty one, darling,' she promised.

'Anyhow, you will look lovely in it, and I shall love you in it.'

'Well, don't be long.'

'Quarter of an hour.'

'Thank you, darling.' She turned slowly and left him.

'And I shall go with *Mrs* Wellard,' said Marmalade, following her.

So Reginald looked a perfect gentleman when the Hildershams were announced—'Mr and Mrs Fairlie Hildersham'—and Sylvia looked so that Grace Hildersham caught her breath and said without knowing it, 'Oh, you lovely thing!' and Reginald murmured to Sylvia, 'She means me.' Then they all laughed—how easily in any social encounter one laughs—and were ready for cocktails.

Fairlie Hildersham was, like his wife, large and pink and fair, and, obviously, was called 'Fairy' when standing drinks. He had, among other qualities, what he called a sense of public duty, which meant that he could only find occupation for his mind from the outside, not from the inside. He was Guardian, County Councillor, Justice of the Peace, Conservator, Vicar's Churchwarden and whatever else was possible, and had a friendly contempt for a man like Wellard who wouldn't even join the Country Gentleman's Association. There was no chair which he would not take, no subject on which he would not speak, no enterprise which he would not declare open, no petition which he would neither sign nor countersign. 'Fairlie always knows his own mind,' his wife would say proudly, but did not add whether there was much to know. She herself had many indecisions, particularly in the matter of dress. Before the evening is over, she will ask Sylvia to tell her frankly whether the apricot velvet suits her. Reginald felt that you couldn't help loving a woman like that. It was as if a man asked you earnestly what you thought of his sense of humour.

'You've signed the petition, of course?' said Hildersham.

'I'm not a very good signer. Which one's that?'

'Bringing water down to Little Malling.'

'Oh, that? No, rather not,' said Reginald. 'I should hate it.'

Hildersham stared at him; looked round at the ladies confidently for support, but finding that they were occupied with each other, provided as best he could his own atmosphere of disapproval.

'Oh! And why?'

'Once you've got water, you'll have bungalows and week-end cottages springing up everywhere. As it is——'

'As it is, in a dry season some of the cottagers have to go a mile for water. As it is, the sanitary conditions——'

'No, no,' protested Reginald, 'not just before dinner.'

'Exactly,' said Hildersham, with an air of sitting down and looking at the jury. 'You can't even bear to talk about it. They have to live with it.'

'Well, then, they've signed the petition, I suppose.'

'Naturally.'

'Well, that's all right. They want the water and they've asked for it. I don't, and I haven't.'

'My dear fellow, isn't that rather an uncivic attitude to take?'

'It seems rather sensible to me.'

'I thought you prided yourself on being a democrat.'

'I am. If the majority wants anything, let 'em have it. But you'll never know whether it is really a majority that wants it, if people start voting for what they think other people want.'

Hildersham looked round at the ladies again, but they were still in a world of their own. A pity, for a little badinage in which they could have joined seemed the best way of meeting these extraordinary arguments.

'Have another,' said Reginald, taking his glass from him.

'No, thanks. It seems to me that a sense of public duty should teach one to consider the public welfare of the neighbourhood.'

'I am. I do. Oh, emphatically. Think of all the horrid little bungalows with water and gas laid on——'

'I don't mean that. I mean one's neighbours. You can think of us all here as a little state in ourselves. What is for the good of the state?'

'You know, Hildersham,' said Reginald with a smile, 'you're always doing things for the good of the public, and the good of the state, but you're always doing it from outside; benevolently. You never realize that you are just one of the public yourself. Now I do. I see myself as a very modest member of the public, and when great men ask me what I want, I tell them. But I don't tell them what anybody else wants, because I don't presume to know.'

'In this case you do know. You know, for instance, what your man Edwards wants. You know that he has certainly signed the petition.'

'How do I know?' asked Reginald, beginning to enjoy the evening more than he had thought he was going to.

'My dear man, it stands to reason that he wants——'

'That he wants the Company's water, of course. But suppose he's being civic and democratic and all that, and saying, "I mustn't think of myself only, I must think of Mr Wellard. Mr Wellard would hate it!"'

Luckily Alice arrived in time to say that dinner was served. 'Shall we go in?' said Sylvia, and in they went.

When Hildersham had absolved his fair moustache from its last suspicion of grape-fruit, he returned, more genially, to the discussion, bringing the ladies into it with his big, charming air of taking them under his protection and seeing them safely through.

'I've been scolding your husband again, Mrs Wellard, but I'm afraid he's hopeless.' He turned to his wife. 'These authors, dear, you know what they are. Can't expect them to see things as other people do. Eh, Wellard? Still, just keep it in your mind. I think you'll find I'm right.'

'What have you been doing, darling?' asked Sylvia in surprise.

'Nothing, nothing, Mrs Wellard. Just a little matter of local politics. Mustn't bother you with it.'

'The water, Sylvia.'

'Oh, yes.' She thought for a moment. 'We don't want that, do we? You did explain to me.' The explanation came back to her. 'Of course the pumping's a nuisance, but it wouldn't seem like country, would it, if you had water and gas and electric light and everything.'

'Well, of course,' said Hildersham courteously, 'there are the cottagers to think of, Mrs Wellard.'

'My dear Sylvia,' said his wife, 'if you'd *been* into some of those cottages——' She threw up her shoulders and her eyes to Heaven.

'Well, but I do sometimes. I stop and look at their gardens, and we get talking, and they ask me in——'

(Of course they do, thought Reginald. Who wouldn't?)

'If you'll forgive me, Mrs Wellard, that isn't quite what Grace meant.'

'Hildersham means you don't really examine the drains, darling.' Sylvia examining drains. What a horrible idea.

'Now, now, Mr Wellard!'

'Pass him something, Grace,' said Hildersham good-humouredly. 'I'm talking seriously to Mrs Wellard.'

Sylvia looked adorably puzzled.

'If you were *behind the scenes*,' said Hildersham with one of his impressive metaphors, 'you would know what I mean. Water, electric light, gas, would simply revolutionize their lives. Revolutionize them.'

'Oh!' said Sylvia.

'And all this from a churchwarden!' murmured Reginald to himself.

'What *do* you mean?' He became heavily and not unattractively playful. 'You go and write another book, old man. Let's see, what are you up to now? Twenty-fifth edition or something, is it?'

'What *did* you mean, darling?'

'Yes,' said Grace. 'Tell us.'

'Oh, nothing very much. Only it always seems to me that the more a man is conscious of the immortality of the spirit, the more he discounts spiritual values in this world. You, Mrs Hildersham, believe that we are preparing our souls for the adventure of the next world. That adventure lasts, you believe, for ever—immortality —and we've only got an infinitesimally short time here for preparation. How shall we spend our time?'

He looked up at Sylvia and found himself caught in the depths of her eyes. Blue, blueviolet, periwinkle blue—how would you describe them? Such a short time here, and only a little of that with Sylvia. She would grow old and be Sylvia no longer; then she would die; and then for ten million years he would commune with her spirit. No, no! What could life beyond the grave be without a Sylvia to see, to touch, to hold in the arms? Ah, but beauty must die. Underneath this stone—how did it go? Underneath this stone doth lie As much Beauty as must die. Oh well, I shall have had my day.

In the silence Sylvia caught Alice's eye and carried it across the room to Hildersham's glass.

'Thanks,' said Hildersham, putting up a finger. 'Thanks. Quite so, I see your point, of course. But surely if we've only got such a short time, it's our first duty to see that we don't lose any of it.'

On the silver-grey table in the silver-grey panelled room in blue glass candle-sticks blue candles stood, waiting to be lit, but as yet unlighted; for the golden sun, now fallen suddenly below the line of the hill, had left that incredible aftermath of beauty behind it, when it is as if each flower had snatched at its last moment of life, to conspire in one glowing intensity of colour. Then, as it were in a breath, the glory will be gone. As much Beauty as must die.

'I see what you mean,' said Sylvia, since Reginald was still staring through the opened windows.

Hildersham, turning himself over in his mind, realized that he was becoming unanswerable.

'In other words,' he said, clinching the matter, 'our first duty is to preserve that life both for ourselves and others.'

Grace agreed. Grace always liked the way Sylvia did her fish. She made a note in her mind to ask her about it again . . . to send on Jimmy's wicket-keeping gloves . . . and to take round those flannels to old Mrs Heathcote. One oughtn't to talk about religion with Alice in the room. It put ideas into her head.

'What are we going to do in the next world?' asked Reginald, coming back with a sigh to this one. 'I'm not arguing, I'm wondering.'

'It will be a different sort of life, obviously. One can't speculate. Presumably our duty will be as clear to us there, as it seems to me to be here.' The words came back to him as he said them: good, measured words. He felt that an intelligent man was weighing his words. Very good wine, too. Lovely woman, Mrs Wellard. He felt sure and at ease.

'Dear, you do have such marvellous fish. Doesn't she, Fairlie? We always say——'

Alice was out of the room now. One could talk about fish and immortality with freedom.

'Do you like it?' said Sylvia eagerly. 'I'll tell Mrs Hosken. She's always glad when you two come to dinner, because she knows how you like things.'

'I like this hock of yours,' said Hildersham to his fellow-man, asserting his sex. 'Very delicate.'

'Do you mind going on with it?'

'Delighted. Much prefer it, in fact. You must tell me about it.' He tasted it again with the air of one listening for something. 'Ninety-seven, isn't it?'

Reginald was tempted to say 'Yes', but decided at random to say 'Ninety-nine'. Hildersham said 'Ah!' accepting the correction as somehow more confirmatory of his taste than confirmation would have been. Grace marvelled again at men's expert knowledge of wine. Reginald marvelled again at the ease with which one gives the impression of expert knowledge. Sylvia said, 'I'm afraid we shall have to light the candles. Do you mind, darling?' And the candles are lighted.

II

They came into the living-room, Grace and Sylvia. Grace with her big, fair, flushed, untidy head and pink neck escaping from the top of an ample apricot velvet which might have hidden anything; Sylvia with her delicate, shining head, no more revealed, no more unrevealed, than the golden body of which it was, this evening, part.

'You don't wear your clothes,' Reginald had said to her. 'You turn into them. Do you ever put one dress on the top of another by mistake?'

Grace, over her shoulder as they came in at the door, said:

'Jimmy's staying with a school friend for the first week of the holidays. Did I tell you? Playing cricket. A Mrs Taylor wrote to me. I never quite like letting them go off like this to people I don't know. But I suppose it's all right. She wrote very nicely.'

'Jimmy's getting quite good at cricket, isn't he? Shall we stay here, or go out?'

'Just as you like, dear. Well, let's sit down for a moment. That is a lovely dress, Sylvia.'

'Do you like it?'

'I think this suits me, don't you? Fairlie doesn't, but men are so funny. Is *your* husband like that?'

'How do you mean?'

'Not liking things, without being able to tell you why. I was wearing a pink chiffon when Fairlie proposed to me—do you remember the fashions then? No, you wouldn't. Nineteen hundred and eight? Almost everything I wear—well, of course their own clothes hardly alter at all.'

'Reginald always notices everything. I mean if I have a new hat-brooch even, or anything. He's lovely like that.'

'Of course, Fairlie's so busy nowadays. And you can't expect to keep your figure after four children. At least, if you're that sort. The thin ones do, of course. Still, I wouldn't be without them. But he always comes back to that pink dress, whatever I wear. That *is* a new ring, isn't it?'

Sylvia slipped it off her finger and offered it for inspection.

'Because of the book. Isn't it lovely? I love the setting so.'

'How do you get paid for a book? So much a copy?'

'Yes. Not very much. Ninepence.'

'Still, it adds up. How many ninepences are there in a pound? That's the sort of thing Jimmy would know at once.'

'Forty sixpences, isn't it?'

'Yes, so that would be sixty ninepences, so if you sold sixty copies—— Oh, no, it can't be sixty, can it? Because if it's forty sixpences——' She gave Sylvia her ring. 'Yes, it's lovely. Did you ever see this?' She pulled off one of her own rings, screwing up her face a little. 'It was my great-great-aunt Ramsay's, that's my mother's great-aunt. I haven't been wearing it lately, I meant to get it made bigger, but I simply had to put it on tonight. Look what's written. Of course today you'd think it wasn't a real stone, but they used to set them like that.'

Sylvia read, written in tiny copper-plate on the gold backing of the emerald: 'Agatha—Richard. Till death.'

'That was her engagement ring. He was killed in a duel on Calais sands the day after.'

'Oh, how awful! About—her?'

'Yes. It was in a club, Almacks or whatever it was, she was rather a beauty of those days and everybody wanted her, I mean wanted to marry her, and Richard Penross, that was his name, came in just as one man was saying—well really, dear, he was betting, well, like they do in Shakespeare sometimes, that he would spend the night with her. Of course nobody knew about

Richard and her—well, naturally, he wouldn't have said it if he had known, and then Richard came in—well, you can imagine!'

'Grace, how awful!'

'It's perfectly true, dear. My mother told me. After I was married, of course. The other man wasn't hurt, but he had to stay abroad. That was what was so unfair about duels, the wrong man got killed—I'm glad they've stopped them.'

Sylvia was still reading that tiny copper-plate writing: 'Agatha—Richard. Till death.'

'Grace, was it true?' she asked; in a whisper, lest the world should hear.

'About being—that sort of woman?'

Sylvia nodded, but at the ring.

'Oh, *no,* dear!' said Grace, shocked at the suggestion. Then, after an interval for thought, 'Well, of course, she was only a great-great-*aunt.* I mean, it was her brother who—and in those days, I suppose—— Well, they're bad enough now from all accounts. Thankyou, dear.' Sylvia had handed back the ring. 'I'd never thought of that. Perhaps she *was.*'

'Did you give me——'

'I gave you yours. It's lovely.'

'Oh, yes.' Sylvia looked at it happily, turning it this way and that on her finger.

'It's very difficult, all that, isn't it?' Grace went on. 'You're lucky, you haven't any daughters. Sylvia, did your mother tell you *anything*?'

'Very—no—well, just—no. Nothing really.'

'I know. That's what *I* felt afterwards. Well, I suppose I shall have to try. They grow up so quickly nowadays. Agatha goes to boarding-school next May, so I can wait till then, anyhow.' Sylvia looked at her with wide-open eyes. 'Well, no, not as it happens. They've had Agathas in Fairlie's family too.' She laughed comfortably. 'So let's hope for the best. What an awful thing to say of one's own daughter, but you know I don't mean it.'

Sylvia nodded seriously.

'You *are* the loveliest, loveliest thing,' cried Mrs Hildersham suddenly, jumping up. 'Isn't your husband absolutely mad about you?'

Secrets, secrets, said the wild-rose in Sylvia's cheeks. She got up and turned away to the open windows. 'Come on, let's go out. It's lovely.'

'It's nice the book's selling so well,' said Grace Hildersham, following her. 'It's really very clever of Mr Wellard. And the children love him, of course.'

III

'Fill up, won't you?'

'Thanks.' Gluck-gluck-gluck. 'Jimmy's just got his colours, did I tell you?' He gave the decanter a circular motion back to Reginald.

'Good man. He's got another year, hasn't he?'

'Yes. They talk of a scholarship, but I've got him down for Winchester. Awkward. I don't suppose he's good enough for that, and I don't want him to go anywhere else.'

'But a scholarship isn't important, is it?'

'Financially, I suppose it isn't vital, but naturally they like getting them. Something to quote.'

'Yes, but you can't send your boy to a school you don't like, just because his private school wants him to get a scholarship for advertisement purposes.'

Hildersham shrugged and drank his port.

'Or can you?' asked Reginald, puffing at his pipe.

'I think the school's feelings must be considered to some extent.'

Is this natural, thought Reginald, or is he getting back at me over the water?

'What's he going to be? Has he decided?'

'No, I haven't quite. The Bar, probably, with a view to politics.'

'Don't you consult him at all? I'm not a father, I'm just wondering.'

'My dear Wellard, he'd like to be a pirate.'

'Well, he'd have plenty of opportunity in the city.'

'Or a professional cricketer. By the way, have you called on the Tylers?'

'I shouldn't think so. Who are they?'

'They've taken Monks Cross.'

'Oh, yes. No; we don't call very well. My fault, I suppose. I hate knowing people for geographical reasons.'

'Mightn't you almost as well say that you hate being an Englishman?'

'No. But not bad,' smiled Reginald. 'I see your idea. As a reward, we will do our good deed for the week and call on the Tylers.'

'Well, that's the point,' said Hildersham, looking at the end of his cigar.

'Oh! I see.' Reginald saw, and hid a smile. 'We don't like our fellow-Englishman. Why not?'

'Englishman!'

'Ah, you have said all.'

'A little Jew pedlar before the war from God knows where. When the armistice is signed, he's a millionaire. That's enough for me.'

'I feel argumentative this evening,' said Reginald. 'I know of a man who was just a little Knight before the war, and as soon as the armistice is signed, he's a belted Earl . . . Name of Haig.'

Hildersham gave a short formal laugh, and said that, speaking seriously, he didn't think Tyler was a desirable neighbour.

'What have you got against him, besides his religion?'

'He made money out of the war. That's enough for me. Technically he may not have made it dishonestly, but he made it. That's enough for anybody. You or I would be ashamed, if we had come out of the war richer than we went in.'

'Sorry to keep dragging in Haig, but didn't he—er—wasn't there some sort of—er——?'

'My dear Wellard, if you think that money voted by Act of Parliament for services to the country——'

'I don't. But, so far, all that you've said about Tyler applies equally to Haig, and a thousand other friends of yours. If soldiers think that war is exclusively a military business, let them run it as a military business, and not come to civilians for help. But if they must call in civilians, then civilians have as much right to profit by it as soldiers have.'

'Only if they are willing to lose by it. Every soldier risks his life.'

'Not every one. If you don't mind my saying so, I think you risked yours much more than Haig did, and made much less out of it.'

'You don't think my services to the country were greater than Haig's?' said a sarcastic Hildersham.

'I don't compare anybody's services with anybody else's. I don't even know whether Tyler provided boots or buttons or bayonets. But if he provided something which the country wanted, he was of service to the country. And if the country is spending five millions a day on things which it wants, it is obvious that a good many people will be richer than they were before.'

'Well, I prefer the company of those who aren't. Unless they've definitely done something to deserve it.'

'Then have another drink, in case it's your last.' Reginald pushed the decanter towards him. 'I am the supreme example of the war profiteer.'

'You? Rubbish!' said Hildersham, feeling a moment of uneasiness.

'On the contrary. I was existing miserably in a bank when war broke out. I had nothing but that to go back to afterwards. But a distant cousin, the son of a very rich woman, was killed in the last week of the war; his mother slowly died of it, and, dying, left her money to her only surviving relation, whom she had seen once when he was a child. Myself. Here I am. And, but for the war, here I should not be.'

Hildersham, greatly relieved, gave a suggestion of a laugh and said, 'Oh, that!' Curious how little one knew of other people. Somehow Wellard had given him the idea of a man accustomed to money. The slightest note of condescension crept into his voice.

'Seriously, though, I think it would be as well if Mrs Wellard didn't call on Monks Cross. I understand that his is a pretty bad case. Please yourself, of course, but as you say you don't call much anyhow, perhaps it is just as well. How's the book?'

'Going strong.'

'Good.'

'Shall we——?'

'Right.'

They got up slowly.

'I met a fellow the other day who was talking about it. He was very much impressed when I told him you were a neighbour of ours.'

'Oh?' (What's the answer?)

'Got another on the stocks?'

'No . . . Let's go out, shall we? I think I saw them.'

'Right . . . Thanks . . . Fifty thousand, didn't I see you'd sold?'

'About that.'

'That's considered pretty good, isn't it?'

'I think so.'

'Yes, I told him you were a friend of ours and he was quite interested. . . . Ah, there they are.'

Chapter Nine

I

In the late autumn they went to London. Life in the country was getting too complicated for Reginald. You stop pulling up weeds for a moment and write a book. The book written, you begin pulling up weeds again. Or so a man would think. Every now and then somebody will say, 'That's a good book you've written, Wellard,' and you will say, 'Oh, do you think so?'—an idiotic question, since he has just told you that he does—and you will add, 'How nice of you to think so,' when you really mean, 'How intelligent.' Then you go back to your weeds. Or so a man would think.

But it was not so. Carruthers and Sons wanted to photograph Mr Wellard. Some lack of co-ordination in the office led them to seek the privilege twice in the same morning. In the one letter Mr Welyard was invited to join their Gallery of Famous Authors, in the other their Gallery of Distinguished Country Gentlemen, lacking Mr Willard, confessed its incompleteness. 'Just make up your minds,' said Reginald in an imaginary conversation which he held with them among the marigolds, 'and then I shall know which pair of trousers to put on.'

The North Finchley Literary and Debating Society was anxious that Mr Wellard should take part in a discussion on the tendencies of modern fiction. It was hoped that Mr Hugh Walpole and Mr Peake would also take part. 'Who the devil's Peake?' said Reginald to the dahlias, and was comforted by the thought that at that moment Peake was probably saying, 'Who the devil's Wellard?'

The Editor of *Home: An Exclusive Journal for Women* would like to talk over a projected series of articles with Mr Wellard at any time convenient to him. Mr Wellard would understand that, while it was obviously impossible just at present to compete financially with more popular journals, it was hoped that Mr Wellard would be sufficiently interested artistically to welcome this opportunity of putting his views before a select public. It might be added that *Home: An Exclusive Journal for Women* was entirely independent of the Newspaper Trusts.

The Secretary of the Incorporated Society of Authors, Playwrights and Composers hoped that Mr Wellard would join the Incorporated Society of Authors, Playwrights and Composers. If Mr Wellard cared to call at the office of the Incorporated Society of Authors, Playwrights and Composers, the Secretary of the Incorporated Society of Authors, Playwrights and Composers would explain to him the advantages which membership of the Incorporated Society of Authors, Playwrights and Composers offered to him. 'Curious', said Reginald, musing to himself among the coreopses, 'how customs change. It seems that if a new comedy is successful, the excited audience now shouts "Playwright! Playwright!" One would like to be there.'

Mr Oswald Chudley was conducting a symposium (at the request of a well-known magazine) entitled, 'How I develop my ideas'. Mr Chudley would be greatly obliged if Mr Wellard would let him have 500 words on this subject as soon as possible, together with a signed noncopyright cabinet photograph. 'How *do* I develop my ideas?' said Reginald, gazing up at the senecio. 'I don't know . . . but I see now how Mr Chudley develops his.'

The Vicar of Lower Beeding begged the favour of a signed copy of Mr Wellard's latest work to be sold in aid of the Restoration Fund, as the present condition of the Church tower, Mr Wellard would be distressed to hear, rendered it unsafe to ring the bells for Matins and Evensong.

Minna Redfern was a little girl eight years old. She had read all Mr Wellard's books and loved them. She had now started an autograph collection of her favourite authors, and would very much like Mr Wellard's autograph.

And so on.

'I shall go for a walk and think this over,' said Reginald to a duck and two drakes, and left his castle by the postern gate. . . .

The trouble is, he thought, I'm so out of it down here. I can't ask anybody anything. I don't want to be a churl, and I don't want to be a fool. If I get all these letters just because of one accidental book, it stands to reason that real incorporated authors must be simply smothered with them. What do they do? Just take no notice? Or write and say 'No' politely? Or 'Yes' eagerly? They couldn't say 'Yes' to everything, of course. Even saying 'No'—oh, but they have secretaries, I suppose. Really I'm just the man who ought to say 'Yes' to everything, because I'm not a professional writer, and my time isn't valuable. What an idiotic expression. All time is valuable, and the time when you aren't working is much more valuable than the time when you are. Well, then, my time *is* valuable, and I'm damned if I'm going to waste any of it indoors, answering these dashed people.

'That's just what I think,' said a lazy voice.

'Hallo!' He stopped suddenly and blinked at her.

'You weren't calling?' said Lena Coleby. She had her arms on the top of the gate, her chin on her crossed arms, and was looking at nothing.

'No. I wasn't much thinking where I was.' He looked about him. 'I suppose I did know you came as far as this? Or don't you?'

'Yes and No. We don't, but we may have to. I was trying to make up my mind.'

'Why?'

'My dear man, you're walking down a nice little lane, and there are no nice little houses on each side of it. So let's put some up.'

'Oh, *no!*'

'That's what *I* say. That's why I want to buy the field. I don't like other people's washing; I see enough of my own. Tom says we can't afford it. I don't suppose we can.'

'What does whoever-it-is—Langley?—what does he want?'

'Six hundred.'

'Six?' said Reginald, incredulous.

'My dear Reginald—we decided that I called you Reginald—use your brain. It's building land now. Much more expensive than agricultural.'

'That's sheer blackmail.'

'Possibly.'

Reginald put his elbow on the top of the gate, rested his head on his hand and looked at her thoughtfully.

'I'm sure Marcus Stone drew us like this once,' murmured Lena. 'A long time ago, of course.'

'Look here, Lena, suppose *I* buy the field?' said Reginald.

'Whatever for?'

'Oh, I don't know. Keep cows in it.'

'Whose?'

'Yes, that's the question. How *does* one keep somebody else's cows?' He was silent, wondering how cow-farmers began.

'What were you worrying about as you came along? I could almost hear you saying "Damn".'

'Oh, silly little bothers. It's this field I'm worrying about now.'

'Why?'

'What does Tom think about it?'

Lena said nothing, made no movement; it seemed as though she hadn't heard.

'I suppose he's right,' sighed Reginald.

'Of course he is. We can't afford luxuries.'

'I hate to think that.'

She gave him a glance—and away again. Then she said lazily, 'I don't think I've ever leant on this gate before. Don't you love looking over a valley? It's the most peaceful gate I've ever leant on. There are your chimneys.'

'So they are,' said Reginald. 'Thank you. That settles it.'

'Made up your mind?'

'Yes. I'm going to buy the field.'

'Oh, I thought you meant—whatever you were damning about. Don't bother about the field.'

'I can't stand being overlooked. I'm not going to have ugly little cottages looking down on Westaways. I'm not——'

'They'd only see the chimneys.'

'That's quite enough. They'd say "Mr Wellard's having a fire in his sitting-room today". Absolutely the ruin of all privacy. No, I'm dashed if I'll stand it.'

'Rubbish!'

'What you mean by rubbish is about the only thing that matters in this world.'

Lena shook her head at the valley. 'We can't leave it like that,' she said.

'Well, what do you propose to do about it?'

'I don't know. That's the trouble. I can't do anything.' After a little she went on: 'Saying "Thank-you" seems so silly.'

'It's idiotic. I'm doing this for my own sake. Or do I represent the Society for the Preservation of Rural Amenities? I'm not quite sure. Anyway, Colebys mean nothing to me. Who are they? I don't know them.'

'Tom would rent it from you. I'm sure he would do that.'

'He won't get the chance. It's my own private field. I suppose I shall have to get some one to cut it for me. Perhaps Tom would do that. I can't afford to pay him anything, but he can keep the hay. And I shan't prosecute you, if you lean on the gate, but you must be careful not to bend it. Thank God we've saved a bit of England today. I feel years younger.'

Lena took a hand away from the gate and, without looking at him, patted his arm once or twice. 'I like leaning on your gate,' she said. 'Give Sylvia a kiss for me and tell her I'm fond of Wellards. Goodbye.' And she was gone.

II

Six hundred pounds, thought Reginald. I could have got Sylvia a diamond necklace for that. No, emeralds. Sapphires. Or suppose I had given her six hundred pounds to get clothes with. Ridiculous clothes. Good lord, I've never even bought her a nightgown. Let's go shopping in London together and buy pretty things. Soft, pretty, *crêpe-de-Chiney*, lacey things. What fun! . . .

What is it that makes a conversation with a woman so different from a conversation with a man? A pretty woman of course. Yes, she's got to be pretty. Or—or something. Feminine. But why? Why do I get that sort of—excitement? Not excitement, that's not quite the word. Why does one get a sort of kick out of it—a tang—a—no, thrill's too strong. A bite. I'm not in love with Lena. Well, of course not. Perhaps it's the feeling that she might be in love with me. Oh, no, damn it. I'm not that sort of fool. . . .

I suppose it all comes from a sort of sexual impulse. The urge to attract; to shine. Nature has this passion for reproducing herself, and does it by making the male animal want to shine before the female animal, so that they come together and produce more animals. The lapwing gets himself another crest— and then lots more lapwings. And we've eons and eons of all that behind us, and we can never get rid of it. Which means that the real reason why I like talking to Lena across a gate is because there aren't enough people in the world already. Idiotic . . . But essentially true, I suppose.

What about Betty Baxter? She's pretty in a way. But do I get any sort of kick out of talking to her? Not the slightest. I suppose she's not my species. Not a lapwing. Grace Hildersham? Lena? Lena—it's different, you see. Yet if Lena died tonight, I shouldn't have one pang, except for Tom. So I can't be in love with her. Well, of course not. Yet if I knew she were going to be leaning over that gate tomorrow I'd walk out this way, wouldn't I? If I didn't feel too self-conscious about it. And there you are: why on earth should I feel self-conscious, if I'm not—if——

And why do I mind telling Sylvia about this six hundred? Well, of course I needn't tell her. Why on earth shouldn't I tell her? Well, I needn't just yet . . . oh, well, of course I will . . . But then if I weren't just the tiniest bit in love with Lena—no, not in *love*. In what, then? He walked on through Beevors Wood, wondering. . . .

'Hallo, darling, I came to meet you.'

She wore a pale-gold jumper and a tobacco-brown skirt; was bareheaded; she was golden-yellow and brown, a wood-nymph, not clothed in this or that fashion, not clothed at all, but herself; this was how she was born you would have said, and lived immortally. This was how she had come drifting through the woods a thousand years ago. . . .

Lena! How ridiculous!

Reginald took a deep breath and called out, 'Stay there!'

She waited, a little smile on her lips, as if it did not matter whether she stayed or moved, now or for ever. He came closer and stood looking at her.

'You did marry me, didn't you?' he said at last.

She nodded.

'You do belong to me, absolutely and always? You're mine, aren't you?'

She nodded again, shyly.

'It's incredible, incredible. Has anybody ever told you that you're the most utterly lovely thing that has ever been created?'

'Only you, darling.'

'Do I tell you often enough? Do I tell you day and night, day after day and night after night?'

Her little shining head went quickly from side to side, as if to make sure that they were alone.

'Do you like my telling you?'

She nodded again, quickly, up and down, up and down.

'Then I tell you now,' said Reginald, and took her in his arms, and kissed her mouth; and then turned her round, and slipped her hand in his arm, and walked off with her quickly, talking quickly.

'I've just been buying a field, back along the lane just below Redding Farm. Langley was going to put up cottages, horrid little things, like those other ones of his. So I bought the field to stop him. Lena told me about it—I met her. Do you mind? Say you don't mind, Sylvia Wellard. It's rather expensive, six hundred pounds. But, you see, we've got the book, that's all extra. And they'd have seen the washing from the Farm. I keep forgetting about the book, I mean the money side of it, so let's go up to London and spend it, I mean really spend it. You see, when you have in your house the most utterly lovely thing that has ever been invented, you must set it off properly, so do you mind if we spend a lot of money on the most adorable clothes in London?'

It seemed that Sylvia didn't mind.

Chapter Ten

I

But before they settled down to London, they had a preliminary taste of it at Seven Streams.

'We've got the Effinghams coming down. Do you know Sir Roger? He's just come back from the Malay States or somewhere like that. Governing. Bertie says that if he's seen nothing but his wife and black women with rings through their noses for six years, it would be a kindness to show him the real thing. Meaning you, dear. I do think I'm the most unjealous woman in Sussex. If it had been any one but you, I should have suggested that even I might be a change after black women with rings through their noses. But of course we understand each other. I shall flirt desperately with your charming husband, and that will leave Sir Roger free to talk to you. I hope he won't be too free. You never know with these hot climates, and the *restraint* they have to practise. The white man's prestige. So important. Eight-thirty, and wear that gold dress, Sylvia. There, that shows you, I wouldn't say that to any other woman.'

'We'd love to come,' said Sylvia, speaking hopefully for her husband.

'There will be one or two other amusing people,' said Betty, also hopefully. 'The Voles woman and Mr Cox. You know Mr Cox, of course. *The* Mr Cox. How lovely your garden's looking. That's your clever husband. One wants the personal touch in a garden. Saturday, eight-thirty, don't forget.'

Reginald was surprisingly calm about it, when the news was broken to him.

'This means a white waistcoat,' he said. 'I've never driven a car in a white waistcoat before. It will be a new experience. Also it will get me ready for London, where I shall live in a white waistcoat.'

'Darling, you are being nice about it.'

'I know.'

'You always used to pretend you didn't like the Baxters.'

'Away with pretence. I adore the Baxters. And I've always longed to meet the Boffinghams.'

'Effingham I think she said, darling.'

'But pronounced Boffingham. It's a very old family. Sweetheart, we're going into Society, and I left a spanner in the tail pocket of my evening coat five years ago. Could you get the bulge out between now and Saturday?'

'Darling, of *course* I'll look after your things for you.'

'Bless you. If it's too late to get the white waistcoat washed, india-rubber and bread-crumbs might help. But anything that occurs to you, sweetheart.'

Sir Roger was small and neat and brown and precise. His eyes behind his pince-nez were pale blue. At Eton (you would have guessed, and guessed rightly) he won a prize for Greek iambics, though not otherwise, noticeably, a poet; at Oxford he won a medal for a Greek epigram, though not otherwise, noticeably, a wit. Whether the ancient Greeks would have been as moved and convulsed as, presumably, the examiners were, will never be known. He gave the impression, quietly, without affectation, of being in all the secrets of the world, which in reality were only one secret: the secret of the conspiracy against British prestige. Everything which happened either had 'a very good effect' or 'a very bad effect' on this or that part of the Empire. Test matches and the fall of the Bank Rate had a good effect; jazz and naval agreements a bad effect. The decline of the classics in our public schools, trade with Russia, the latest crash in the City, the modern novel, dirt-track racing, the death penalty, the Prince of Wales, lengthened skirts and the reported agreement of the University golf captains to waive stymies—each fell into this or that side of the balance, and made Sir Roger's task the more or the less difficult. 'Ask Charlie Winter, ask Lulu,' said Sir Roger quietly, 'they'll tell you the same.'

'I always say', said Mr Cox, 'that the Bank Rate is the Barometer of Empire.'

Fancy *always* saying that, thought Reginald.

Sir Roger looked across the table at plump little Mr Cox (*the* Mr Cox) and considered him thoughtfully for a moment. A friend. 'Yes, in a sense, yes,' said Sir Roger. 'You in the City bear a great responsibility.'

'When you say prestige,' put in Reginald, feeling that something must be done about this, 'what you mean is impressing the native with the importance of the Englishman?'

'The White Man's Burden,' explained The Mr Cox.

Sir Roger looked across his hostess at Mr Wellard, and considered him thoughtfully for a moment. An enemy?

'I should say the integrity of the Englishman,' he corrected.

'Well, put it that way if you like——'

'That is how I do put it,' said Sir Roger quietly.

'Though I don't see what a large Navy and a low Bank Rate have to do with integrity.'

'Financial integrity,' murmured Mr Cox.

'Anyway, what it comes to is that you want to impress inferior races, as you naturally consider them, with the mental or moral or material superiority of the British.'

'There are only two ways of governing, Mr Wellard. By respect or by fear. The British way is by respect.'

'Yes, but is the respect of one's inferiors a very great prize? If I made it my life-work to impress my gardener, or, let us say, to win his respect, no doubt I should have to show certain good qualities, but I should have a ridiculously restricted life. And if God said to me on Judgement Day, "What have you done with the talents I gave you?" and I said, "Impressed my gardener, Lord," well—I wonder.' After saying which, Reginald drank half a glass of champagne and wondered if he had impressed Sylvia. He also wondered if he hadn't made a mistake in introducing God to Betty Baxter.

Sir Roger stopped chewing his lips, and said, 'I hope I shall be able to answer that I have done what I conceived to be my duty.'

The damn fellow makes me respect him, thought Reginald, that's the trouble. He's so admirable and so absurd. English, in fact.

'What do you consider to be your duty, Mr Wellard?' asked Betty, beginning to feel a little anxious.

'Mine are all negatives, I'm afraid.'

'Come on, Wellard,' said his host, 'give us a lead, and we'll all try and follow you. The whole duty of man in a negative. Needn't be too all-embracing or too true.'

Well done, Bertie, thought his wife. Now we're safe.

'Well, for a start,' smiled Reginald, 'here's one. Not to acquiesce in ugliness.'

'Good. Here's mine. Not to set a higher standard for others than one sets for oneself. Now, Lady Effingham?'

'Not to speak without knowledge,' said her ladyship, and Reginald realized that he had been given notice.

'Not to do things just because other people do,' said the Voles woman.

Everything seems so terribly personal, thought Reginald. I wonder what Sylvia will say.

'Whole duty of man, I mean woman. Go on, Sally,' said an Unknown Young Man, nudging the Unknown Young Woman next to him.

'To make your own mistakes.'

'Negative, you idiot.'

'All right, then. Not to let other people make them for you.'

'Mine's, not to wait for things to come to you. Because they don't.'

'Nor people,' said Sally.

'Well done, children,' said Baxter. 'Go on, Betty.'

'Not to miss anything.'

Not bad, thought Reginald. I wonder what Sylvia will say.

'Not to expect anything,' said The Mr Cox.

And I didn't expect anything nearly so good, thought Reginald. So that's all right. Oh, Sylvia, think of something!

'Mine', said Sir Roger, 'is the converse of our host's. Not to set a *lower* standard for others than we set for ourselves.'

'Good,' said Baxter. 'Now, Mrs Wellard.'

Every one looked at Sylvia. Oh, Sylvia darling! The wild-rose deepened.

'Not to be afraid,' said Sylvia.

II

Reginald went into the drawing-room feeling very proud. It was not only that the Unknown Young Man had whispered to him, 'Who was the Sheikh's Dream of Paradise sitting next to the Black Man's Burden?' It was that in that game they played she had given the best answer of all of them. 'Not to be afraid.' I'm always being afraid, he thought. Sir Roger spends his whole life being terrified. Terrified of anybody thinking differently from the regulation way. Betty is perpetually afraid of doing the wrong thing. Baxter— what is Baxter afraid of? Come to think of it, I hardly know Baxter at all. I've thought of him as just a stockbroker. Stupid of me.

In the drawing-room somebody had turned the wireless on.

'They're playing all the old waltzes,' said Betty. 'Lady Effingham and I can hardly bear it. Of course Sylvia and Sally hardly know what a waltz is like.'

'The collars I used to ruin,' said The Mr Cox. 'It takes me back to those collars. I always used to say that I was a three-collarman.'

'Bertie, I'm sure we used to dance this one together. Come and hold my hand. I feel quite sentimental.'

'There *is* something about them,' conceded Sally. 'Waltzes.'

Sir Roger moved across to his wife. They smiled at each other. Perhaps that tune had some private memory for them. He sat down next to her. Holding her hand, thought Reginald; or no—her hand in his arm, as he leads her to the conservatory.

'Bertie, wake up!'

Baxter was standing in the middle of the room, his head on one side, listening to the whisper of old-fashioned frocks on a polished floor. Somewhere.

'Bertie!'

Baxter woke up, walked across the room and turned off the wireless as a new waltz began.

'It's rather a divine tune,' said Sally. 'Anybody know its name?'

'Gracious, no,' said Betty.

'Sizilietta.'

'How much?' asked the Unknown Young Man.

'Fancy your remembering, Bertie. What is it again?'

'Sizilietta,' grunted Baxter. He walked round with a box of cigars; then lit one for himself, giving it all his attention.

'Tell us about her,' said Sally.

'Sally, you're the limit.'

'Is it a story, Bertie? You've never told me, have you?'

'Yes to the first, Betty, and No to the second. I've never told anybody.' And then after a pause. 'There's nothing to tell.'

'Please Mr Baxter,' said Lady Effingham.

'I shan't be jealous, Bertie. You know I never am.'

'I say, that sounds bad,' said the Unknown Young Man.

'Don't be silly, Claude,' said Betty sharply.

Claude and Sally, thought Reginald. Now I know everybody.

'There's nothing to be jealous about. Who ever married the girl he first fell in love with? I mean first thought he was in love with. Bridge, Sir Roger?'

'Aren't we to have the story?'

'Please!' said Sylvia.

'It isn't what *you'd* call a story, Wellard. Just—oh, nothing. Do you really——? Oh, well. It's a silly story.' He lay back in a chair and puffed at his cigar.

If only people would stop drinking just at this point, thought Reginald. Just where Baxter is now. Just at the point where you have lost nothing but self-consciousness.

'I was about twenty-two. If Betty has given you the idea that I was the nephew of the Duke of Argyle and the grandson of the original Rothschild, forget it. My father was a country G.P. He just managed to send me to Cambridge; I came down and read for the Bar. Later on a sort of cousin took me into his firm in the City, but that was only because his son died and he wanted to keep the name going. At first I knew nobody in London, at least nobody who showed up. One day I was lunching at—what's the place—Grooms, I was just going when somebody called out "Hallo!" I turned round and saw a face I thought I knew. "It's Baxter, isn't it?" he said. I couldn't place him for the moment; then I remembered. We'd been at a private school together. Fellow called West. I sat down and had a cup of coffee with him. And we talked—what happened to *you*, what are you doing now, that sort of thing. At least I talked; he didn't say much. Then he suddenly asked, as if he'd been thinking of it all the time, "Are you a dancer?"

'In those days dances were dances. Solemn, organized affairs, and no gate-crashing. I'd danced a bit at Cambridge, but I'd really taught myself in London. Saturday nights at the Kensington Town Hall or the Empress Rooms, dancing with shop-girls, and dashed good dancers too, and dashed nice girls. All I could get; I didn't know anybody. We did weird things called waltz cotillions, great fun. Well, it turned out that West had promised to bring a man down with him for the Bicester Hunt Ball. Would I be the man? A friend was putting us up for the night, and so on. Of course a Hunt Ball sounded a bit terrifying to me in those days. The impression that Lord Lonsdale and I were boys together in Newmarket, which some of you may have, is a mistaken one. We weren't. I hardly knew one end of a horse from the other. And of course I knew that I was only a stop-gap; somebody had let West down. But I wasn't proud, I was very keen on dancing, and I think I had a vague feeling that I should so endear myself to the county that they'd all bring actions against each other, and employ me as their counsel. So I said "Right", and arranged to meet West at Paddington the next evening.

'It was winter, of course, January, dark and cold and wet. We were met at Bicester, and driven to the house. Horses; took about an hour and a half. A butler received us, and showed us to our rooms, and we dressed and came down just as they were beginning dinner. Whatever introductions were made meant nothing to me, I didn't catch a single name. There were about ten or a dozen of us, all the men in pink, except ourselves, and all the girls in pinks and blues and greens, clashing horribly. All except one sensible one in black. My neighbour on the right asked me what pack I hunted with, and, hearing that I didn't, lost interest in me until the sweet, when she forgot and asked me again. My neighbour on the left also asked me what pack I hunted with, as did my hostess across the table. On hearing that I didn't, they also lost interest in me. It was rather a dull dinner.'

'Poor Bertie, I should think so.'

Baxter blew a cloud of smoke from his cigar and watched it form slowly into a grey veil which hung motionless at the level of his eyes. Then he brushed it suddenly away with his left hand, and went back to his story.

'The girl in black. How does one describe anybody? She was tall and slender, and she had a look as if she were waiting eagerly for somebody or something; expecting something to happen.

She had—it sounds absurd—a sort of arched nose, and a very short upper lip. It was that upper lip being so short which made her look expectant, I think; made her mouth almost come open, and show the smallest, whitest teeth. And her face didn't come down straight as most faces do, but was at an angle; and she had high cheek-bones, freshly coloured but with the colour seeming to be underneath the skin, and not laid on outside with the wind and rain. You could watch the colour coming and going. . . . You see, Sally, this was before the days when everybody's colour came and went. Only actresses made up then, and other immoral women.

'I'm sorry I can't describe her better. I was frightened of her. She looked so proud and so eager and so thoroughbred. All the other girls were prettier, I dare say, but, to use their own language, she was out of a different stable altogether. I kept looking across at her at dinner and wondering if I should dare to ask her to dance with me.

'As soon as dinner was over, we were hurried into carriages, a carriage and an omnibus. I was in the omnibus with my hostess and a couple of pinks and blues and two men. We drove back to Bicester, I suppose, an endless drive anyway, and engaged ourselves on the way for various dances. When we had unpacked ourselves and got on to the floor, I looked about for the girl in black. She seemed to know everybody. When I reached her, she had only one dance left. The last. Number twenty on the programme. We had programmes then, Sally.

'It was an appalling dance. There wasn't a girl in Derry and Toms who couldn't have wiped the floor with the lot of them. As for the men . . . I suppose they weren't actually wearing their spurs, but they seemed to be. They kept raking you down the ankle. Ghastly. Every now and then I missed a dance, and had to hang about with a cigarette as if I was waiting for somebody; well, anyway, I wasn't trodden on then. Luckily I had a supper partner—my hostess; I suppose somebody had let her down.

She was some sort of relation of West's, and kept asking me about him—I didn't like to say that I hadn't seen him since he was twelve. Once or twice she asked me what pack I hunted with, and said "Oh, no, you don't, of course, you told me"; I suppose I ought to have worn a placard on my chest to make it quite clear.

'We came to the last dance, and I found the girl in black. I was utterly tired and bored by then, and I should think she was too. Anyway, we danced like it. We went wearily round and round the room until at last the music stopped. Then we stood and clapped wearily, and I hoped to God that the band was equally sick of it and would play the National Anthem and let us get away. But it didn't. It started a new waltz— Sizilietta. . . .

'That was the first time I had heard it played; probably the first time it had ever been played at a dance. Perhaps the conductor wrote it himself and tried it out on us just at the end, to see how it went. It was one of the well-known London bands. We began to dance again, and this time we danced. You couldn't help it. There was never a more beautiful dancer than that girl; there were never two people in more complete harmony. Our faces were almost on a level, and whenever I looked at her, I looked into her eyes, and there was a sort of rapt expression in them, as if at last it had happened what she had been expecting so long. . . .

'They must have played that tune for nearly an hour. It made even the spurs dance decently, and they wouldn't let it go. She and I went on and on and on, too happy to say a word to each other, just giving each other a little smile now and then, as if to say, "You understand." Then it was over, and our host was bustling up to say that the horses couldn't be kept waiting any longer and we'd better get back the same way as we came. Which meant that I was with the pinks and blues again.

'We got back to the house about four. The carriage had been ahead of us, everybody had gone straight to bed and we followed them. West had to get back early, which apparently meant that he and I were having breakfast at seven. It was the first I had heard of it. When I said good night and thank you to my hostess, I waited hopefully, but with no result. If she had asked me to stay for a later train, of course I should have stayed, but I suppose she thought West and I were inseparable. Once more we made that journey to Bicester in the cold and dark and wet, half-asleep this time; we slept and woke and slept again to Paddington, and then West said, "So long, old boy," and hurried into a hansom. I went back to my rooms and thought of the girl in black.

'I would write and ask her to marry me. No, that would be absurd, of course, but I would write and ask her to meet me, and then later, a day later, a week later, I would ask her to marry me. Anyhow we must meet again, soon, very soon.

'I sat down to write to her. Dear—— And then I remembered that, absurdly enough, I didn't know her name. Well, I should have to get it from our hostess. But how? I couldn't just say that I liked that girl in black, and who was she? I thought of all sorts of excuses, and finally decided that this girl and I had talked about a book, which I had promised to send to her; so would she very kindly give me the name and address? And then I thought that this would be rather a good way of writing to the girl herself, sending her, not a book, of course, but the music we had danced to—Sizilietta. I had found out its name from the conductor.

'So I sat down to write to my hostess. Of course I had to write to her anyhow, a bread-and-butter letter. This was Wednesday, I ought to get an answer by Friday, and if I wrote at once, then I might get a lettter from the girl in black by Monday. Maddening to lose those three days, but it couldn't be helped. Dear—— And then I remembered that I didn't know the name or the address of my hostess.

'More delay. But still, it was easy now. I had to write to her anyway, so it was only natural that I should ask West for her name and address. I sat down and wrote to him; said how much I'd enjoyed the dance, and that I felt I wanted to say "Thank you" to our hostess, but didn't quite know how to address the letter. Sorry to bother him, and I hoped we'd meet again soon.'

Baxter got slowly up and stood for a moment in front of his chair, whistling the first few notes of Sizilietta gently to himself. Then, with a sigh, as he moved across to the fireplace, he said, 'That's all. That's the end of the story.'

There was a sudden gasp from his audience. 'But *how*——' cried Sally.

Baxter threw the end of his cigar into the fireplace.

'I didn't know West's address. I couldn't remember his initials, I didn't know his profession or anything. I never saw West or my hostess or the girl in black again. Now then, Sir Roger, what about Bridge?'

Betty got up and put her arm in Bertie's, and gave it a squeeze.

'Poor old boy,' she said. 'Still I'm glad you didn't. Now who's going to play?'

III

The Baxters and the Effinghams were playing Bridge, the children had gone off together to the billiard-room, and Mr Cox was telling Sylvia the story of his life. Reginald moved across to Miss Voles.

'Let's go outside,' she said. 'It's stifling in here.'

They sat on that of the many Baxter verandas which Betty called the *loggia* and looked out on to the sweet stillness of the night. 'Do you mind?' said Reginald, holding up his pipe, and she shook her head. He filled and lit it.

'Aren't people stupid?' she said suddenly.

'I'm wondering whether I'm just a complete ass or——'

'Or very clever?'

'Well, moderately intelligent.'

'How are you going to find out?'

'By asking you a question.'

'Well?'

'If I am a complete ass, will you forgive me?'

'Well?'

'Oh, well, I'll risk it. Here it is.' He glanced at her and looked away again. 'Do you always wear black?'

For a moment there was no answer. Reginald wondered if she had heard, or, hearing, had understood. He smoked and told himself he had been a fool.

'Baxter,' she murmured. 'Fancy waiting for nearly thirty years to find out the name, and then it's only Baxter.'

'You weren't waiting all the time,' suggested Reginald.

'Oh, no!'

'How long? I beg your pardon. Do you mind my asking questions?'

'I'd always wondered how it was. I felt certain he couldn't just have left it like that.'

'I don't see what he could have done, do you?'

'No . . . How did you guess?'

'I saw that the tune meant something to you too. And then— but, of course, his description. It seems incredible to me that he wasn't describing you as you sat there.'

'Thirty years ago,' said Miss Voles with a scornful little laugh.

Compliments chased themselves through Reginald's mind and left him silent.

'He hadn't an idea, of course,' Miss Voles said.

'Oh, no. Had you, until he began?'

'No. Not until he said the Bicester Hunt Ball. Then I felt certain suddenly.'

'It must have been uncanny listening to the story after all those years.'

'Uncanny. Yes. I felt that you had guessed. I think you were the only one. Unless——' She went back into her thoughts.

'Oh, I'm sure I was the only one,' said Reginald confidently and rather proudly. He imagined himself adding, 'But then I'm a novelist, it's my job to study people,' and shuddered to think of the things that one might say. Instead he asked, 'Did it mean very much—anything—to you at the time? I often used to wonder, when I went to dances and got rather keen about somebody, whether girls get keen like that too. You know what I mean; interested. At first sight.'

'Oh yes, I expect so. Not so often, I imagine. Men are so much more alike, aren't they? I mean one man is just like another so often. Types. Particularly in a hunting country. Mr Baxter wasn't—then. He's a stockbroker now, isn't he—to look at? The sort of setness, and the careful little moustache and everything. He used to be—more like you.'

'My type in fact,' laughed Reginald.

'Well, but it's rarer . . . in a hunting country.'

They were silent again. I suppose if I were really a writer, thought Reginald, I should make a story of this. She must be— what? Forty-five, anyway. And yet I could see her as the girl in black all the time Baxter was talking.

Miss Voles began to speak, almost as if she had forgotten that Reginald was there; as if she were the girl in black again, telling middle-aged sympathetic Miss Voles just what had happened.

'I watched him at dinner. Our eyes never met, but I was conscious of him. I knew he was different from the others; I thought I was different from the others too . . . until I found that I wasn't. I suppose he was right about my waiting for something to happen. If you live in that set, and—and are different, you're bound to feel that it can't go on for ever. That there's a way of escape . . . when you're young.

'I didn't mean to look proud . . .

'I tried to keep some dances in case he asked me. I did mean to. And then it was only the last one. I was terribly tired when it came, and it was a stupid tune. I didn't think he danced very well, and he didn't talk. I kept wanting to say something, to see what he was really like, but everything seemed so obvious and futile. I felt that if I opened my mouth I should ask him what pack he hunted with. . . .

'Then they played that tune, and it was as if we both came to life again. I felt I knew him suddenly and it was all right. He was different; I was different; we had met at last. Can you fall in love like that? Not really, I suppose. Just sentiment.

'Or perhaps . . . I don't know . . .

'Of course I thought I should see him in the morning. I wondered what we should say to each other. You see, we hadn't said anything. Just looked at each other, and I had been in his arms for a second . . . for an eternity. That's silly, of course. I know. The whole thing was silly.

'I said at dinner not to do things because other people did them. Girls used to wait in those days, didn't they? Doing nothing, just waiting. So I did nothing. Just waited for him to come back, to write to me. And he didn't.

'Then I thought I had imagined it all.'

She was silent again. Then very gently she began to croon that ridiculous tune to herself. Silly sentimental stuff, thought Reginald, and yet—— He could just see the glimmer of her face, he could imagine her eighteen again, waiting so eagerly for something to happen, all the romance in her, all that she had read and thought and imagined in that alien country stirred suddenly into life. Would she have stayed happy with him? Not this one, the settled, comfortable one, but the one that might have been?

'I don't see what you could have done,' he said prosaically.

She broke off her crooning to say, 'Written to Mr West. Easy,' and picked up the tune again.

'Did it—did it make much difference to you?'

She stopped her music, laughed and said, 'Oh, don't let's be sentimental about it. In a way I suppose it did. I was more afraid to let myself go, to trust my instinct. I never thought of marriage as just a thing you did, it had to be just everything to me. I suppose we all have one chance and miss it, and then have to put up with the second-best. Well, I couldn't. I felt I'd missed the best and that was the end of it for me.'

'But was it the best if he—— I mean you must have felt that he'd failed you.' Baxter the best!

'I felt that he was very shy and very modest about himself, and in strange country. It was I who ought to have done something.' Baxter very shy!

'Let's go in, it's cold out here,' said Miss Voles. 'I'm not so young as I was.' But before she got up, she said, 'Did you love your wife absolutely and completely the first time you met her—even before you spoke to her?'

'Utterly,' said Reginald emphatically.

'Yes. Ah, well, of course you would.' She got up. 'You won't say a word, of course. It's our secret. Rather fun.'

'Of course not,' said Reginald as he followed her into the house. 'At least, what about Sylvia? I never feel I can promise about her, because—well——'

'Is she a talker?'

'No. At least, I don't think so. How little one knows.'

'How little.' Miss Voles looked at him with an odd smile. 'Tell her tomorrow if you like. Or Monday. After I've gone back.'

So Reginald said nothing to Sylvia as he started the car, and nothing as he went cautiously up the drive, but, as he got on to the main road, Sylvia said:

'She was the girl, wasn't she?'

'What girl?'

'The girl in black.'

'Who?'

'Miss Voles.'

'Who said so?' asked Reginald sharply.

'Nobody,' said Sylvia dreamily. 'I just sort of knew. I thought she might have told you when you went out. It *was* all right, wasn't it, darling? I mean, you did enjoy it?'

IV

Sylvia lay sleeping, her right hand under the pillow, as was her way. The light bed-clothes had taken on her shape, so that in the midnight she seemed to be lying there unclothed. It was, to Reginald, as if nothing could come near her without rejoicing to become part of her; as if her physical beauty were such that it could never cease to express itself. No sound, no movement came from her. She had left her loveliness there to await her return in the morning.

Reginald lay on his back, awake, thinking. Of all men, Baxter! Well, but what had he done? Fallen in love, and been fallen in love with, as a very young man. Was that anything? Weren't millions of young men doing it every day? But she was a very special sort of girl, and evidently she thought him a very special sort of young man. Baxter! 'And one to show a maiden . . . ' what was it? Two faces?—two people?—two souls? Wait a bit . . . 'One to face the world with'—that's right. 'And one to show a woman when he loves her.' He has two somethings, one to face the world with, and one to show a woman when he loves her. Two faces? But you wouldn't have face twice—yes, you would if you had two faces. . . . I mustn't go to sleep before I get this right. Pull yourself together. Isn't it funny how one can *feel* one's brain slipping away at night? What about front, that would do it. He has two faces, one to front the world with, and one to show a woman when he loves her. Got it! . . .

Baxter's got two faces. We've all got two faces. Sylvia has one lovely face, and one I've never seen. Or have I? I don't know. Betty's got two faces. I liked Betty this evening. Lots of wives would have been jealous of that story, just because it happened before they knew their husbands. Part of the past which they have missed. But she was a dear. Betty, of all people! Three faces really. One to front the world with, one to show a woman—or man, of course—and one which nobody but God ever sees for more than a moment. . . . A three-faced man . . .

But Baxter! Typical man-of-the-world . . . Man-about-town . . . Clubman. What's the difference between a man-about-town and a man-of-the-world? And a Clubman? I'd sooner be a man-of-the-world. No I wouldn't. I'd sooner be . . . I'm in a club . . . on a club . . . getting bigger and bigger . . .

Reginald turned on to his side, his hand touched Sylvia's shoulder, and he fell asleep.

Chapter Eleven

I

Somewhere in the Hinterland north of the Thames, between the settlements of South Kensington and Gloucester Road, there is, on the very edge of modern civilization, a sign-post, one of whose arms points to the Hub of Empire, London, and the other, at right angles, to the uncolonized territory of Hayward's Grove. Who erected the sign-post is not known; probably Hayward. To the burgesses of South Kensington, and more particularly, to their wives, this mention of London is a source of irritation; for how can they persuade themselves that Town is 'full' or 'empty', according to whether they are or are not in residence, if Hayward continues to assert that 'Town' is, in fact, somewhere else? But to the freemen of Hayward's Grove it is a source of pride that they should have a sign-post to themselves, and, on a wet night, a satisfaction that it should be so visible to their charioteers. For, left to himself, no cabman would take a gentleman in evening-clothes, a captain possibly, into so unpromising an alley.

By some accident the freeholds of the twelve houses of Hayward's Grove are in possession of twelve owners, all of whom live, or, as agents say, reside there. But for this, no doubt, the Grove would now be a block of delightful flats with a frontage into Eastney Street; or a day-and-night garage; or the Wire-netting and Garden Accessories Department of Hankey's Stores. From time to time Mrs Carstairs, at Number 6, had expressed a willingness to be a twelfth part of the Wire-netting Department, but her situation, in the middle of the Grove, prevented the negotiations from crystallizing into anything like a firm offer, and she had to be content with an occasional 'let' to a 'thoroughly satisfactory' tenant.

One may be allowed a glimpse of her in bed before she goes to Buxton. She is wearing her 'boudoir cap' and the grey shawl, the one sent from Shetland by a grandson who had gone there to fish. 'Let us hope', said Mrs Carstairs, as her maid unpacked the parcel in front of her, 'that his taste in fish is better. I shall wear it when breakfasting, Parks, on the understanding that you do not express admiration for it. Nobody else is to see me in it.' Parks expressing immediate admiration of its warmth, Mrs Carstairs added, 'By the way, *when* is Mr Harold's birthday? Tuesday? Strange!'

However, now she is in bed, breakfasting and opening her letters, while Parks stands by.

'A Mr Wellard,' she is saying. 'Apparently he has written a book called *Bindweed*. I must have read it, because I read every book which comes out, and I don't remember a word of it, so it can't have been a good one. Apart from writing a bad book, his references seem satisfactory.'

'I remember the gentleman coming,' says Parks. 'He looked a very nice gentleman.'

Mrs Carstairs raises her eyebrows, and says, '*You* will be with me in Buxton.'

'Yes, madam,' says Parks meekly.

'I am leaving Stoker, and they bring a maid with them. A man is coming today to take an inventory. If you noticed the gentleman, Parks, no doubt you noticed the lady also. Any comments?'

'She didn't come the first time, madam, and the second time was my afternoon out.'

'Ah! Go and look at yourself in the glass, Parks. No, the long one.'

Parks goes wonderingly.

'Think yourself pretty?'

Parks blushes and says, 'No, madam.'

'You mean Yes, madam.'

'Yes, madam,' says Parks, looking quite pretty now in her confusion.

'But no brains.'

'No, madam.'

'And brains last longer.'

'Yes, madam.'

Parks having heard in the kitchen that the visitor was 'a lovely one', wonders if all this about brains refers to Mrs Wellard or to herself. Anyhow, who wants silly old brains?

'Would you have said that I was good-looking as a girl?'

'Oh yes, madam,' says Parks eagerly.

'Well, you would have been wrong. I had a complexion. Nowadays you can buy them, but in my day you had to grow them. Much more difficult. A complexion, and a figure; which really meant a figure in those days, and not just an absence. That and brains. Brains, Parks. Mrs Wellard, poor dear, is just beautiful— but, my God, how beautiful. All right, now you can send up Stoker.'

After which she goes to Buxton, and we lose her.

II

They came up to London on Tuesday, Reginald and Sylvia in the car, Alice by train with the luggage.

'But can we use the car in London, darling?' Sylvia had asked.

'No, but we shan't feel so far away from Westaways. We can pop down any time we feel like it. I don't know how you "pop down", but I'm sure it can't be done by train. Not our sort of trains. Besides, I want to drive up.'

'Are you sure you can, darling?'

'No, I'm almost sure I can't. By Tuesday I shall know for certain.'

'Of course you can, darling.'

It's very odd, thought Reginald. Just now she implied that I couldn't.

'Of course I can. Somewhere in the heart of South Norwood, possibly among the shoppers on the pavement, I may suddenly feel tired, and hand the wheel over to you for a bit. And when you have reversed out of the perambulator, dodged the lamp-post and missed the two trams and the policeman, I may feel refreshed again. I don't know. I'm full of hope.'

But when he began to wake up on Tuesday morning something was hanging over him. He was either going to the dentist or making a speech. Oh no, he was driving the car up to London. Not quite so bad. Not at all bad, in fact. Rather fun. In fact, great fun. Ridiculous for a grown man, who had been asked for his autograph, to feel nervous about a little thing like that. He splashed loudly in his bath, and introduced a note of gaiety into his vigorous towellings. . . .

'Aren't you hungry, darling?' asked Sylvia at breakfast. Most annoyingly.

'Much as usual,' said Reginald crossly. 'Why?'

However, he did it. Alone he did it. No, not alone, he thought. Without Sylvia's 'It's all right, darling' at the anxious moments, I should never have done it. It ought to be possible to carry a very small Sylvia about with you everywhere; in the waistcoat pocket; so that wherever you were, you could take her out and feel her loving warmth in your hand, and hear her say, 'It's all right, darling.' . . . And then, of course, if you liked to put her back in your pocket when you were discussing the Theory of Relativity at the club, or talking rather cleverly and humorously to—well, to Lena, or to— well, Miss Voles, say, then you could— if you wanted to.

'Damn,' said Reginald to himself. 'Why do I keep thinking these things? And what does Sylvia think about *me*? What a hell this world would be, if we knew each other's thoughts!'

Alice and tea were waiting for them in Mrs Carstairs' drawing-room. 'Hallo, Alice,' said Reginald gaily, as one back from the Pole and greeting a long-absent friend. Luckily Alice knew the right answer to that. 'Good afternoon, sir,' she said respectfully. But when she was out of the room, Reginald began to laugh.

'What is it, darling?' smiled Sylvia, happy that he was so happy.

'I was just thinking how surprised we should have been if, when I said "Hallo, Alice", Alice had said "Hallo". The natural answer.'

'Oh, but she wouldn't,' said Sylvia, almost shocked.

'No, but it would have been funny,' persisted Reginald. Dash it, he thought, you *shall* see that it's funny.

Sylvia poured out the tea, frowning to herself. . . . Then she smiled. . . . Suddenly she began to laugh. . . .

Oh, my darling, I like to hear you laugh. Your laugh is as beautiful as the rest of you. How little you have laughed with me, Sylvia, my lovely. You who have been so generous with your other treasures. Give me your lovely laugh, sweetheart, for there is none other like it in the world. . . .

All the same, he thought, as she went on laughing, it wasn't as funny as that.

III

Settled down in London, Reginald naturally asked himself why he had come there. What was his programme? The evenings would look after themselves; one could do all the things one did in the country (which was hardly anything) and then all the other things besides. But what of the mornings, what of the afternoons, what of that delightful interval between tea and the evening bath? 'There' demands so much less provision than 'here'. 'O, to be in England now that April's there': one could think so in Italy without definitely focusing one's occupations between breakfast and luncheon, luncheon and tea, tea and dinner. No need then to say 'O, to be talking to Mr Tennyson in

Freshwater at 11.30 on April 7th!' England, April, the two words were enough. But once disembarked, one could not just go about crying, 'I am in England, it is April, hooray!' One would have to take advantage of it somehow.

London in late October. What did one do in London in late October? One met people. Why else had he come to London? He was 'out of it' at Westaways, now he was 'in it'. Right. He would 'meet' people. How?

It was a sparkling October morning. (Heavens, why had they left Westaways!) Sylvia at the moment was 'meeting' Mrs Stoker in the kitchen. He could picture her half-sitting on the kitchen-table, making one of her natural conquests. Mrs Stoker was suggesting a nice sole, but really telling herself that never in all her life had she had to do with one of them that easy and pleasant, and as for looks, why, the Queen of Sheba herself in all her glory would have felt sorry for herself next to Mrs Wellard. But they would go on talking about what Mrs Carstairs had fancied, and what Mr Wellard might be supposed to fancy . . . and Hayward's Grove . . . and Westaways . . . and, no doubt, the late Mr Stoker, for a long time yet . . . until at last Sylvia would put on a hat (again a matter of time) and go down the road and round the corner to wherever Mrs Carstairs went round the corner, and dazzle a fishmonger by promising him that he could continue to send round to Number 6, and stimulate now the brain of the author of *Bindweed*. Yes, Sylvia's time was accounted for. Already she was 'in it'. But what about Mr Wellard?

'*I* know,' said Reginald suddenly. 'What fun!'

So he, too, put on his hat (a matter of no time at all) and went off to Bingley Mason's, saying doubtfully to himself as he went, 'It *is* Bingley Mason's, isn't it?'

For though Bingley Mason, A. H. Pratt, Miller and Peabody, Stauntons and Weatherby Bell all sell the most enchanting things for ladies, yet there are ladies and ladies. Great ladies, real ladies, pretty ladies, undoubted ladies, and women who shudder at the word lady, all of them made more great, more real, more pretty, more undoubted, more womanly by one or other of these gentlemen. And though the windows through which all these ladies are irresistibly drawn are equally eye-opening to a man, yet to his wife one only is the opening to Paradise. At the others she shrugs her lovely shoulders and says, 'Oh! Stauntons,' or, if in kindly mood, 'Wonderfully good for Weatherby Bell,' knowing by instinct that Bingley Mason's alone carries the hall-mark of class. 'At least,' said Reginald doubtfully, 'I think it's Bingley Mason's.'

In the days of man's financial innocence, before the war, it was possible for a respectable citizen to offer a respectable cheque to a respected tradesman without feeling uncomfortable about it. The tradesman had no doubts, the customer no uneasy realization that he was doubted. The time may come when those of us who suit the figuring of our cheques to our balances will hold up our heads again, and face our temporary creditors without shame; but now any sudden absence of cash moves us to a stammering apology for our default, and a nervous resort to our cheque-book, which only densifies the atmosphere of suspicion. We feel just as we imagine the accredited swindler must feel, though he, surely, would show his feelings less openly. In short, we are no longer ourselves, but an imagined projection of ourselves on the plane of another's thought.

So, doubtless, in the days of man's sexual innocence, whenever that was, it was possible for a husband to buy, unembarrassed, the pair of cami-knickers which his wife, equally unembarrassed, could then have done without. No harm, of course, nowadays in buying underclothes for your wife . . . and yet, said Reginald to himself outside Bingley Mason's, will the girl in the shop believe that I am buying them for my wife? No? Shall I look as if I believe it myself? No. And even if we both believed it, isn't it still rather embarrassing? I mean these things may have gadgets which— well, I mean—oh, but dash it, I can't be the first man to have done it. They must know in the shop just how technical the conversation can be allowed to become. Or shall I stick to stockings?

At least he would begin with stockings. He began on the ground floor with a dozen pairs, fearing that his nerve, subsequently, might fail him. The young woman (young lady? girl? what do you call them?) smiled at him in friendly fashion, warmed by the pleasant October morning which came in by report with each new customer. Silk stockings? Certainly, sir. What size?

'Oh!' said Reginald. 'Well, I don't—— I quite forgot—— I mean I never thought—— They're for my wife,' he explained, as if the trade should now be able to make the necessary calculations.

But the young woman was still in need of *data*.

'What size shoe does Moddam take?'

'There you've got me again.' He tried to visualize Sylvia's pretty foot. 'Fives? I really don't know.'

'Is Moddam about my height?'

Reginald looked at her thoughtfully.

'Yes, just about, I should say.'

'That would be nine and a half, then.'

'That sounds a delightful size,' smiled Reginald, feeling immensely at ease. And the wife-idea, he thought, came in most convincingly.

'What colour would Moddam like?'

Very unfair, just when they were getting on so well.

This is much more difficult than I thought, said Reginald to himself. Isn't there a colour called 'elephant's breath'—or am I thinking of a cocktail? Anyway, they have frightful names like 'nude' and 'nigger' which simply cannot be said aloud.

'Show me a lot,' he commanded. 'All colours. The latest and the most beautiful. And the most expensive. And I'll have a dozen pairs.'

By the time they had agreed on the most beautiful, and Reginald had accepted his colleague's authority for the lateness and the expense, they were on such good terms that the mildest curate could have given the conversation a kick in the direction of nightgowns. And by the time the young woman had said, 'That will be upstairs, sir,' all his new-found courage was gone. Upstairs meant that instead of following a conversation along its natural lines with an intimate friend who knew all about one's wife, one would crash into the startling topic of nightgowns with a complete stranger. And from nightgowns—where then? Still a higher floor, and a more daring flight into the unseen?

'You are a man-of-the-world,' said Reginald. 'You are a man-about-town. You are a clubman. Pull yourself together.' Pulling himself together, he went upstairs. . . .

Five minutes later he was thinking: If I were a woman, I should live here. Nothing would ever drag me away from this floor. If I were a leader of fashion, I should insist on bare legs, so as to leave more money for the other things. Stockings! Good Heavens, what a waste! When I had spent all my money, I should fake the household accounts. When my husband was bankrupt, I should become a shop-lifter. Yes, I'll have that and that and those. And those and that. Oh and this. And what about that? Only seven guineas? The *set*? You mean that and that *and* those? It's giving it away. Have you another set just like it in pale green? *Eau-de-Nil*, that's it. Look here, we've got rather carried away. We were just talking about nightgowns when we got led on to these things. Going back to them for a moment, what about a pale green one and a pale gold one? Sorry, *Eau-de-Nil*. And does Moddam wear pyjamas? No, but I suppose she could. Let's have one very exciting pair. The absurdest pair you have. And would you be frightfully annoyed—I mean, is it simply not done at all?—if I asked you to be so terribly kind as to choose a—a set or whatever you like, for yourself? I mean, it seems to me simply damnable that you should live among these lovely things, and not—or perhaps you—well, I mean anyhow one couldn't have too many of 'em. Would you really? I say, thanks awfully. It makes the day so much happier for everybody, doesn't it?

Feeling ridiculously proud and pleased with himself, Reginald raised his hat and marched away.

The two parcels came after tea. 'Is that all?' said Reginald, forgetting by how many 'practically nothing' must be multiplied to make anything at all. He took them up to Sylvia's room, cut the string impatiently (Sylvia would have untied it) and laid the lovely things out on her bed. Then he went down to her.

'Just come upstairs a moment, Sylvia. I want to show you something.'

She came, unsuspecting. He opened the door for her and waved a careless hand at the bed.

'A little present for you, and don't say I've got all the wrong ones.'

But for a moment she did not say anything, but stood looking in wonder. Then, as she touched this and that, little exclamations came from her, and catches of the breath, and suddenly she would see something else and dart round to the other side of the bed, and cry 'Oh!' again, and pick up the pretty thing to hold against her cheek; and the wild-rose grew deeper and deeper, and her eyes larger and larger, until they overflowed into tears which entangled themselves in her lashes, and had to be winked away.

'Darling, do you love them so much?'

She nodded eagerly, shaking the tears down her face, and had to laugh at the foolishness of her tears when she was so happy, and at the way she had shaken them down her cheeks, and she said, 'Oh—I love *you* so much.' And then she said, 'Shut your eyes,' and when he opened them again at her 'Ready!' there she was in this or that one of her new treasures, looking so adorable that each time he had to take her in his arms. . . .

'Happy?' whispered Sylvia.

'Absolutely,' nodded Reginald, and wondered whether he was.

IV

For London, as Reginald was beginning to discover, is the most uncomfortable place in which to do nothing particular; you must either work or be bored. In the country you are never quite sure whether you are working or idling, for the one is as engrossing as the other. After breakfast you light a pipe, and stroll into the garden. You may be getting your thoughts into order before beginning your chapter on Polarization and Transversality of Light Waves, or you may be going to see if the dianthus cuttings have had a good night; in either case you stop for a moment at the zinnias and thank God for so much beauty. But who, having praised zinnias, could shut his mind to the butterfly prettiness of the coreopsis, the velvet of the salpiglossis, the flaunting dahlias, the blue mist over the ceanothus, the golden mass of marigold and nasturtium and eschscholtzia; who could not feel that, beside all this, the transversality of light waves was, for the moment, a little thing, so that, putting this lesser thing on one side, he must continue his walk through the garden . . . until he comes to the nursery beds and ascertains if the dianthus cuttings have had a good night? But at the nursery beds we are on territory of which at best we are no more than suzerain. Edwards or Challinor comes lumberingly or sharply up; there is talk, idle-seeming at first, but leading here or there; a swarm to be taken, a fence to be mended, seeds to be ordered, drainage to be put in hand. And if by lunch-time there is no more of our chapter on its new page but the heading, do we reproach ourselves? Have we been idle; have we wasted our morning? Why, no, when we have been living so luxuriantly.

But in London what can we do but go deliberately to our room, close the door, pick up a pen, and—work? (Or look at the wall-paper?)

Sylvia was busily happy. A talk with Mrs Stoker; a talk with Alice; getting ready to go out; ordering this and that in a leisurely way; stopping for a moment at this or that shop-window; home again; getting ready for lunch; lunching; arranging flowers; going to the library and changing books; home again; getting ready to go out to tea or to welcome a friend to tea; going out to tea, or giving a last touch to flowers and cushions; tea; chatter; showing Laura or Letty the latest purchases, or being shown; goodbyes; home again, or feet up on the sofa for half an hour; leisurely bath; leisurely dress . . . and the evening with her husband.

And when you think, said Reginald, that that allows no time either for the weekly permanent wave or for the permanent weekly wave, you realize what a very busy woman she is. Half-past twelve; I'm going to the club.

Curious how few people at the club realized that one was now a Londoner, and lunching there every day. And if, when he had lunched there every day for a year, he were to go to Patagonia for seven years, curious how few people would realize that his lunches had seemed so much less regular. 'Hallo, where have you been these last few weeks?' The more observant might give him this much greeting on his return.

He turned round, hair-brushes in hand, at the sound of a voice.

'It *is* you,' said Ormsby. 'Thought so. Difficult to be sure of a face in a mirror. Ever noticed that? I come in here sometimes and see three blighters brushing their hair, and I say, "Three more damn fellers got their brothers into the club." '

Reginald laughed and said that there should never be more than one member of a family in a club.

'Right. Funny about that. Got any brothers?'

'No.'

'Well, if you had a brother and he was George the Fifth and George Washington and George Robey all in one, do you know what I should say?'

'No.'

'I should say "Of all the damned anaemic imitations of Wellard—— " See? The first one you meet is the family; the others are just trying to be like him and making a heluva bad job of it. Crippen's brothers would have been just as disappointing. No character of their own at all.'

He tossed his towel into the basket, and began to manicure his nails.

'Look here, I've got some blasted soap-boilers lunching with me. But come and have coffee up in the little smoking-room at 2.15. I'll have got rid of them by then. So long.'

He nodded and went confidently off.

How wonderful, thought Reginald, to be as certain as that. 'Hallo, you. You look as if you wanted to lunch with me. Well, you can't; but, as a special treat, we'll have coffee together.' And then to walk off, taking it for granted that the other will be there. I suppose that's how millionaires are made. That utter single-mindedness and certainty.

For the other was there, as Ormsby knew he would be. At 2.15 they were having coffee in the little smoking-room upstairs, and the secret of Hayward's Grove was out.

'You must come and have supper with us one night,' said Ormsby. 'I'll tell her ladyship to drop your missis a line. Don't suppose you want to bother with formal calls and that sort of jiggery.'

Ormsby and Sylvia! What on earth would Sylvia make of him? And what would he make of her, being what he was?

'Like to write for me?' And then as Reginald began to speak, Ormsby held up a delaying hand, and said, 'I know. You weren't going to write any more. Your first and your last, eh? And I said, "That be damned!"'

Another essential of the millionaire's makeup. Memory. Everybody you meet may mean something to you later on, and therefore, when you meet him again, you must know at once whether the occasion has arrived.

'Really,' said Reginald, 'I don't quite know why we did come to London. There was talk of making the book into a play, and there was an American publisher I wanted to see, and—and one thing and another. Things which seemed rather important when I was some miles away from them, and less important now I'm closer. I should imagine that—well, I must do something. It isn't like the country. Only——' He hesitated.

'My papers, aren't quite your style, eh?'

'Well——' and Reginald smiled apologetically.

'Go on. Be frank. I'm nothing to you, and you're nothing to me. We shan't die if we never see each other again. What the hell does it matter what we think of each other?'

'All right,' said Reginald suddenly. 'Then, frankly, Ormsby, your papers really do make me shudder sometimes. I mean the daily ones—I don't quite know which of the weeklies *are* yours. The—the vulgarity of them! Oh, God!'

'Vulgar, eh?'

'Frankly, yes.'

'Finished your pipe? Then have a cigar.'

As Reginald took one, he began to laugh, and then explained, 'When I was sixteen, I was office boy in a firm of printers, small stuff, bills of sale, "Lost, a Pekinese puppy", that sort of thing. Fulham way. The local rag was having one of its periodic bankruptcies, and I went round to see the proprietor—*and* editor he was, and printer and the whole bag of tricks. Sudden idea of mine. Sixteen, hair plastered down the middle, very high collar, black satin tie with crimson horse-shoes on it. I must have looked foul. He said, "What the hell do *you* want?" I said, "I've come to buy your paper." He looked me up and down—there wasn't much of me, so it didn't take him long—and said, "Well, why don't you? Plenty of copies." I said, "Don't be funny. Why should anybody want a copy of the damn thing? I'm negotiating for the transfer of all rights." "You're *what*?" he said. I said it again, I was rather proud of the phrase. "You're not serious?" he said. "Absolutely. My bankers are Lloyds and Co." I had taken my fifteen pounds savings out of the post office that morning. He said "My God!" took a cigar out of his waistcoat pocket, pinched it, got it half-way to his mouth, hesitated suddenly and then handed it to me, saying, "Here, shove that in your face, and tell me all about it." And for years afterwards I used to say, "Here, shove that in your face," whenever I offered anybody a cigar. I thought it was a heluva smart thing to say.'

Reginald stared at him.

'Is that really how you began?' he asked.

'Yum. That's why I was laughing, wondering how vulgar you'd think me if I said, "Here, shove that in your face!" '

'That's different.'

'Don't think *I'm* vulgar then?'

'You've got character. Nobody with character is vulgar.'

'And how many people who can read and write have character? You don't think I sell my papers to a million different people every day? If I sell 'em to ten, I'm lucky. And each one thinks like the ninety-nine thousand, nine hundred and ninety-nine others in the herd.

They're vulgar people, and they want a vulgar paper.'

'I wonder.'

'Ever listen in?'

'I have sometimes.'

'Concerts and Hallelujahs?'

'Cricket results, I'm afraid,' smiled Reginald.

'Then perhaps you've heard what they call their News Bulletin?'

'I don't think——'

'You're lucky. I'll tell you what it's like. Now just imagine a million people, two million, three million, all sitting in their little bloody sitting-rooms with their damned ear-phones on, looking like God knows what, all waiting to be thrilled. And then suddenly a refined gentlemanly voice tells them that owing to the drought in Alabama President Hoover has postponed his visit to Ohio, that the Finnish Prime Minister unveiled a statue to Professor Winkelstein, that there has been an unprecedented fall of snow in Eastern Rhodesia, and that Major-General Foxtrot has passed away peacefully at Southsea at the advanced age of a hundred and one. And who the hell cares? Well—that's refinement. Telling people something with no guts in it.' He looked at his watch and got up. 'Trouble is, Wellard, life's vulgar. Being born's vulgar, dying's vulgar, and as for living, well, three-quarters of it is stomach, and stomachs are damn vulgar. My God, when you think of what goes on in your stomach.'

'Yes, yes, but that isn't what I mean by vulgar. What I mean——'

'Sorry, but I've got to go now. You'll come to supper. I'll tell the missis. Hayward's Grove, you said. What number? You'll like her ladyship. She's a very remarkable woman.'

'Six. But——'

'Right. So long.'

And that, thought Reginald, is the last essential quality of the millionaire. Knowing when to say, 'Sorry, but I've got to go now.'

Chapter Twelve

I

As his lordship said from time to time, Margaret Ormsby was a very remarkable woman. But this was not surprising; for her father, John Fondeveril, had always been a very remarkable man.

John Fondeveril was one of those unworldly souls who 'might have been anything' if they had really cared about it, but who, unfortunately for their country, preferred to go on being accountants in a tea-broker's. At Philpot Lane, saying 'Yes, sir' and 'No, sir' to the partners, Mr Fondeveril could wrap himself up in his illusion of greatness without subjecting it to any strain. His appearance helped him; a magnificently whiskered six-foot-three was obviously Somebody. No doubt his name helped him too. To hear that this magnificent gentleman was Mr Smith would leave one unmoved; to hear that he was Mr Fondeveril set one asking, 'Who *is* Mr Fondeveril? I know I've seen him somewhere.' He was lavish with his name. He would give it to a chance acquaintance before the other had time to ask for it, adding, as a matter of popular interest, 'Always the same, always game, John Fon Deveril.' Possibly somebody had so toasted him in the 'eighties; possibly not; but he was assured by now that so they had always toasted him. His romantic interest in himself never wavered.

He married a Miss Stokes from some small Midland town; 'a Stokes of Leicestershire, the great hunting country', as he would explain to his friends, adding, with one of his inevitable flights of imagination, 'Ah, she misses it now, poor girl.' Certainly she had felt the loss of the country, if not of the sport, and after ten years of the Kilburn end of Maida Vale, she returned, in the picturesque phrase of her husband, 'to the happy hunting-fields'. Mr Fondeveril bore her loss bravely. His friends knew his motto:

> Always the same,
> Always game,
> John
> Fon
> Deveril.

Perhaps he realized that six-foot-three of magnificent mourning had lost nothing in romantic interest for the travellers on his omnibus. Descending from his seat next to the driver (his almost by right) he would make for Philpot Lane as for an exit up-stage, leaving, as he well knew, the driver and the other front-seat passenger in conversation. 'That's Mr Fondeveril I was talking to, just lost his wife, poor gentleman,' the other passenger would hear, and 'Dear, dear' would say, wondering, as everybody did, who Mr Fondeveril was. And sometimes Mr Fondeveril himself would wonder. This transmigration of souls which that fellow had been talking about. What more natural than that the soul of (say) the great Alexander should return to earth, seeking suitable quarters? He hummed lightly to himself at the thought, and returned the salute of the commissionaire with the preoccupied but military gesture which Alexander would have given it. An Alexander who had just lost a general.

He had been fond of his wife, in the rather absent way in which great men are fond of their wives, and faithful to her, for she had been a good listener. Fortunately she had left an even better listener behind her: a nine-year-old Maggie. On Sundays he and Maggie would walk out to Hampstead Heath together, Mr Fondeveril explaining on the way what he would do if the King suddenly decided to make him Lord Mayor of London, 'but with real power, Maggie. Power', and he made a semicircular movement with his free hand, 'to sweep away this or that. Power to say NO!! or YES !! as the case might be. For instance, dear, just to give you a small example of what I mean, I might —' he looked round for inspiration—'well, now, the Leg-of-mutton Pond here, just take that as an example. I might decide to—sweep it away. Well, of course that means—plans have to be made. It's a question of drainage—and—er—seepage, and so forth. It would have to be emptied, filled-in, levelled and so on. I should give the necessary instructions. And then when it was done I should decide what I was going to have here instead. A cricket ground perhaps. If so, I should of course be prepared to take the best advice. I should,' he made a beckoning movement with his finger, 'I should say to Dr. Grace, "Just come here a moment, Doctor. Now if *you* were—— " You see what I mean?'

'Yes, Pa,' said his daughter meekly.

'The point is I should have Power. Real power. They want men with power at the helm, that's what it comes to.'

On other Sundays, when Maggie was a little older, he would take her to Queen's Hall, where he gave without difficulty the impression of one who might have been a Great Conductor if he had thought of it. 'I won't say I should have taken that movement differently, Maggie, not the actual movement,' he explained on the way home, 'but I should have Built it Up more, if you see what I mean. As it was, it just lacked that something. Technically perfect, of course, I should be the last to deny that. My complaint is that he didn't Go About it in the Right Way. The first thing I should say to myself would be, Now how am I Going About This? Once you have decided on that point, the rest is easy. You see what I mean?'

'Yes, Papa,' said his daughter quickly.

'We have been attending a concert, my little girl and I,' Mr Fondeveril explained to the driver.

'Ah!' said the driver. 'That so?'

'I suppose I oughtn't to say it,' said Mr Fondeveril in a carefully lowered voice to the driver, 'but that little girl of mine—there's really no saying *where* she mightn't get to. Right to the top of the tree. So they all tell me.'

'Ah!' said the driver. 'Pianner?'

'That, too, of course, but I was thinking rather of the human voice. There's a purity about it, they tell me, an unforced purity——' He sighed and added, 'A pity that her mother couldn't have lived to see the day.'

'Mother dead?' said the driver. 'Ah, that's the way it is.'

'A Stokes of Leicestershire,' explained Mr Fondeveril. 'The great hunting country.' And added, almost unconsciously, 'Wonderful seat.'

Which brought them, it might be, to the latest little frontier war, and gave Mr Fondeveril a chance of explaining that War was not just a matter of Pushing Forward Pickets, but of Large Vision. 'Now if I had been in command, I should have sent for my—er—my chief-of-staff, and I should have said "Now, look here". Hallo, this is where we get down. Come on, Maggie. Good afternoon to you, driver.'

It was in this atmosphere that Lady Ormsby was brought up. She knew all about Great Men; she had listened to them all her life. She was twenty-five when Bob Ormsby fell in love with her; her father was still the Great Man that he had ever been, her lover was a Great Man in the making. She had grown to be tolerant of Greatness, whether Greatness in retrospect, or Greatness in prospect. Mr Fondeveril spoke mostly of the days when he had been, or might have been (he made it sound much the same thing), Prime Minister; Mr Ormsby spoke of the days when undoubtedly he would be. In either case one said, 'Yes, dear.'

For what were Great Men? Children, to be humoured.

So, for twenty-five years, Maggie Ormsby had humoured her Bob. For twenty-four of these years he had been unfaithful to her. So, too, had been Mr Fondeveril. Her father (how often!)

had promised her this or that, and in the greatness of his thoughts had forgotten about it. Was that being faithful? But you forgave him because he was a great man, and great men cannot be bothered with the silly little things which seem important to the ordinary. So, too, you forgave Bob. You had to. What was the good of divorcing him? Would he be happier for it? Would you? If she had been his mistress, and he had dared (as he so often did) to take another mistress, he would have deserved her indignation. But she was his wife, a very different thing. As his wife she had no rival. The Great Man's wife—and nursemaid. A very remarkable woman.

II

Supper at the Ormsbys was, to Reginald, something that had taken place, or was about to take place, rather than something that was ever actually happening. For a week he had wondered what it would be like; for another week he was trying to remember what it had been like. The supper itself had never seemed quite real. It had that lack of continuity so noticeable in one's dreams.

However, there were impressions which could be developed.

They had wondered whether to go to a play first or to wait quietly at home. If they went to a play first, then the question of 'tidying up' arose. It seemed silly to come all the way back to Haywards Grove for a wash and brush-up, yet where else could Sylvia go? But if they stayed at home with a book, then how still more silly to turn out sleepily at eleven o'clock just when they wanted to be going to bed. . . . Much discussion about that. In the end they went to a play.

The Ormsby house. Big, but, surprisingly, not grand. A long, low dining-room with a number of round tables—four? five? six? (what a bad detective he would make)—each table with six (eight?) people at it.

Lady Ormsby. Small, eager, rather wistful. (Eager to please.) A nice little face framed in pale brown hair with threads of grey. (Threads of grey. Bad. *Cliché*. But anyway I'm not a novelist, thought Reginald, so why bother whether it's good or bad. It's true.) Eager to please, but I don't mean nervously anxious; no, just wanting everybody to be happy; hoping eagerly, and rather afraid they won't, as if she had hoped so much once for herself, and now knew that it never happened.

Their arrival. Straight into the dining-room. About twenty people at the tables, eating and chattering, half the seats unfilled, no sign of Ormsby, Lady Ormsby getting up to welcome them; rather wistfully, as if saying, 'I can't get more enthusiasm into it, because you see, I don't really know who you are, but you do understand, don't you, and I hope you'll have a nice time.'

Introductions at Lady Ormsby's table, and Sylvia dropped there. Reginald guided to another table—a string of names—how d'you do, how d'you do, how d'you do—departure of Lady Ormsby—Reginald sits down.

A girl on his left in pale green, dark, sulkily beautiful, mechanically listening to her other neighbour, her thoughts elsewhere. A girl on his right, determined to be pretty, talking with all the assurance of a pretty girl, talking with all the assurance of the life and soul of her circle, obviously not pretty at all, yet giving the air of one who was accepted in her circle as pretty.

'Good lord, not *the* Mr Wellard?'

'The cricketer?' said Reginald. 'No, I'm afraid not.'

'My dear man, do I look as if I hoped you were a cricketer? You wrote *Bindweed*. Confess it.'

'Have you read it?'

'He asks me if I've read it!'

'Well, you'd have to pretend now, wouldn't you?'

'Definitely. And then you would never know. The uncertainty would gnaw at your vitals. It is the vitals they gnaw at, isn't it?'

'I believe so.'

'I suppose you've come here for copy for your next book. We *are* rather a menagerie. Well, do your worst, we're not afraid. Only *do* give me black hair. I've always wanted black hair.'

'Of course you'll have black hair,' said Reginald. 'And then when I'm accused of libelling you, I shall say, "But, good Heavens, I wasn't *thinking* of her—she's got *fair* hair!"'

'Oh, definitely,' said Fair Hair.

And so on. Always the faint assumption that her personality was impressing itself on her companion; the assumption that any exchange of thought must have this personal reference to her.

The distinguished-looking man, who might have been an ex-Cabinet Minister (or still in the Cabinet? Reginald was vague about that body) who was talking to the absent girl in green. Six-foot-three, white hair, white curled moustache—Bismarck with a touch of Bancroft.

'If the King had sent for me, I should have said, "Very well, sir. Since you put it like that, of course I have no option. But with all respect, sir, I must make it quite clear that, if I am to form a Government—— "'

An ex-Prime Minister apparently. But which one? Reginald wished he could have heard more, but Fair Hair was being vivacious again.

Ah, there was Ormsby, and there had he been, no doubt, when they came in. At the far end of the room, next to that extremely pretty actress whom Sylvia and he had been watching that evening. Was she the latest? So he had heard, but, listening to her across the footlights, had found it hard to believe that sentiments so moral could have been expressed with such morbid enthusiasm by one for whom they must have so little meaning. What a cad the man was to bring her here. What an interesting, likeable cad.

Fair Hair talking to the man on her right. Her property. Heavy-shouldered, young, red face, short clipped moustache. Obviously she had brought him with her. He interrupted his eating to say, 'Sorry,' when she spoke to him, and 'Quite,' when she had finished. So much was demanded by good manners, since she had brought him.

How was Sylvia getting on? Every one at her table looking at her. How natural. Every one listening to her, and apparently laughing. How odd.

Then he was at another table, having fruit salad again. The room was filled up. He had stood for a moment, talking to Raglan, who had just come, and somebody had taken his chair—(the man for whom the girl in green had been waiting?)—and then somebody had found him another chair and some fruit salad. One had to eat something. He was next to a young man now; unpleasant young man. Imagine a subaltern in the Guards, close-cut regulation hair, close-cut regulation whisker, close-cut regulation moustache, who has been out in the rain for a week, and has then stood in a very hot sun and sprouted, so that the hair on scalp and cheek and lip has suddenly got luxuriantly, but genteelly, out of control. The result, thought Reginald, was not so much hairy as an assertion of hairiness. It was as if a maiden lady in a cathedral town had suddenly begun to swear, using language by many degrees less coarse than that of a corporal, but infinitely more revolting.

'I am so glad to meet you, Mr Wellard,' said this young man, 'because I have always wanted to ask you whether you loathed *Bindweed* as much as I do.'

Reginald gave a little gasp of surprise, and began to think rapidly.

'Well, it's really a secret,' he said, 'but we'll exchange confidences. I'll tell *you*, if you'll tell *me* something.'

'What is it?'

'Do you loathe young men with whiskers as much as I do?'

Then the young man was gone, and the large-eyed, large-mouthed, pleasantly comfortable woman on his right was saying:

'Was Claude Ashmole being as rude as usual?'

'Who is he, what is he, how rude is he usually? I don't know anybody.'

'Well, he used to think he was a poet, and tried to catch the eye by looking like a man-about-town. But now that all his rich relations have died and he has become a man-about-town, he tries to look like a poet. It's his passion for avoiding the obvious.'

'Isn't that rather obvious in itself?'

'Extremely, I should say. But then where are you to stop? As soon as it becomes rather obvious to avoid the obvious, then it begins to become rather obvious not to avoid it, and so on. Most difficult and circular.'

'Yes, I see.'

'It's like the differences in the classes.'

Reginald considered this and said, 'No, you're too difficult for me. I'm from the country.'

'Well, the lower-classes behave in a certain way, and the middle-classes have a whole lot of rules to distinguish them from the lower-classes, and the upper-classes have a whole lot of rules to distinguish them from the middle-classes; the result being that the upper-classes find themselves behaving just like the lower-classes again. Another circle.'

'Example, please.'

'Oh, that's not fair on the spur of the moment—but, well, take family life. The lower-classes simply ooze family. None of them would dare to speak disrespectfully of Uncle Alfred. If Liz marries Bert, she marries Uncle Alfred too. So does Lady Elizabeth, if she marries Lord Herbert. But in the middle-classes you find people becoming more and more independent of the family. Or here's an easier one. When one of Bert's relations drops in, Liz offers her a nice glass of port wine. Middle-class calls it port. But the good old crusted families say "port wine" again.'

'Good,' said Reginald. 'And, taking it a step further, Royalty says "port".'

'Probably. Anyhow, Royalty's definitely middle-class, isn't it? We're all terrified of being mistaken for what we've just missed being, so we pretend to be something which nobody could mistake us for.'

'Life seems very difficult,' sighed Reginald. 'Couldn't we, just for this evening, cast away pretence altogether? I am sheer middle-class, called by courtesy upper-middle-class. At least I suppose so.'

'Right. And I'm definitely a Countess, who went on the stage by way of the beach.'

'Oh, no! Why, of course, you're Coral Bell!'

'Yes. Well, don't be so surprised. Somebody had to be.'

Coral Bell! That would be twenty-five years ago. He had come up, by special leave, to see a dentist, and by some mistake, not altogether accidental, found the appointment was for the Wednesday after. So there he was in London. Of course one might have got back to school by an earlier train, but of course one didn't; one preferred to explain that one had spent the afternoon at the Natural History Museum. So he went to see Coral Bell. His house was Coral-mad; he was sixteen, on the verge of his house eleven, and had never seen Coral. . . . He saw her. . . .

What was that song?

> There are girls who marry titles,
>   And a villa down in France,
> There are girls who give recitals,
>   There are girls who act and dance.
> I'm a spinster willy-nilly
>   And the pier is more my style . . .
> But—if a thing is silly
>   Then I simply have to smile.

And then the wordless chorus hummed with closed mouth slowly widening into a ridiculously happy smile.

> I know I'm not a lady,
>   And I'm not a Beauty Queen,
> My pedigree is shady,

> *And my manners can't be seen.*
> *I haven't any money,*
> *And my brain is half-and-half . . .*
> *But—if a thing is funny*
> *Then I always have to laugh.*

And then the chorus again, her laughter, adorable music in itself, set to this enchanting melody; trills and gurgles and bubbling happiness coming out of this absurdly attractive face —large eyes, large mouth and very little else.

The last verse. Sung very solemnly, with a tremendous effort (after each two lines) to keep control.

> *At a sermon of the Vicar's*
> *My attention was profound . . .*
> *Till I saw his sister's knickers*
> *Slipping slowly to the ground . . .*
> *I was grave as Mrs Grundy*
> *As the first instalment showed . . .*
> *Then, although it was a Sunday,*
> *Well, I couldn't help explode.*

An explosion of helpless laughter, the tune of the chorus abandoned . . . and then magically caught up again into the trills and bubbling happiness of the second verse . . .

Coral Bell. . . .

Then he was at another table, and back to lobster again. Ormsby's own table.

'Hallo, Wellard. D'you know Mr Wellard, Ruth? Reginald Wellard. You've read his book. Miss Fairfax.'

A remark of Reginald's that he had met Miss Fairfax that evening across the footlights. Interest in Mr Wellard, unroused by mention of his name, now faintly shown. How did he like it? Naturally he liked it enormously. Miss Fairfax charmingly and modestly calls attention to the marvellousness of the leading man—with whom she is not on speaking terms. Reginald agrees that he is marvellous.

Miss Fairfax, hiding some slight annoyance, tries again. Isn't Dolly Perkins divine? Reginald ecstatically agrees that Dolly Perkins, whose scene Miss Fairfax tries nightly to ruin, is indeed divine. Miss Fairfax lets cold eyes wander off him and round the room, and then returns them to Lord Ormsby. So that's the famous Miss Fairfax. Fancy choosing it when you're a millionaire. . . .

Supper then becomes a sort of musical chairs. At some time in the game Reginald is back at his old table. Only two people there now: the ex-Prime Minister and his hostess.

'All right, dear?' she is asking anxiously.

'Quite all right, thank you, Maggie.'

'Ah, here is Mr—— You did meet my father, didn't you?'

'Wellard,' he explains.

'Mr Wellard, of course. We've had your lovely wife at our table. Father dear, this is Mr Wellard.' Her face lights up at a sudden achievement of memory. 'You wrote that book! Father, he wrote that book.' Then to somebody else, 'Oh, must you *really* go?'

'My name', says the Elder Statesman with dignity, 'is Fondeveril. One so rarely hears a name.'

'Ah!' says Reginald, wishing that he had taken more interest in politics. (Gladstone's last Government?)

'They used to have a silly rhyme about me,' said the Elder Statesman with a reminiscent chuckle. 'I dare say you've heard it. Let's see, how did it go? "Always the same, always game, John Fon Deveril." Something like that.'

Reginald smiled, and tried to look as if he remembered it well.

'Great organizing power my daughter has. Now a party like this. I doubt if we realize, Mr Wellard, that in its own way a party like this requires as much organization as—well, let us say a campaign. There are some who think that organizing power is hereditary. No doubt it is to some extent. It's a question of Having One's Fingers on the Threads of—er——' He indicated with his white, long-fingered, deeply veined hands the conclusion of the sentence. 'You see what I mean?'

'Undoubtedly,' says Reginald, and wonders if he could walk in a perfectly straight line to Sylvia, and tell her the time. Half-past three.

'That ability to Feel the Pulse of—of whatever it is. To Know by Instinct. Instinct—well, that was what I was saying. It's hereditary. I suppose I oughtn't to say it, but others would tell you. Ask them in Whitehall—in the City. Ask them', said Mr Fondeveril darkly, 'in Wall Street. Ask them', said Mr Fondeveril, emptying his glass, 'on the Bourse.'

'Yes,' said Reginald.

And almost as soon as he had asked them on the Bourse, it was four o'clock, and Sylvia and he were in the hired car, driving back to Haywards Grove.

'*Wasn't* it fun?' said Sylvia, sparkling with excitement.

Reginald agreed sleepily.

III

Coral Bell! Twenty-five years ago none had been so Coral-mad as he. She was in all his day-dreams. When he was batting, she was watching; when he was in his form-room, she was waiting in the Yard outside, and as he crossed it, would ask him the way to the Headmaster's house. It would appear that she didn't want to see the Headmaster very much, for when he suggested an afternoon on the river, and tea at the Rose and Crown, she agreed at once. It meant cutting cricket, and perhaps trouble afterwards, but how gladly one would suffer for her sake.

He was sixteen. Legally you could be married at fourteen, but they might have to wait until he was twenty-one. Five years, and everybody else in the house wanting to marry her too. But if they were wrecked on a desert island together . . . If only. He would have to take a sea voyage of some kind these holidays. It could be quite a small one (and his heart leapt, as he realized suddenly that it need only be a small one) because your boat might be run down by an ocean-going liner, to which you would be transferred, and Coral Bell would be looking down as you came up the side, and then the liner could be wrecked properly in the tropics. Really, a cross-Channel trip would do it. He would suggest it to his father . . . something about improving his French. . . . Once he had left the pier at Folkestone, then the palms and the blue sky and the white sand, and Coral Bell by his side, were easily within reach.

That was twenty-five years ago, thought Reginald, and now I have seen her again. I suppose she's forty-seven. I wish I'd been funnier last night; I don't think I made her laugh once. I wonder if she still laughs like that. I was right, you see. She wasn't just the empty-headed little fool that everybody said. A most interesting, intelligent woman. I wonder if she's read *Bindweed*.

It would be rather fun if Sylvia asked her to dinner. Can you just ask a Countess to dinner when you've met her once, like that? Oh, but Coral Bell! It's not like an ordinary Countess. She'd understand. . . .

She doesn't look forty-seven.

Extraordinary what a lot of interesting, intelligent women there are about, really. Lena . . . and that Miss Voles . . . and Coral Bell.

Chapter Thirteen

I

A Mr Filby Nixon was to dramatize *Bindweed*. In fact, he was coming to see Reginald that morning.

'A play? What fun!' said Sylvia, when she was told at breakfast. 'But couldn't you do it yourself, darling?'

Having wondered for some weeks whether he oughtn't to try to do it himself, Reginald was naturally annoyed at the suggestion.

'My dear Sylvia, it's a very technical job. Not a thing that *anybody* can do. There's a lot of craftsmanship and so on wanted. You've got to know the theatre from the inside.' So he had been telling himself for these last few weeks, not believing a word. Now for the first time he began to think that there was something in it.

'Isn't there craftsmanship in writing a book, darling?'

'Of course. But of an entirely different kind. That's the point. It doesn't follow that, because a man can write a book, he can write a play.'

'Yes, I do see that, darling, but I'm sure *you* could.'

'Oh, Sylvia, what *is* the good of saying that?' he burst out; and then added, 'Sorry, but——' and got up, cup in hand, as if he were bringing it to be refilled, and said, 'Sorry,' and kissed the back of her neck while she refilled it.

'Thank you, darling,' said Sylvia. 'Of course I know I don't understand much about these things, but I know it's all right what I'm really trying to say.'

'Go on, darling, say it,' urged a penitent Reginald.

'Well, I said Isn't there craftsmanship or whatever it is in writing a book, and you said Yes, and I suppose it didn't follow that because you—you—because I love you, that you had that craftsmanship, but you *had*, and even if it doesn't follow that you *can* write a play, it doesn't mean that you *can't*. Like the book, I mean.'

Perfectly true, thought Reginald.

'You're absolutely right,' he said, blowing her a kiss, 'but I expect the answer is this. I might write a play, but I couldn't turn my own book into a play, because I should be thinking of it as a book always, and not wanting to leave out the best bits.'

'I see, darling. Ought you to leave out the best bits?'

'Not necessarily,' said Reginald patiently, 'but the best scenes for a book mightn't be the most effective scenes for a play.'

'*I* see, darling. And is this Mr-what-did-you-say a very good man at knowing?'

'Filby Nixon? Oh, rather, everybody says so. He's one of the leading dramatists. Tell Alice, will you? I mean that he's coming this morning.'

Mr Filby Nixon was tall, and handsome in a very correct style, and extremely well dressed. He knew everybody in the theatre by his or her Christian name, and everybody in the theatre called him Phil. If you went into almost any leading lady's dressing-room on almost any night, you would find Mr Nixon there. Sometimes the leading lady would be saying, 'Hallo, Phil, darling, when are you going to write me a play?' and sometimes he would be saying, 'Hallo, Mary, thought you'd like to know I've got a play coming for you.' Business seemed always on the verge of being put through. He was a great figure at the Theatrical Garden Party, helping with dignity, and without getting too hot, at this or that stall. Young women from the outlying parts of London, seeing him there, knew that he was a famous dramatist, because he was obviously not one of the famous actors whom they did know, but when they asked each other afterwards what plays he had written, they could only remember *Halves*, *Partner*, and immediately became uncertain of that, because, don't you remember, it was written by somebody who died the very day it was put on—there was a bit about it in the paper only last Sunday, how ironical it was?

Mr Nixon was also among those invariably present at memorial services to stage favourites, where his manner of giving and returning salutes while keeping his thoughts on the dead was particularly correct. This manner was useful to him sometimes at first nights; but he did not attend these regularly, lest he should jeopardize his position as a real member of the stage brotherhood, and be mistaken for one of the many types of hangers-on.

From time to time the headline 'Mr Filby Nixon's New Play' would be seen at the top of a theatrical column. The subsequent paragraph announced that

'Miss Mary Cardew' (or some other), 'who, as we have already informed our readers, is the latest actress to go into management, and has obtained a lease of the Apollo, has decided to commence operations with a revival of *The School for Scandal*. This will be for a strictly limited run, after which she will present either *Four Square*, in which she will take her old part of *Sally*, or a new play by Mr Filby Nixon to which he is now putting the finishing touches.'

On one famous occasion the headline had been 'New Nixon Plays', and readers were informed thus:

'It seems probable that Mr Filby Nixon, the well-known dramatist, will shortly have four plays running simultaneously in the West End. As we have informed our readers, Miss Mary Cardew is following her revival of *The School for Scandal* with a Nixon play, and it is probable that the new comedy which Mr Wilmer Cassells commissioned from Mr Nixon some months ago will now be ready for the opening of his season at the

Garrick. When we add that Mr Herbert Stott has practically decided on a revival of *Halves, Partner* at the Globe, and that *Yes, Papa*, which has been doing such good business at Southsea this week, is only waiting for a suitable theatre before coming to London, it will be seen that Mr Filby Nixon is likely to be very much on the theatrical map this coming autumn.'

And even if, owing to some unforeseen circumstance, Mr Filby Nixon did not actually make any geography at all that autumn, he would still be found in dressing-rooms, being asked urgently for a play, or heralding its long-awaited approach; he would still attend memorial services; and still you would feel that all the best plays of the last twenty years had, somehow or other, been Nixon plays.

For the reputation which *Halves, Partner* had brought him would never be left behind. It is true that there had been a collaborator, now dead; it is true that that collaborator, like every other collaborator, had been convinced that he had done all the work; but it was also true that, long before the play was sold, the collaborator had sickened of *Halves, Partner*, and had offered all his rights in it to Filby Nixon for a fiver. Nixon had behaved with a sort of correct generosity. A legal assignment of rights had been made, the consideration being, not the suggested fiver, but twenty pounds, almost all Filby Nixon's savings at that time. Moreover, at first, the names of both authors had appeared, with whatever visibility was available, on programmes and bills, although this was not insisted upon in the agreement. Also, up to the time when that 'bit' in the Sunday paper had misrepresented the position, ten pounds had been sent every Christmas to the dead man's only relation, a dipsomaniac uncle who lived at Blackpool and had never seen his nephew. And on the remaining earnings, London, provincial, American and amateur, of *Halves, Partner*, Mr Filby Nixon had lived comfortably and correctly ever since.

He had only one vice. He kept on writing plays.

It was Wilmer Cassells who had 'put Phil on to *Bindweed*'. He said afterwards, 'jokingly, of course, my dear fellow,' that he ought to have had his ten per cent, but with his constant explanation of it the joke began to evaporate, leaving behind a suspicion that he would have taken his commission if it had been offered to him.

Mr Wilmer Cassells was one of the earliest admirers of *Bindweed*. In the intervals of being an actor-manager—or, more accurately (since there are no intervals), while continuing to be an actor-manager—Mr Cassells read a good deal by proxy. It so happened that his wife, his family, his secretary and his business and stage-managers were, all of them, for their different ends, enthusiastic subscribers to Libraries and Book Clubs. Between them they covered the ground, and gave him the impression, to be shared generously with the next comer, that he was covering it too. Whether it was Wertheim on Banking, Born on Relativity, the latest detective-story or the longest chronicle novel, somebody in the orbit of which he was focus could speak of it with authority, an authority which passed, naturally and as by right, to the Great Man himself. 'Have you read *Bindweed*?' he would say suddenly to a nervous young woman in search of an engagement. 'You must get it at once. I'm in the middle of it— marvellous book.' And the aspirant would assure Mr Cassells, almost with tears in her eyes, that she would buy it that very evening, hoping thus to give him proof of her eagerness to profit by him.

Thus had he read *Bindweed*. Dear old Phil he had known for years, of course. A dozen times he had asked old Phil for a play, and two dozen times old Phil had brought him one. Mr Cassells still felt that the next one would be just the one he wanted, but growing up in his mind was a conviction that Phil's real genius was on the technical side of play-writing; so that he was now in the habit of referring young dramatists to Filby Nixon as to the master of stage-craft whom they should study before bringing him another play. 'In fact,' he would say, 'if you and Phil got together he could show you at once how to put *this* right.' He fluttered a few pages. 'I'll tell you what. Come to lunch one day and I'll get Phil along.' The young dramatist thanks him warmly, and waits for the rest of the invitation, but to the actor-manager the luncheon is already over, and the thanks merely those of the departing guest.

Feeling like this about Nixon, Cassells handed him back the twenty-fifth play with his usual charming apologies, explaining at even greater length than usual that he would have loved to do it but for this, that or the other, and that Phil was really rather lucky as it was obviously just the play for what's-his-name; and then went on:

'I'll tell you what I wish you *would* do for me, Phil, old man.'

'What's that?' asked Nixon, without any real enthusiasm.

'Get me a play out of *Bindweed*.'

'Ah!' said Nixon as if thoughtfully, knowing it as a weed rather than as a book, and wanting more information.

'Read it?'

'Not yet.' And he added a little resentfully, 'I've been pretty busy lately, Wilmer.'

'Of course. Well, you read it. There's a damn good play there. All the time I was reading it, I was saying "Phil could get a damn good play out of this".' He gave his pleasantly deprecating laugh and said, 'Nearly had a shot at it myself, but of course you'd do it a million times better. Just your line.'

'Who's the author?'

'What's that fellow's name? *You* know. I've got it here somewhere, I think.' His eyes wandered vaguely round his dressing-table, and went back to the mirror, and he gave another touch to his cheek-bones as he said, 'Oh, no, I took it home. But you get hold of the book, and then get hold of the fellow and fix it up, and then I'll——' He held out his hand and said suddenly, 'I'm on in two minutes. *Bindweed*. Don't forget. A hell of a play there, and you're the one man in England to do it. So long, Phil, old man.'

So now Reginald sat in his room at Haywards Grove, and waited for Mr Filby Nixon to call upon him. How wise of them to have come up to London. One couldn't sit in one's office at Westaways and expect famous dramatists to come down in search of one. But in London how easy all this was; how natural. Business in the morning fixing up dramatic rights, or something; a picture-gallery, perhaps, in the afternoon, nodding to Coral Bell and other friends; dinner and a play; and then supper at the Ormsbys or somewhere. How full life was in London. Never a moment to oneself.

Sylvia seemed to be busy too. Having people to lunch . . . and going out to lunch . . . and going out to tea.

'Mr Filby Nixon.'

Handshakes, how d'you do's, do sit downs, smokes.

'First of all,' said Mr Nixon, 'may I congratulate you on *Bindweed*. One of the most delightful books I have read for some time.'

'How nice of you to say so,' said Reginald.

But why, he thought, are people always so indefinite when they praise you? Why, since this sort of praise is obviously formal and insincere, and anyway is of no value coming from a stranger of whose tastes one knows nothing, why not be definite over some part of it anyway? '*The* most delightful book I have read for such-and-such a time'—or, if you prefer it, 'one of the most delightful books I have *ever* read.' So much more gratifying.

'I gather from my friend Wilmer that you would like me—you would be willing for me to try my hand at getting a play out of it. I don't know if Wilmer has said anything to you——'

'Wilmer?' said Reginald vaguely. 'I don't think I——'

'Wilmer Cassells.'

'Oh, Cassells,' said Reginald hastily. But somehow he did not confess to a lack of all acquaintance with the great man, but left it to be inferred that their friendship had just not reached the Christian-name stage.

'I'll tell you my usual methods in these cases,' said Nixon.

There's a sort of pathos about him, thought Reginald, watching Nixon's face as the explanation went on. He's handsome and he's well dressed and he's popular and he's established, and he's a man-of-the-world and a man-about-town and a well-known clubman; he's everything that a gossip-writer admires and a Judge respects— and yet he's wistful. Why, I wonder? I suppose he's missed something which he really wanted. If I patted his shoulder and said, 'My dear old fellow, I'm damned sorry,' I wonder what he'd do. Be utterly staggered, I suppose, and wonder what on earth I was talking about. Or would he burst into tears? I shan't risk it.

They got down to business.

'I don't know if you have an agent?' said Nixon.

'Agent?' said Reginald vaguely. 'No. Ought I——'

'As it happens, it's just as well. Wilmer, as you know, has commissioned this play, but I don't care about discussing business with a personal friend. I have a very good man who does it for me, if you're prepared to leave it in his hands——'

'Of course, of course,' said Reginald warmly. 'You know all about it. I know nothing.'

Nixon gave his brief, courteous smile with, as it still seemed to Reginald, something wistful at the corners of it, and said, 'Then as to terms between ourselves, I suggest fifty-fifty all through.'

'Again I know nothing,' said Reginald. 'Is that usual?' *My* book, he was thinking, and this fellow gets half.

'Well, naturally, it depends on circumstances, but it's the usual basis on which to start. In the case of a dramatist at all well known——' Reginald interrupted with a little bow, and Nixon acknowledged it with that little smile— 'it is very often two-thirds and one-third. On the other hand, in the case of a well-known book like yours, which has already made a public— — So I think that fifty-fifty would be fair to us both.'

'That's very nice of you.'

'By all through, I mean, of course, in all countries, if translations are made, in the provinces, America, amateurs and so on.'

'Quite.'

'And film-rights, of course, too. That is, if you have had no inquiries for them on the strength of the novel.'

'None,' said Reginald, shaking his head. 'It's hardly that sort of book.'

'Just so. But it may be that sort of play. Almost any successful play is pretty sure to be made into a talkie. We may have to let the manager into a share; Wilmer is sure to ask for it; but as between ourselves, we divide all the profits from film-sales equally. Does that meet your views?'

'Quite,' said Reginald again.

So a formal fifty-fifty agreement was sent to him to sign. And as soon as it was signed, there was a paragraph in the papers to say that Mr Filby Nixon was dramatizing Mr Reginald Wellard's well-known novel *Bindweed*. And a fortnight later there were paragraphs to say that, as already mentioned, Mr Nixon was writing a new play for Mr Wilmer Cassells, the theme being taken from the novel, *Bindweed*. And just when Our Theatrical Correspondent was announcing that the new Nixon play *Bindweed* was likely to be one of the events of the season, Reginald met Coral Bell again.

II

They met at the corner of Piccadilly and Sackville Street. Reginald was on his way back from a prolonged luncheon at somebody else's club, and at the corner of Sackville Street had stopped suddenly, wondering whether to call at his tailors, since there he was, and choose a new suit or two. London seemed more exigent in the matter of clothes than Westaways. But no, he must have Sylvia with him. Sylvia loved choosing his clothes. A roll of cloth meant nothing but a roll of cloth to him; as such it might be of a more pleasing colour than another roll of cloth, but he could not see it with legs and arms, and himself inside it. Sylvia, it seemed, could. Possibly a pretty pretence on her part, possibly one of her many strange gifts. Anyhow, they had always gone to Sackville Street together, and made of each visit a happy little memory.

So he had suddenly turned back into Piccadilly again, meaning to continue his long walk home, had bumped into somebody, apologized abjectly, and then exclaimed, 'Oh, it's *you!*'

'Yes, it's me,' said Coral Bell. 'And too much of me, as usual. Are you—do I—— Yes, I do. Now don't tell me.' She put her chin up in the air, and looked at him with half-closed eyes. 'Ormsby. You were—*I* know! Reginald Wellard.'

'Right. How wonderful of you.'

'Wonderful? Why, you were the darling who—— Shall we withdraw into Sackville Street? We're taking up all the room here, and people are beginning to walk *round* me. I do hate that so.'

They escaped into the quietness of Sackville Street.

'Now then,' said Coral Bell. 'You were the darling who fell in love with me when you were sixteen. That was—are you any good at arithmetic?'

'Pretty fair as it happens. I was in a bank once.'

'A bank! Oh dear! Then if you happened to know how old I was when you fell in love with me, you'd *easily* be able to work out how old I am now?'

'No,' said Reginald, shaking his head. 'Mine was one of those banks where time grew very wild. You couldn't depend on it at all. One might have been eighteen twenty-five years ago, and just about thirty now.'

'And if one had been twenty-two then?'

'Then one could easily be looking twenty-nine in Sackville Street.'

'Good. Then that's all settled and we needn't refer to it again. What were you dodging in and out of Piccadilly for?'

'I was wondering whether to order some clothes. I've got a tailor here who makes a pair of baggy flannel trousers for me every three years, and apparently does very well out of it.'

'And the three years are up today? How exciting! Quite an occasion.'

Coral Bell began to laugh. Just in the old style, thought Reginald.

'Oh, come on,' he urged. 'I haven't heard you do that since—however many years ago we agreed that it wasn't.'

'Do what?' she asked, genuinely surprised.

'Laugh. You've smiled, and now you've laughed. Any hope of your bursting soon?'

She laughed again, as Coral-like as ever.

'Every hope if you go on being ridiculous. Come along.'

Mr Hopkins, small and neat and grey-bearded, with his spectacles on the end of his nose as usual, bowed himself into an angle of a hundred and thirty-five degrees, said 'Good afternoon, your ladyship,' and 'Good afternoon, sir,' and 'Very inclement weather we are having', and waited disinterestedly. Reginald said that he wanted two lounge suits, one loud and the other almost completely silent. Mr Hopkins smiled at her ladyship as if to say, 'Mr Wellard is always a little quaint,' and went off for materials.

'I suppose everybody in London knows you,' said Reginald.

'I've been here with Charley once or twice,' explained Coral Bell, fingering cloth.

That's the husband, I suppose, he thought. I'd almost forgotten about him.

'His lordship is keeping well, I hope,' said Mr Hopkins, returning with a bale or two.

'Very fit, thank you.'

'We shall be getting another inch off the waist, perhaps, in the spring. I shall look forward to that. Now, Mr Wellard, here is a material which will make up very well. Not *too* adventurous and yet at the same time cheerful. How do you feel about it, Lady Edgemoor? Mr Wellard would look nice in that, I think?'

Lady Edgemoor was in no great hurry to decide. Mr Hopkins, smiled upon by her ladyship, was in no great hurry for a decision. Reginald was in less hurry than either of them. They examined roll after roll. . . .

'I suppose', said Reginald when at last they came out, 'it would be quite ridiculous to ask you to have tea with me somewhere.'

Coral Bell looked at him with a sudden smile.

'You see the point,' he said. 'If it isn't ridiculous, then you'll come, which would be heavenly; and if it is, then you'll burst, so I shall have that anyway. Any hope?'

She shook her head doubtfully.

'It looks as though you lose both ways. I should like to come, but I've promised to go and see Lady Collingbourne. Do you know her?'

'I told you I didn't know anybody.'

'Then we can't run her down together. Or anybody else. So what could we possibly talk about if I did come to tea?'

'You will?' he cried eagerly. 'Bless you.'

'I don't meet an old admirer every day.'

'Nonsense, you're always meeting them.'

They had tea at Stewarts, and never stopped talking.

'You know everybody,' he said. 'D'you know Filby Nixon?'

'Phil? Rather! What's *he* been doing?'

'He's dramatizing a book of mine.'

'Oh, have you written lots?' she asked with an air of innocence.

'You won't believe it,' he laughed, 'but I was trying to be unassuming; and it's terribly difficult. If I'd said "He's dramatizing *Bindweed*", it would have assumed that you'd read *Bindweed*, and knew I'd written it. If I'd said "He's dramatizing my book", it would have assumed that you know what the book was, or, if you didn't, were interested enough to ask the obvious question. Besides "*my* this" and "*my* that" always sounds egotistic.

So I said "a book of mine", because, you see, I couldn't very well say "the book of mine", could I? And, anyhow, how did you know I hadn't written lots?'

'I know more than you think.'

'Of course you do. So tell me about Nixon. Is he pretty good?'

'Phil? Oh, he's all right. Poor old Phil.'

'Yes, I felt "Poor old Phil" myself. But . why?'

'Did you ever see *Halves, Partner*?'

'No. Was it so bad?'

'Bad? It was brilliant.'

'Sort of *Charley's Aunt*, wasn't it?'

'No, that's just what it wasn't. It probably set out to be, and got spiritualized somehow. The result was a sort of ethereal farce. It's funny that it should have been so popular, I mean in the provinces and America and places like that. And London too, for that matter. There's not much to choose between them, really. I dare say the ethereal quality has evaporated a bit by now—well, it must have. But you would have loved it as it was first played.'

'And I suppose the collaborator really wrote it, and Nixon stole it, and remorse gnaws at him, and——'

'Ah, there you are!'

'Why? Did he?'

'Nothing so romantic. I had it out with Phil once. We'd had a very good supper together, and I was feeling, and I expect looking, because of course I can't help it now, extremely maternal, and he was a very small boy who had drunk too much. The original idea was his, and then they made additions and things between them, mostly Phil's. The final writing was all his, and perhaps four-fifths of the original writing. The other man was always trying to turn it back into a knock-about farce. It went the rounds for three years, and the other man, who always blamed Phil for its lack of success, finally sold his rights in it for twenty pounds. And Phil's never made less than three thousand a year out of it since.'

'Then why poor Phil?'

'Because he's mad on the theatre, and mad to do it again, and, poor darling, he can't. And he gets horrible fits of feeling that everybody thinks he's a fraud—just as you did—and that the other man—Stenning, that was his name—wrote the first play. That's why he's so terribly keen on doing it again, so as to prove that he did it before. But he can't and never will. It was an utter fluke, and he hasn't got the ghost of an idea how it happened. Poor old Phil.'

'But isn't he pretty successful still?'

'No. Never has been, except for that one play. But he's so much part of the London theatre, that people never seem able to realize it. Luckily for Phil.'

'And perhaps not so luckily for me.'

'Oh, he may do that quite well. I do hope so, for both your sakes. Anybody else you want to know about?'

'Yes. Coral Bell. Tell me, do you like knowing everybody?'

'Love it. Do you like knowing nobody?'

'Love it.'

'Sure?'

'I think that's just how men and women are different, don't you? A man instinctively dislikes new people, and then finds to his surprise that half of them are quite charming. A woman likes meeting new people, and then finds to her disgust that half of them are detestable.'

'No, you're wrong. People do divide up into those two classes, but not by sex. It's the public-school type and the other. Most women are not the public-school type, which is why you get more of them in the second class.'

'Coral Bell,' said Reginald suddenly, 'you keep sounding to me like a very wise woman. Did you—is it——' He broke off and asked, 'May I be horribly rude?'

'You may try. I don't suppose you'll find it easy.'

'Were you always as wise as this, or have you learnt a terrific lot since you married into the peerage?'

She laughed happily.

'You forget that I was performing on the beach when I was eight. You forget how I was brought up. You're thinking of the stupid, pretty girl from the stupid, middle or upper midde-class family, who goes on to the stage at seventeen, because she is too stupid and too pretty to do anything else. That's where the silly, vain, nothing-in-the-head actresses come from. Thank Heaven, I was never pretty—or stupid. Lord, Lord, what fun I've had out of other people.'

'I expect so. You've simply had to laugh,' he quoted.

'Ah, but now you're making the usual mistake of the amateur. You're confusing the part with the player. I'm a serious person, really. By "fun" I mean interest, excitement. I've had what I call fun listening to Einstein.'

'You've met him? Yes, of course, you would have.'

'Well, I don't know about "of course", but I have.'

'You're right, you know. I did think of you as just like the song. Always gay and laughing and—and adorable. But then how else could anybody of my age think of you?'

'That's why it's a mistake to marry actresses.'

Reginald was silent for a little, and then asked:

'Which surprises you most—that so many marriages are happy, or that so many are unhappy? I can never make up my mind.'

'That's rather a good question,' said Coral Bell, adding approvingly, 'I've never thought of it like that. I think——' She put her head on one side, and thought—'I think that so many are happy. It's terribly difficult, marriage, isn't it?'

'Why is it so difficult? That's silly, of course. I mean—what do I mean?'

'The really difficult thing is knowing when and how to fall *out* of love.'

'Oh, come! There *are* people who stay in love with each other all their lives.'

'Of course, and we all hope that that's what our own marriage is going to be like. And it's because people will go on hoping when there's obviously no hope, that there are so many failures. You see, if you're in love, every little difference has to be made up before you're happy again; if you're "out of" love, you can quarrel as often as you like, and still keep happy and friendly.'

'On a lower plane.'

'Yes. But it's in the descent from the higher plane to the lower that most marriages crash. If only they can get safely on to the lower plane, they're all right. And of course to stay happily on the higher must be heaven. But how few manage it.'

'But once you let yourself down on to the lower plane, what's to prevent you falling in love with somebody else?'

'Falling in love? Or being what they call unfaithful?'

'I suppose I meant that.'

'Well, what's to prevent you doing anything disloyal or hurtful if you want to do it very much? What's to prevent you promising to do a thing and not doing it? *I* don't know.'

'Nor I. In fact, here's another good question for you. Which surprises you most: that people are so good, or that people are so bad?'

'I'm sorry, Mr Wellard, but I'm dining early tonight. When I've got a year to spare, we'll go into it. All I say now is, that you can't go to Brighton for the week-end with somebody else's wife without knowing that you're doing it. And you don't do anything without working out, subconsciously perhaps, one of those balance-sheets of yours. I must be going. I've enjoyed my afternoon tremendously. Thank you so much.' She opened her bag and looked at herself.

Large eyes, large mouth, a face wise, generous and friendly.

III

Reginald went home on the top of an omnibus; and for a little while he was thinking with pleasure of his pleasant afternoon;

all the things he had said to her, all the things she had said to him. He felt that he had been successful; almost like somebody in a book, talking to a Countess, talking to a stage favourite, interesting, interested, easy-mannered, carrying off an adventure with an air. I can't have looked too bad either, he thought, putting up an automatic hand to his tie; Sylvia always says I look nice in this suit. . . .

He remembered suddenly how Sylvia and he had chosen 'this suit' in that September heatwave. She had come up from Westaways with him; he had driven to the station—she by his side, saying 'Well done, darling, it was much better', as he changed gear. She was lunching with Margaret, he was lunching at the club, they were to meet afterwards at Hatchards. She was there first, looking so cool, so still, so fresh and lovely, her eyes turned down at some new-found book, on which the tips of her fingers gently lay. There were other women there, hot, unrestful, turning over untidy pages, chattering, bustling, blown by some hot gust into this oasis from the burning pavements outside; but she was part of it.

As he came in she was aware of it instantly and turned her face to him and, as always at any meeting with him, there came that sudden faint accession of colour up to her eyes, giving her eyes that shy, eager, welcoming look which he loved so. They had made a pile of books with that careless grandeur which came over him in bookshops sometimes, and then, leaving the address behind them, had crossed Piccadilly, for safety hand in hand. And from time to time as Mr Hopkins was stroking amicably this or that roll of cloth, his hand was finding hers under the counter, and secret smiles would pass between them, smiles for the innocence of Mr Hopkins, who supposed that they were a staid old married couple, long past the apprenticeship of holding hands.

And now—what had happened to him? He had let another woman take Sylvia's place; he had robbed himself for ever, he had robbed her for ever, of that half-hour's remembrance. No longer would either of them be able to think, 'We always go together. One of the things we always do together.' I've spoilt all that, thought Reginald. . . .

How childish, he thought. It's just as Coral Bell said. As long as we are in love, the silliest little things hurt. Would Coral Bell mind if her Charley went to his tailors without her? Of course not. They have got safely and happily on to that lower plane. But I shall be fighting always not to get there. That's the way marriages crash, she said. I don't care. If Sylvia and I are not in love with each other, we are nothing to each other.

It's funny, he thought, as he walked the last few yards to his house, I feel as if I'd let Sylvia down in the most horrible way, and it's all too childish for words really. I shall go and tell her all about it and ask her to forgive me.

Laughing at the idea, he let himself in. Alice appeared in the hall from nowhere, just as he had noticed a hat which wasn't his.

'Lord Ormsby is upstairs, sir,' she explained.

'Oh!' said Reginald. 'Thanks.'

He did not go upstairs. He went into his own room, the morning room, and tried to read *The Times* again. He felt extremely ill-used.

Chapter Fourteen

I

So nothing was said about Coral Bell for the moment. At times during the next few days Reginald would think, Rubbish. I'm always doing things and not telling her about them. One can't tell another person everything, and if it comes to that, she's always going out to lunch and tea, or having people to lunch and tea, and not saying anything about it. Then he would wonder if that was quite fair. Nothing is ever really the same, he thought. There are no absolute parallels in life. It was easy, then, for his mind to wander back to Coral Bell, by way of Einstein, who agreed with him about absolute parallels. She's delightful, he thought, and it isn't reasonable to suppose that a man can cut all delightful women out of his life just because he's married and in love with his wife. . . .

All the same, if Ormsby had spent the afternoon with Sylvia, helping her to choose clothes, and had then taken her out to tea—oh, but that's different. There *are* no parallels.

It was Mrs Stoker's evening out. Every Wednesday, wet or fine, foggy or clear, she took an extraordinarily unattractive combination of busses, trains and trams to some remote corner of Willesden and had supper with a widowed sister-in-law. She did this more as an assertion of her right to an evening out than from the pleasure she got from it. A long-standing feud between the Stoker brothers, into whose intricacies, never fully explained to the wives, she and Jane had married, had caught up the Stoker widows in the emotional period of their mourning and held them as deeply involved as ever their husbands had been, but with presumably less knowledge of what it was about. Wednesday's supper, which began with cold mutton, tomatoes and a re-statement of the case for the younger Stoker, in as far as Jane could remember whether it all started with his falling off a bicycle on to his head at the age of eight, or with his being expected to be a girl eight years earlier, and ended with cold sago pudding and a statement by Mrs Stoker that if Rights were Rights some people wouldn't be talking to their neighbours about Reel Meogany Wardrobes, had long since ceased to be an improvisation, and had attained the dignity of a stage performance in which the protagonists were word-perfect. So, too, with the exit lines. 'Likely I'll see you next Wednesday,' says Jane without enthusiasm, and with an equal lack of enthusiasm Mrs Stoker replies, 'Likely you will.'

On Wednesdays, then, the Wellards dine out, and on this particular evening they were at the Ivy; not dressed for dinner or the play, but wondering if they would drop in at some cinema on the way home. Over the top of Reginald's head as he bent over the menu Sylvia's lovely smile flashed across the room, leaving some faint note of its passing in his consciousness. He looked up at her, saw the smile still lingering there, and said, 'Who?'

'Mr Fondeveril, he's just gone past. No, he went on inside, darling.'

'Fondeveril? That's Lady Ormsby's father, isn't it? He was at the supper. I didn't know you'd met him. What about oysters? That gives us time to think about something else.' How many oysters, he thought, die in this cause?

'All right, darling.'

'Two half-dozens, and you might bring me the wine-list.'

The waiter speeds off.

'I didn't meet him at the party, but he was at lunch the other day.'

'Where? . . . Oh, thanks. What shall we drink, Sylvia?'

'I don't want anything, darling. Couldn't we have that—what was it?—we had in Italy?'

'Chianti?'

'It had rather a lovely name.'

'Oh, you mean Lacrima Cristi?'

'That was it. But just as you like, darling. At Lady Ormsby's it was.'

'I suppose they've got it,' he said doubtfully. He looked, and ordered a bottle.

'Lord Ormsby was there, and him, that was all.'

'I didn't know you'd lunched there. You never told me,' he said, a little surprised, a little hurt.

'I expect you were thinking of something else. I did tell you, darling.'

This seemed to be Coral Bell's cue.

'Did you see Lady Edgemoor at the supper? No, of course you didn't. I told you about *her*, didn't I?'

'Not at the supper. I have seen her since. Lady Ormsby brought her to tea.'

'Oh?' Again he felt a little surprised and a little hurt. 'I didn't——' He broke off and said casually, 'She's a dear, isn't she?'

'She's a lovely person.'

'I met her quite by accident in Piccadilly the other day, and—— Oh, thanks.' The oysters were put before Madame, before Monsieur. 'Well, she didn't seem—— Thanks, thanks.' Brown bread and butter, lemon, etceteras.

'What will Monsieur have to follow?'

'Oh, curse this,' murmured Reginald. 'Darling, what will you have?'

'I don't want much,' said Sylvia, looking vaguely at the menu.

'Have a kidney omelette and fried potatoes and a Japanese salad?' said Reginald in one brilliant inspiration.

'All right, darling.'

'Two, then,' said Reginald to the waiter, and, turning to Sylvia and his story, saw Filby Nixon coming in, as beautifully as any hero of his plays.

'Well, she was—— I say, there's Nixon. I must just introduce him to you.'

Nixon caught his eye and came up to them.

'Sylvia, this is Mr Filby Nixon. My wife.'

They shook hands with a smile.

'We have met,' said Nixon, 'though perhaps Mrs Wellard doesn't remember. At Lady Edgemoor's at lunch the other day.'

'Good Heavens,' thought Reginald.

'Of course I remember,' said Sylvia. 'I told you, darling, didn't I, and how well the play was going on?'

'Of course,' said Reginald. What *has* happened to us, he thought. I suppose I was thinking of something else again. Or reading the paper at breakfast. 'I say, sit down a moment, can you, and tell us some more about the play.'

'I'm waiting for Ethel. I'll just sit down till she comes if I may. She's always late. I expect *you've* found that.'

'Is that Ethel Prentice?' asked Sylvia. Damn it, thought Reginald, that's the actress. If you know her too, if you know everybody, and I'm just the country cousin who knows nobody, I shall scream.

It turned out that Sylvia only knew her by name.

'I'll introduce her if I may. As a matter of fact, she's rather keen about playing *Sally.*'

If she's to play *Sally*, thought Reginald, she must be as lovely as Sylvia, for Sylvia was *Sally*. Well, in parts. Only *Sally* was—well, of course she had a sense of humour. Well, I mean——

'You see *everybody* here,' Nixon apologized, making his fourth bow since he had sat down. By everybody he meant everybody in the theatrical world, his world.

'Who *was* that?' asked Sylvia. 'I know his face so well.'

'Willie? The tall, thin one? Willie Evans. The writer.'

'Oh! No, then I don't know him.'

'You mean it wasn't his face, darling.'

'Well, it's awfully like somebody. An actor or somebody.'

'It's a bit late for the actors,' explained Nixon. 'Unless they're out of a job, or rehearsing.' He looked at his watch. 'Ten past eight. We're getting near Ethel's idea of eight.'

'Isn't Miss Prentice acting now?' asked Sylvia.

'Luckily, no. That's why she wants *Bindweed*.'

'Has she ever acted with Cassells before?' asked Reginald. 'They'd make a very popular pair, I should think.'

'Well, as a matter of fact,' said Nixon, 'Wilmer—I saw him last night as it happens. He's terribly sick about it, but he's under contract to do that French play. We could wait, of course, till he got through with that, but I thought——You know, I'm not really certain that he's the right man. And as Ethel—ah, here she is.' He got up and went to the door. Sylvia gave Reginald the briefest possible glance of excited anticipation, and touched his foot lovingly with hers under the table.

Reginald got up. Introductions were made. The men hovered uncertainly. Miss Prentice, well up-stage, stayed there firmly while delivering her lines. She adored *Bindweed*. Aren't you very proud of him, Mrs Wellard? 'Very proud. Are you really going to play *Sally*?' Ah, well! Of course she'd *adore* to, but she might have to go to America. And there was a film she'd been asked to do. How d'you do, how d'you do, how d'you do, how d'you do— smiles to four tables. But she would have *adored* to. Phil darling, we mustn't be late—*how* d'you do—and we're keeping Mr and Mrs Wellard from their oysters. Don't you *adore* oysters? Goodbye, Mrs Wellard. *Goodbye,* so delightful to meet you, it will make a *divine* play. Another radiant smile, snapped off the moment her face began to turn away, and she was gone. Nixon bowed his farewells with an added courtesy, as if to apologize for her, or perhaps for stage-folk generally, in that their excess of charm shows up so plainly all that it seeks to hide.

'I didn't know you knew Nixon,' said Reginald, still a little resentfully, as he sat down.

'Yes, darling. He was at lunch at Lady Edgemoor's.'

'Yes, but I didn't even know——'

'I did tell you, darling, but you were reading *The Times*.'

'When was that?'

'Last Thursday was the lunch, but I said at breakfast——'

'Thursday. Oh, then that was after.'

'After what, darling? Was that what you were going to tell me?'

'Yes. You see, I happened to meet her in Piccadilly just as I was——'

'She told me she'd had tea with you.'

Reginald felt ashamed suddenly.

'Sweetheart, I meant to tell you. I'm awfully sorry. Say you didn't mind.'

'It's all right, darling. There doesn't seem to be so much time for telling in London, does there? And I love to think of her having tea with you. She's sweet, I think.'

'Did she tell you what we did?'

'No. Except about tea.'

Reginald made his confession.

'You do see how it happened, don't you?' he urged. 'There she was, and there I was, and there Hopkins was——'

'Of course, darling. Do you think I shall like them?'

'I expect so,' said Reginald coldly. He felt absurdly annoyed because she was so little hurt. Were all their happy little memories memories for him only? But at the back of his mind he knew that, if she had been even a little hurt, he would have been annoyed at that too.

'I should have hated it if we had been in the country,' said Sylvia. 'I do so love meeting you at that bookshop and then going on with you. But it's different in London.'

'Yes, it is,' agreed Reginald, feeling much happier suddenly. You darling, he thought, now you've said exactly the right thing.

'There are so many other people.'

'I suppose that's it.'

He wondered suddenly if Sylvia compared him with all the other people, as he compared her. The thought was rather disturbing.

II

Mr Fondeveril was dining at the Ivy tonight with his daughter. She was late. He strode magnificently from the inner room to the swing-doors, stood a moment while country cousins asked 'Who's that?' and strode magnificently back to his table, looking at his watch in the manner of one who had been kept waiting on a certain historic occasion by Paul Kruger, and was amazed that the lesson he had had to teach the fellow had not been learnt by others.

Lady Ormsby and her father were much in each other's company. Ormsby had an amused tolerance for his father-in-law, which sometimes, to his surprise, degenerated into a sort of affectionate admiration. The old boy was as mad as a hatter, of course, but he was distinctly a figure. It seems absurd that a man of fifty-five, and Robert, first Baron Ormsby at that, should have a father-in-law at all, but if he must have one, let him be anything rather than a nonentity. Everybody in London knew Mr Fondeveril by sight; everybody was either impressed by him or amused. Of how many fathers-in-law could that be said? Ormsby could afford to show his gratitude.

He showed it. Mr Fondeveril became a feature of the official Ormsby establishment. Maggie was encouraged to have him about the house, to display him at parties, even to console herself with him at week-ends when Bob was, unfortunately, called away. Better keep a room for him, eh, old girl, and any time you feel lonely——? And *I'll* see to it that he's all right. By all right he meant had money to spend. It was as well that he did see to it, for the pension from the tea-broker's might just have kept its late accountant in dress-shirts for the innumerable supper-parties, but would do no more. Ormsby, feeling an unaccustomed virtue in the action, furnished a flat for his father-in-law in New Cavendish Street, the district being chosen with the good-humoured mischief of one who knew his man. Mr Fondeveril could imagine himself, if he liked, a man-about-town with a West End address, or, just as easily, if he preferred it, a fashionable consultant with a home elsewhere. Mr Fondeveril did both. Ordering this or that from a stationer's, he might choose to say, 'I think you had better send it to my consulting-rooms', and then, raising his hand and frowning to himself, 'No! On second thoughts to my flat,' or he might say, 'Send it round to my flat—no, no, what am I thinking about? To my consulting-rooms'; but in either case he could give an address which carried conviction.

In a sense they really were his consulting-rooms, for in them he consulted freely his dictionaries and encyclopaedias. A successful newspaper proprietor can always pension off a father-in-law without hurt to his feelings or harm to the public. For many years the column in *Ormsby's Home Elevator* entitled 'The Wonderful World We Live In' was written by a John Fondeveril who (as a Public Man) preferred to use the *nom-de-guerre* of 'James Fountain B.A.' The subject exactly suited his *oratio recta* style, for in these weekly articles he could take his reader by the hand and introduce him personally to the subject. 'Now supposing I were a Bank Manager, and you came to me and said "Ah, good morning, Mr Fountain, I want to raise Ten Thousand Pounds". Well, I should say, "Very good, Mr Smithers, but what *Security* can you offer me?" '—and so on, in 'This Week's Talk on Banking'. The B.A. at the end of his adopted name was put in by the editor, who thought it would inspire confidence. Mr Fondeveril, a little shocked when he first saw it, confided to his son-in-law his doubts as to the propriety of it, seeing that he was not 'strictly speaking' a Bachelor of Arts; to which replied Ormsby genially, cigar in mouth and a bottle inside him, 'But I expect you were a Bloodyrotten Accountant, old boy.' So the matter was left over, and it was not long before Mr Fondeveril was talking, with regret for the time wasted there, of his College days.

With the coming of the *Cinema de Luxe* and the *Palais de Danse,* the number of people who were willing to elevate themselves at home was insufficient to pay a dividend, and James Fountain, B.A., died in his hood; one Thursday explaining loosely, but with an air of being largely responsible for it, the Reason Why his readers saw their faces upside-down in a spoon, the next Thursday back for ever into the void from which our Wonderful World had itself once emerged. For a little while the allowance made by Ormsby to his father-in-law was regarded between them as a retaining fee, and it was almost developing into a pension to James Fountain's dependants when, just in time, the Cross-Word fever took possession of the country. Always the same, always game, John Fondeveril returned to business as 'Macedon' of the *Sunday Sun.* The new office suited him no less well than the old. Writing, as the clue for '13 *across*', 'I am a gasteropod with a trochiform shell and a low visceral hump' he could lose himself in a world of speculation as easily as when, in the old days, he had imagined himself Mr Gladstone or Sir Garnet Wolseley, as easily as when, in later days, he had assumed a personal share in the laws of banking or refraction.

He looked at his watch again as Lady Ormsby came quietly up to his table.

'I'm sorry, dear,' she apologized. 'I stopped to talk to the Wellards.'

'Eight-fifteen,' said Mr Fondeveril, snapping his inscribed gold hunter and lowering it back into his pocket with both hands. 'Eight-fifteen, Maggie.'

'Ah, then I should have been late, anyhow. Did you see the Wellards?'

'I bowed to Mrs Wellard. A charming woman.'

'Lovely.'

'You don't remember Mrs Langtry in her prime? No, no, of course, you wouldn't. Ah, there were beautiful women in those days. I have ordered a few oysters to begin with, bearded in their shells. Will that suit you?'

'Thank you, dear.'

'I always used to say that Mrs Langtry, Lady Randolph Churchill and your mother were the three most beautiful women I knew. Mrs Langtry didn't hunt, of course. Her beauty was more exotic. We used to stand on chairs in Hyde Park to see Mrs Langtry go past.'

'They wouldn't now, would they? Father, I'm a little anxious about Bob.'

'Bob?' said Mr Fondeveril, affecting surprise. 'Oh? Ah!' He busied himself in the wine-list.

But though he was not surprised that Bob had been causing anxiety, he was surprised that Maggie should have referred to it in front of him. He knew all about Ormsby's love-affairs, of course; who didn't? But there had always seemed to be a sort of understanding between Maggie and himself that he didn't really know—not officially. If he had known, surely he would have said something to his son-in-law; something virile; something as man to man; or, perhaps, something, though now much less, as man-of-the-world to man-of-the-world. But definitely something. Awkward, of course, to have to tell your son-in-law, who was supporting you, that he was a cad; so awkward that the convenience of not realizing that he was a cad, and therefore, of not having to put yourself in this awkward situation, presented itself to the mind almost without conscious thought. It had only to present itself at the portals of Mr Fondeveril's mind to be made thoroughly at home. He was convinced that he did not know; that as a Public Man it was his business not to know; or that, if he did know, his silence was an heroic sacrifice of his own happiness, even of that of his well-loved child, to the public weal.

'I'm sorry, dear,' said Maggie, with one of her wistful little smiles, understanding so well his discomfort. 'But you *are* so helpful to me sometimes.'

He patted her hand forgivingly.

'My dear Maggie, I regard you as a sacred trust. I told your dear mother so, when she lay dying. "A sacred trust, Caroline," I said. "My constant care. I cannot, alas! afford her the advantages which you had as a child, the beautiful and stately home, the constant life in the saddle, but I will devote myself to her, be sure of that." She knew. She died happy.'

Maggie pressed his hand and let it go. 'I know, dear.'

'And we did have good times together, didn't we?' he asked with a pathetic eagerness. 'Didn't we, Maggie? D'you remember how we used to go to the Zoo and Madame Tussaud's, and Rams-gate, wasn't it, that first summer, and the niggers, and I got talking to one, and we brought him back to tea, and he sang his songs to us——'

'Rather, darling! Of course I remember,' said Lady Ormsby, her face lighting up, so that she looked almost like that little Maggie for a moment. 'Why I can remember the songs he sang. One was "Hi-tiddley-hi-ti" and one was "I asked Johnny Jones and now I know", and——'

'Ah! Yes,' said Mr Fondeveril, also remembering. 'A certain robust humour, perhaps——'

'Darling, I loved them, and didn't understand a word of them. We've had heavenly times together.'

'Well, well, what is it about Bob?'

Lady Ormsby hesitated, and then said, 'Oh, nothing really. It's just——' She gave a nod towards the outer room. 'Those two.'

'Tut-tut! You don't mean——'

'No, I don't mean anything. I'm just a little anxious. She's so lovely, and so—innocent.'

'But——' Mr Fondeveril began on a note of expostulation, and turned it into a perturbed cough. What he had been about to say was, 'Surely Bob's women are always—er—professionals? Nobody falls in *love* with Bob.' He remembered in time that he knew nothing about Bob's habits.

She read his thought, as she always did.

'It isn't that,' she said. 'It's just that people will talk, if they go about together. His reputation—it's a pity. She's so sweet. And people are so horrid.'

'Are they—do they go about together?'

'Well, they hardly know each other yet. She came to lunch, and Bob was there some of the time—I didn't know he was going to be, and he did say he'd seen her since.'

'Oh, well, if he *said* so,' said Mr Fondeveril, eager to reassure himself.

She shook her head. 'You see, I know Bob. I've seen him looking at her. I don't think he would—' she hesitated, and ended, 'well, he never has yet. Not my own friends. Besides, *she's* quite different, and much too much in love with her husband to think of anybody else. But anybody as lovely as that—— Poor Bob! He fancies himself, you know, and yet he always has to pay. It's rather sad.'

Mr Fondeveril wanted to express horror at his little Maggie's calm acceptance of her husband's infidelities, but didn't quite see how he could reconcile it with his own ignorance of them. So he said:

'I don't think there's much to worry about, dear. You saw them together just now. As happy a married couple as England has to show.'

'It's only that I know Bob. There'll be talk. And the nice little Wellards will be hurt.'

'Little!' said Mr Fondeveril, seeing a chance of diversion. 'From a shrimp like you!'

'You know what I mean, dear.'

So she had not quite finished. Well, well, he must sum the matter up.

'As I see it, you think he will want to be seen about with her, and that if he is, people will put an utterly unjustifiable construction upon it. Well, why not say a word to him, in a friendly way? Or to her? Or even to Wellard?'

Lady Ormsby looked at him with the loving smile with which she always thought of him. The idea of telling a woman you had only just met that she will lose her reputation if she is seen about with your husband was rather funny.

'Bless you, dear,' said Maggie. 'Now, what were you going to tell me?'

Mr Fondeveril told her. And the country cousins said, 'Who *is* he? I know I've seen him before.' And the Wellards consulted the menu again, drank coffee, and went off to the Rialto.

III

But it is doubtful if they ever got there. The Wellards' London was widening daily, but would never catch up with the geography of the Film Magnate. Reginald had started half a dozen Rialtos behind, and did not seem to be making any ground. As soon as he could say confidently to himself, 'This is the Taj Mahal,' the Louvre would flash its new-found lights at him, and leave him with the dazzled feeling that it was somewhere else. 'No, darling, that's the Bargello. The Louvre—or am I thinking of the Rialto?' And though it was certainly of the Rialto that they were thinking when they left the Ivy, and of the film which everybody said was so good, it was at the Giant Pyramid, as likely as not, that they passed the evening.

In the company of two-dimensional husbands and wives. Which surprises you most, Reginald had asked Coral Bell, that so many marriages are successes, or that so many are failures? The surprising thing, surely, was that so many were successes. Do we ever stop fouling the domestic nest? If a writer is to be serious about married life, there is only one way for him to be serious; the marriage must be a tragic failure; sordid, unlovely; a vulgarity of body, mind or spirit. If a writer is to be humorous about married life, there is only one way for him to be humorous; the marriage must be a comic failure; but still sordid, still unlovely; vulgarity holding both its sides. Tragedy, comedy? A man loses his faith, his honour, his loved one, or he loses his hat; he is a theme for tragedy or comedy; but not if faith and honour and the loved one are never kept, not if all the world is mislaying its hat. Surely, thought Reginald, even in a film there should be a suggestion that marriage might be a lovely thing, that here was a beauty worth striving for, even if so many missed it.

That couple in front of us. Perhaps they have been holding hands for two years, watching a film like this once every week— a hundred films like this, and now they are to be married! How easy it makes it for them! How well-remembered, how right, the infelicities of marriage will seem! And if the children of their sordid house should fail to bring them honour, how inevitable to blame those other pictures, of the adventurous and the lightly clothed, for contaminating their young minds. . . .

Things aren't moral and immoral, thought Reginald, they're beautiful and ugly. Ugliness is the only thing which ought to be censored. . . .

From underneath the bed the husband's head came cautiously out. Its jaws worked silently, chewing gum. There was an extremity of terror on its features, and as these became smaller and more distant, the cause of their apprehension came backwards into focus, a harsh-faced little woman with a rolling pin in her hand, seated opposite the door, waiting grimly for her husband's return. Like that of some anxious tortoise, the husband's head moved forth and back, like some misinformed hawk the wife waited to pounce on what was not there, on what was behind her, unseen, unsuspected. From wife to husband, from husband to wife, four thousand eyes were conducted, backwards and forwards, backwards and forwards, lest any implication of the misunderstanding should be overlooked. Wife waiting for Husband; Husband already there. Wife resolute to wait all night. Husband, under bed, doomed to remain all night. . . .

A Bedroom Scene. Fortunately not one of those Bedroom Scenes which corrupt the morals. All clean, healthy fun. . . .

Sylvia is laughing. (How curiously insensitive women are.)

Reginald is laughing. (Ugly, horrible; but, after all, it *is* rather comic.)

Chapter Fifteen

I

Undoubtedly Sylvia was, as they used to say, leading her own life. She was no longer Westaways, the Westaways that was invited to lunch or tea or dinner, to tennis parties or cricket matches; she was no longer the Wellards. 'You' now meant herself, 'you' was Sylvia Wellard, that lovely Sylvia Wellard, singular not plural. In the country 'you' was honestly you, in London, it seemed, 'you' was as often as not an invidious thou. How many husbands, not aware of this, have dragged in unnecessary wives, or wives unwanted husbands?

Of course Reginald also was leading his own life; very much thou. But this was natural. It was he who had written *Bindweed*, he who was part-author (if you called it that) of a play now in rehearsal, he who lunched with Mr Pump in order to discuss the next novel. Sylvia had nothing to do with all this. Sylvia's activities were social, in which Reginald might well have been asked to join; Reginald's were business, in which Sylvia had no part. No wife could possibly object when Reginald became 'thou', but the most understanding husband might feel a little hurt (surely?) at the constant familiarity of this second person singular with Mrs Wellard.

Reginald was hurt. Unreasonably, of course, but that made it no less painful. What I really want, he thought, what every man wants, is a harem. Three wives. One to look after me, one to talk to, one to love. And the loved one must be sacred. Nobody must see her, nobody come near her, but myself. Or is that nonsense?

Yes. I think it is. Damnably unfair, anyhow. . . . If I were one of three husbands, what would Sylvia choose me for? Perhaps I shouldn't be chosen at all. Yes, I should, I should. Shouldn't I, Sylvia? You do love me still?

In the golden light of memory what a succession of lovely pictures the past threw up! Every shared experience at Westaways seemed now as some precious infinite moment in a dream, a realization of happiness never truly to be held, perhaps never again to be touched. There had they sat, there stood, there held hands; met, walked, kissed, looked into each other's eyes; played, laughed together. This day, that day, when this had happened, when that had happened, each memory, however commonplace, brought now its sudden vivid, overwhelming picture of himself and Sylvia as one, inextricably twined. She was the lovely flower, on whose beauty he lived.

Was it only her physical beauty which kept him alive, only her body which he loved? Ridiculous! As seen thus in retrospect, every thought of hers, every misunderstanding, every incomprehension was part of the Sylvia to whom he was bound, the Sylvia to whom he had been unfaithful. There is an unfaithfulness of spirit, he thought, no less than of body. I have been unfaithful to Sylvia. God help me, I have even despised her. No, I haven't, he thought quickly. . . . And then, Yes, I have.

I am being damnably jealous for no reason at all. Why can't she go her way, I mine? And then we meet in the evening . . . at night . . . and are one again. I have my secret thoughts—why should not she? I have my friends, my activities—why should not she? It's this damnable possessive instinct which men have. I want to be free, but I want her not to be free. And yet I am less free than she is, for I have that faint uneasy feeling of disloyalty to her when I am with another woman. Does she have that feeling? Of course not. Why should she?

I wish I could be on a desert island with her for ever and ever. . . . He laughed as he remembered that he had once wished to be there with Coral Bell.

I wish we had never come to London. (And never met Coral Bell? Certainly.)

I wish—oh, God knows what I wish. Only I love you, Sylvia, and *don't* enjoy yourself too much without me, and—oh, let's go back to Westaways soon! We were so terribly happy there.

But, as he came to the Green Park, he had altered it to 'I mean, *I* was terribly happy there', and, as he left the Park, again to 'I mean, I seem *now* to have been terribly happy there', and by the time he reached the theatre he was thinking that London wasn't a bad place after all, when exciting things like this were happening.

'This' was Reginald's first approach to a theatre through the stage-door. Miss Ethel Prentice, that popular favourite, was to be presented by Mr Augustus Venture, that extremely popular impresario, in an entirely new play by Mr Filby Nixon, that popular dramatist, based on that remarkably popular novel *Bindweed*. 'It might amuse you to drop in to a rehearsal,' wrote Nixon. 'We start on Monday.' And on Thursday Reginald felt that he could delay his amusement no longer.

So here he was, not quite knowing how to take the first step. Ask for Mr Nixon? But then ought one to drag him away from the middle of rehearsal? Push through the swing-doors and hope for the best? The problem was settled for him.

'Yessir?' said a head, popping out of its cage.

Reginald explained, with that air of apology which somehow seemed natural to the situation.

'There's no rehearsal called for this morning, sir.'

'Oh!' (What had happened?) 'They *have* been rehearsing here, haven't they?'

'Yes, that's all right, sir, but there's been just a little trouble, as I understand it. Mr Nixon's up with Mr Venture now. Shall I tell him you're here, sir?'

'Oh, well, I don't suppose he wants——'

'No harm in letting him know, sir.' He picked up the telephone.

So, a little later, Reginald was shaking hands with Mr Augustus Venture, and was by him being introduced to Lattimer. ('You know Lattimer, of course?')

Though of no more than middle height Mr Venture was probably the widest man in London. As he wore pale fawn waistcoats, and was fond of putting his thumbs under his braces, he seemed even wider than that. He had a reddish-brown suit, a red carnation in his button-hole, a high collar with a red bow tie, and a cigar in the middle of his round red baby face. Mr Lattimer was black, and apparently in the Church. Even with this aid, thought Reginald ridiculously, Mr Venture was much too wide to get into Heaven.

'I'm glad you've come, old man,' said Nixon again. 'It concerns you in a sort of way.'

'And four heads are better than three,' murmured the clergyman sardonically.

Mr Venture said something indistinctly through his cigar, and nodded to Nixon.

'It's like this,' began Nixon.

Mr Venture removed his cigar.

'See here,' said Mr Venture, who had moments of wishing you to think he was an American. 'See here, Mr—— Sorry. Didn't get your name.'

'Wellard, Reginald Wellard,' prompted Nixon in a distressful whisper. 'The author.'

'Well, see here, Mr Willard——' He inhaled deeply from his cigar, held it for a moment in two fat fingers, blew out a large cloud of smoke, returned the cigar to his mouth, and said to Nixon with the lethargy of a man who has now done his share, 'You tell him.'

'It's Ethel. You know. Playing Sally.'

'The world's worst actress. You know,' said the clergyman.

An inquiry as to who wanted her to act seemed to come from Mr Venture's cigar.

'Damn it, Lattimer, what's the good of saying that?"

'He's said it,' mumbled the cigar.

'Exactly. And here's the result.'

Mr Venture suddenly gave the impression that he was about to make a speech, and the clergyman's instinctive 'Oh, my God', gave the impression that he had already heard it.

'Mr Willd,' said Mr Venture earnestly, keeping his thumbs under his braces, and speaking with difficulty through his cigar, 'I got a lill codge in Kent, and erry wick I dry to that lill codge, and I par thounds lill houses, and all the thounds peel in those thounds lill houses go to the thear, paps once a year. Annie ersary, birsday, weng,' tever it is. And warray go to see? Atser point. Not *warray*, but *hooay* go to see?' He took the cigar out of his mouth, blew out a cloud of smoke, and said very distinctly and firmly, *'That's* the point.'

'And now that you know all about it,' said Lattimer, extracting a gold case smartly from his hip-pocket, 'have a cigarette.'

Something in Lattimer's movement revealed him to Reginald as of the stage. Of course! Lattimer the producer. Not the clergyman. Idiot not to have seen it before. Well, that explained it.

'Miss Prentice has thrown up her part, is that it?' he asked.

'We shall have to wait for the Sunday papers,' said Lattimer. 'She has either been called up suddenly by a film company which has an exclusive option on her services, or her doctor has ordered her to Madeira for a rest-cure.'

'There's simply nobody else,' said Nixon, 'except Letty——'

Mr Venture withdrew a hand from his braces, and made a movement which put Letty, whoever she was, back to wherever she came from.

'Then there's nobody.'

'I know a little girl,' began Lattimer, but Mr Venture made another movement, which returned all little girls to the Provinces, the Sunday Societies and the Academy of Dramatic Art.

'Gussie feels, and I think he's right,' explained Nixon, 'that you *must* have a name.'

Reginald looked round anxiously for Gussie, saw Mr Venture's braces, and identified them as (of course) Augustus.

'Not warray, but hooay go to see,' said Augustus.

'Is there really nobody?' Reginald asked Nixon.

'Nobody except——' Mr Venture began to unhook a thumb, and Nixon withdrew the exception with a shrug. 'Nobody.'

Reginald looked appealingly at Lattimer, and the ex-clergyman whipped out his gold cigarette-case again. Reginald shook his head, and asked him, 'Well, what are you going to do?' In his heart he was saying, 'Oh, let's go back to Westaways.'

'I've told 'em my idea, Mr Wellard. Naturally it isn't popular, because it means more work for Nixon and less money for Venture.'

'Damn it, Lattimer, there *is* a book after all. I owe some loyalty to Mr Wellard. Besides, she wouldn't come.'

Mr Venture took his cigar out of his mouth, and said, 'What would she want?'

'Eighty.'

'Money has nothing to do with it in her case,' snapped Nixon.

'Make it forty, then,' said Mr Venture, returning the cigar.

'Besides, she isn't a name at all in your sense of the word.'

'Nay in bess sess o' wor',' said the cigar.

'I don't care a damn about that,' said Lattimer. 'She can act. And I've got a little girl for Sally, and *she* can act. And then we're all happy.'

I suppose I'm helping, thought Reginald, but I don't quite know how.

'If Mr Wellard doesn't mind,' began Nixon doubtfully. 'Of course it *could* be done,'

'What?'

'After all, it's your book.' And then, as Mr Venture seemed to be emphasizing that he had bought a play, 'I know, Gussie, I know, but there *are* limits.' He turned back to Reginald. 'It's Aunt Julia.'

To Mr Venture, stiff in his chair with his thumbs under his braces, waiting to be photographed, a secretary came, spoke, continued to speak in monologue. She went out, leaving him still gazing rigidly at the opposite wall. Lattimer, half-sitting on Mr Venture's desk, was idly turning the pages of a theatrical *Who's What*, and murmuring 'God, what faces'. Filby Nixon explained, without prejudice, the Aunt Julia problem.

'So really, old man, what it comes to is may she marry Andrew? If so, I can write in a scene quite easily. Of course, her part will have to be strengthened all through, well, that's all right, I can do that, and there's just a question whether she ought to be an aunt at all, well, I don't mind the aunt so much, but I think she ought to be a widow. I mean any one so charming as she'll make her must have been married before, don't you think? It'll shift the focus a bit from Sally, but then that's just as well if we have one of Lattimer's young girls. I know 'em, clever as the devil, but you want more than that to carry a long part. So really, you see——'

'I see,' said Reginald coldly. 'It's hardly my affair at all, is it?' Sally—Sylvia—to be made a secondary character! And played by some clever young devil with a long nose.

'Legally, I suppose not, but between authors there are other considerations. I'm in your hands entirely.'

'That's very decent of you. I'm bound to say——' He broke off, and asked, 'The idea being, I suppose, to get a name for the aunt as you can't get one for the niece? Let's have it clear.'

'Exactly. A play wants all the help it can get nowadays. If you get people saying "I *must* go and see so-and-so——" '

'Well, who is she? See if it makes *me* say that.'

'Coral Bell.'

'*Who?*' cried Reginald.

'Coral Bell. I don't suppose you remember her on the stage. She's Lady Edgemoor now, that's why Gussie takes to her. You've met her, haven't you? Mrs Wellard——'

'Yes, yes, but *would* she come back?'

'Well, that's the point. Lattimer thinks she would.'

'By Jove,' said Reginald softly, 'it would be marvellous if she did!'

Mr Augustus Venture, coming to life suddenly, explained that he had a little cottage in Kent. Every week he drove to that little cottage, and passed thousands of little houses, and all the thousands of people in those thousands of little houses went to the theatre. Perhaps once a year. An anniversary, birthday, wedding, whatever it might be. And what did they go to see? That was the point. Not *what*, but *who* did they go to see? That was the point.

Reginald nodded. They would go to see Coral Bell. Who wouldn't?

II

Meanwhile Lord Ormsby was going to see Sylvia Wellard again.

'Hallo!' said Sylvia with her friendly smile. 'Tea, please, Alice.'

'Not for me, Mrs Wellard.' He shook hands heartily, and sank into a chair. 'But I'll watch you.'

'It's nothing really to watch, you know.'

'I *don't* know. Ever heard of Byron?'

Sylvia wrinkled her forehead and wondered if she had ever heard of Byron.

'He was a poet. Lived about a hundred years ago.'

'Oh! How funny!' She was laughing.

'Go on laughing, I like to hear it. Don't care how often you laugh at me, if you laugh like that.'

'I wasn't laughing *at* you, only—— You see, I thought you meant somebody in London, some friend of yours. Of course I've heard of *Byron*.'

'Ah! That's the worst of being self-educated, Mrs Wellard. You know what you know a damn sight better, sorry, than the other man, but you don't know what *he* knows. See what I mean? All you educated people, you've all had the same governesses, and been to the same schools and colleges, and you all know the same things at the same time. Now I was talking to a woman about a hell of a feller, sorry, called Beckford, heard of him?'—Sylvia looked vague—'no, neither had she, but how's an outsider to know that Byron's in the curriculum, and Beckford isn't? See what I mean?'

'I always expect that everybody knows everything that I know, *and* lots more,' said Sylvia.

'Don't you believe it. And look here, I'll tell you something. Education. Latin and Greek. I'm not saying anything against swells like Raglan. But why do we teach small damfool boys in Eton collars, sorry, Latin and Greek? To educate them? No. Just so's small damfool boys who haven't got Eton collars won't know Latin and Greek. See what I mean? I'm not a Socialist, because you can't run my sort of papers on Socialism, and anyway it's bunk, and I wish to hell I knew Latin and Greek, sorry, like Raglan does. But don't think I don't see through it.'

There had been a time when conversation with a woman other than one of his chosen had seriously cramped Ormsby's style, for certain words would keep obtruding themselves if he were not on the watch for them; and it was not until he had fallen into this habit of slipping in a neutralizing 'sorry' as soon as convenient afterwards that he was at ease again. Today it might be that even a nice woman like Mrs Wellard wouldn't feel the need of apology, but apology was now so automatic that the omission of it would have cramped him just as badly.

Alice came up with the tea.

'Sure you won't have any?'

'No, thanks. Now what were we talking about?'

'Education.'

'Yes. No. What the—— Oh, I know, I asked you if you knew Byron.' He frowned, a little annoyed.

Sylvia laughed happily.

'Of course! And I thought you meant—— Well, the answer is Yes. Why?'

'That's it. Seems so damn silly to come back to it. Like capping a feller's story in the club, and some damn feller, sorry, sorry, comes up just as you're getting to the point and smacks the other feller on the back, and says, "Hallo, old man, haven't seen you since God knows when, how's the family?" and they swop their blasted—they swop families for five minutes by the blasted—by the clock, and then your feller turns back to you, and says, "Sorry, what were you going to say?" And the whole thing's as cold as a—as a——' He groped for a substitute for the 'bloody ham-sandwich' with which alone he could express its coldness, failed to find it, and ended with a shrug and a 'See what I mean? Sorry'.

'You're making it worse,' said Sylvia. 'Because I feel I must know about Byron now, and the longer you put it off the colder he gets.'

Ormsby laughed, his eyes kept on her with the unwinking absorption which had been his passport through the defences of women. Sylvia turned her head away, and made a lingering choice between indistinguishable pieces of bread-and-butter.

'Byron couldn't stand seeing women eat,' said Ormsby slowly. 'He thought they ought to do it in private—like—well, he thought they ought to do it in private.'

'How funny of him,' said Sylvia coolly.

'That was just his romantic idea of women, Mrs Wellard.'

'And you're not romantic, Lord Ormsby?'

'Not in that way,' he said with a chuckle. 'The more I see of women, the more I like it.' He chuckled again. 'Whatever they're doing,' and his eyes were fixed on her, still, unwinking; suggesting, challenging.

A little sigh came from Sylvia, and she turned her shining head, and let her lovely eyes rest on him, meeting first his eyes and then, unhurried, seeming to travel over him and through him and beyond him to some world out of Ormsby's reach. Often with his greedy relentless eyes he had made intimacy with a woman, so that she felt naked and ashamed (or naked and unashamed), but never had he stripped her so of her defences as now he felt stripped. Every ugliness, every physical grossness, seemed to be laid bare by that look. He was naked, hideous, obscene, a shuddering offence against love, against the mystical beauties and intimacies of love. It was not, he felt, his soul which she had seen; it was his actual body; seen, rejected, left contemptuously lying for him to pick up. She turned lightly away, and he struggled back into it, red-faced.

'I'm so sorry,' said Sylvia, coming back to him; 'do smoke.'

'No, thanks. I really came to give you these.' He brought his hand out of his pocket, and held out an envelope to her. 'The show tonight. I thought you and your husband might be amused. The Palace.'

'But isn't it the first-night?'

'Well, of course. That's why I thought it might amuse you. Ought to have sent 'em along before, I'm afraid, but only remembered about the damn thing, sorry, this morning.'

'But I thought,' stammered Sylvia, 'I thought all the seats, I thought——'

Ormsby laughed back a little of his self-respect, and explained how it was that to the Ormsbys of this world the ordinary suppositions did not apply.

'Oh, I *wish* we could, it *is* nice of you, but——'

'Engaged?'

'Yes. Reginald's got to go to some play—he rang up from the theatre—to see somebody, some actress, I think. He said they wanted him to see her. What a pity! I've never been to a first-night.'

'You haven't missed much.'

'But it must be thrilling, wondering what it's all about, and everybody else wondering, and the dresses and everything.' She looked thrilled as she said it.

'Oh well, people seem to like all that.'

'It *was* nice of you to think of us. Thank you so much.' She had taken the envelope, and now she gave it back to him. 'You must go and ring up some other lucky person. Quickly.'

Ormsby took the tickets, looked at them a moment, and said humbly, his eyes still on the tickets, 'I suppose you wouldn't care to come with me. To let me take you. I'd call for you, we'd have dinner or—or not, as you wished. I could tell you who the people were, if that sort of thing interests you. If you think you'd like that sort of evening, it seems bad luck to miss it.'

And not knowing how she knew, Sylvia knew that this was the invitation which he had intended when he came into her drawing-room; and, not knowing how it had happened, she knew that at some time he had abandoned that intention and had made way for her husband; so that now he only offered himself humbly in that husband's default. And not knowing how she knew, nor how it had happened, she knew that she was utterly safe with Lord Ormsby from now onwards. And London was a heavenly place.

'I should love it,' said Sylvia, her face alight with happiness. 'It *is* kind of you. But I think I'd better have dinner at home, it won't be such a rush.'

Ormsby got up.

'I'll call for you at a quarter to eight. Can you manage that?'

'Easily. Thank you so much.' She held out her hand.

'Thank *you,* Mrs Wellard. Quarter to eight, then.'

And as he went downstairs he was thinking, Why in hell didn't I have a daughter like that? If Maggie had known her job—— Damn it, nobody can pretend it's *my* fault. . . .

And Sylvia was thinking, Perhaps the green . . . I suppose Lady Ormsby won't be there . . . Lady Edgeworth's seen it. . . . Of course she mightn't be there, and anyhow we mightn't see her. And I expect I shall keep my cloak on, and she hasn't seen that. . . . 'All right, Alice, I've finished.'

'Mr Wellard has just telephoned, madam,' said Alice, as she took the tray. 'He's very sorry he won't have time to get back to dinner, and he'll get something out.'

'Oh! Oh, well, that makes it easier. I want something at seven. Will you tell Mrs Stoker? Just the fish, I think, and the sweet. I'm going to the first-night at the Palace, Alice.' She laughed. 'Palace, Alice. Doesn't it sound silly?'

'Fancy,' said Alice.

Chapter Sixteen

I

When Coral Bell was in her hey-day, adored by all the curly young opera-hats which supped nightly at the Savoy, she received one afternoon two proposals from the same man. She sat in her dressing-room after the *matinée,* a colourless wrapper pulled round her body, a white shiny face looking back at herself from the glass. Ned Lattimer, hands on top of his stick, chin on hands, gravely watched the face in the mirror.

'Now you know just how beautiful I am,' said Coral Bell.

'You've got such good bones,' said Lattimer, 'you'll always be all right.'

'Gracious, you can't see them, can you?' She threw down the rag with which she was busy, and gave the wrapper another pull.

'I meant the bones of your face.'

'Oh! You're welcome to those,' she said, and went back to them. He watched her silently.

'I'm having a season at the Circle,' he said suddenly.

'How do you mean you're having a season at the Circle? What as?'

'Producer. Part Manager. Hoffman and I.'

'Really? I say, you *are* getting on, aren't you? Why, you can't be a day more than sixty-seven.'

'I'm twenty-eight this year.'

'I thought you were sixty-seven. When were you nine?'

'Eighteen years ago, I should think.'

'Don't tell me that eighteen years ago you were running about and shouting and singing———'

'I was.'

'And laughing and bowling a hoop?'

'Probably.'

'And then your white mouse died, and you never smiled again?'

He smiled now, and said, 'Life hasn't been too easy, you know.'

'Good Heavens, why should it be?'

'True. . . . Coral, there are two things I want you to do for me.'

'If I can.'

'I think you can. One is, Marry me. And the other is, Play Rosalind for me.'

She turned round on him with a jerk, clutching her wrapper round her with both hands.

'Are you serious?'

'You say I always am.'

'What do you expect me to answer?'

' "No. No." But then I'm a pessimist. What I hope you'll say is "Yes. Yes". '

'Must the two go together?'

'Not necessarily.'

She stared at him for a little longer, and then turned back to her mirror.

'Why do you want to marry me?' she asked quietly.

'Because I love you more than I thought it was possible to love anybody or anything.'

'Oh, Ned, Ned, I'm so awfully sorry.'

'I suppose they all say that.' He meant 'all the people who propose to you'.

She shook her head.

'They may use those words, but they don't make them sound like that. Oh, Ned, do forgive me.'

'What for? Come and play Rosalind, and I'll bless you for ever.' She sighed and said nothing. 'Well?'

'My dear man, I'm what they call a musicalcomedy soubrette. Why not get an actress?'

'You can act all their heads off.'

She turned back to him with a wide, happy smile.

'You really *are* a genius! How did you know that?'

'Oh, don't let's ask each other how we know our jobs. You'll come?'

She shook her head slowly; a little sadly.

'It's too late.'

'Contracts? I can——'

'No, no. This is quite, quite private for the moment. You're the first to know.' She hesitated, as if even now she oughtn't to give away the secret, and said, 'I'm leaving the stage and getting married.'

'Ah!' He got up. 'Well, that does settle it, doesn't it!'

'Ned!'

'If ever you come back——'

'Ned!'

He went to the door, turned, a little as if in a play, said with a laugh, 'Another white mouse dead,' and went out. And if, later on, Coral Bell married Lord Edgemoor, and Joan Hedley made a great success of *Rosalind*, and Lattimer, from time to time, married some other woman, yet there had been that scene between the two of them, which one of them could never quite forget.

She remembered it now as she held out her hand to him.

'Thank you for letting me come,' he said. 'Is this where the aristocracy live?'

'You've had plenty of chances of finding out, if you had really wanted to know.'

'I never go to parties.'

'You certainly never come to mine.'

He looked round the room appraisingly.

'It would make rather a good stage set.'

'Copy it if you like.'

'Is that your bedroom in there?'

'Yes. Do you want to see it? You could hide any amount of people there in the Second Act.'

He ignored that, and walked over to a table in the window.

'These are good,' he said, fingering one of a pair of candlesticks. 'I was looking for something like this in *Lady in Blue*. Where did you get them?'

'Italy.'

'They're not Italian.'

'They don't speak it, if that's what you mean. But the man who made them was an Italian. I'm sorry. He was. And we met him in Italy, and he works in Italy, and he made them in Italy, and we bought them in Italy. That's why I said "Italy"—like that.'

He came back to her, a smile trying to lose itself in the corners of his disillusioned mouth, and said, 'I offered you a job once.'

He had offered her two, thought Coral Bell. Rosalind and Mrs Lattimer. She said, 'I've always been grateful for that.'

'Now I've come to see you about another. You'll say no, of course, but I've told that fat cocoon Venture that I thought you might if I asked you nicely. Nixon's keen. So's Venture, if that doesn't put you off. Well?'

'What are we all talking about?' asked Lady Edgemoor plaintively.

So he told her . . . and three-quarters of an hour later Coral Bell was saying, 'All the same, it would be rather fun, you know. Shall I? Shan't I? Well, I must cable to Charley.'

Charles, Lord Edgemoor, was on his way to Thibet, looking for Monterey's Ibex. Some weeks earlier the last survivor of this noble and otherwise extinct species had wandered into a hill village, looking as if it were looking for Lord Edgemoor. As soon as the news came through to him, his lordship took up the challenge and hurried out. The cable caught him at Darjeeling. He cabled back, slightly under the influence of the East, 'Your pigeon, old girl.'

So that was that.

II

To hear her saying the words which he had written, that was wonderful. To hear her, as happened more often, saying the words which Nixon had written, that, though not quite so wonderful, was still wonderful. Even, thought Reginald, to hear her, as happened most often of all, paraphrasing a speech which she had forgotten in words which no self-respecting writer could possibly have written, even that filled him with content.

But, he had to admit, he was also very well content to listen to Lattimer's Young Girl (whose nose was not nearly so long as had been feared) playing her love-scene with the young cousin, what time Coral Bell sat among the ruins of the current attraction *(Act I, Scene 2, The Castle Terrace, Midnight)* chattering gaily—('Coral, *please*! How *can* we get on if——' 'Terribly sorry, Ned. I'm sorry, Miss Masters')—talking, then, in hushed whispers to the Defaulting Solicitor. At least he would have been content if Coral Bell had joined him in the stalls, or, alternatively, if he had had the nerve to join her on the terrace. It was her conversation, her intelligence, which he admired so much, which he grudged so much to others. In looks she could not compare even with Miss Masters.

Quite early on, Reginald had had to come to an agreement with himself as to what he was doing there at all. Obviously nobody wanted him. Equally obviously, if he didn't interfere, nobody minded him. Mr Venture had bought a play; Lattimer was producing that play; Nixon (undoubtedly) had written that play. Mr Venture knew nothing about a book called *Bindweed*. With the air of one conferring distinction on the non-reading public, he emphasized that he never read books. He was a Theatre Man. But of course if Mr Wellard was a friend of Phil's, that was all right.

So, for a few days, Reginald came to the theatre as a friend of Phil's. 'Do you mind, old man, if I bring a friend in?' Some would, some wouldn't. Mr Venture didn't. But it seems a little odd never to be able to attend rehearsals of your play without the support of a friend, the same friend, and hardly an intimate friend at that. So Mr Nixon's friend came no longer, and, instead, there entered a gentleman, Reginald Wellard, who was 'studying the theatre'.

'Do you mind,' he said to Lattimer, and he almost added 'old man' to show what an apt pupil of the theatre he was becoming, 'do you mind if I sit about at the back somewhere and watch you do this? It seems rather a chance to get to know something about——' Could he say it? He could—'er—technique and—er—stage-craft and—and so forth. I mean if I ever tried to write a play— You see, it's all so new to me.'

Very few men can resist the attraction of the novice.

'Of course. Come as often as you like. There's a lot to learn.' And from time to time the great man himself would stroll round to the back of the stalls and say to an uplifted Wellard, 'You see what I'm getting at? You see how——' and make embracing gestures with his hands. 'Rather,' said Mr Wellard. 'It's wonderful.'

Mr Venture sat in the middle of the front row of the stalls, smoking his cigar from the middle of his mouth. From time to time he mumbled something. Nobody heard, or, hearing, understood, or, understanding, regarded him. From time to time his secretary hurried across the stage and down the bridge, whispered earnestly in his ear, and was herself unregarded. Filby Nixon sat at the end of the third row of stalls. From time to time he jumped up, hurried after Lattimer, and waved his hands. Lattimer said, 'Right . . . Right. I've got that in mind,' and went on as before. Meanwhile the players split their infinitives, suspended their nominatives, and said, 'Just give me that,' to the prompter.

Then one day Coral came down to talk to Lattimer, found him talking to Reginald, and cried, 'Why, it's Mr Wellard.'

'Just a moment, darling,' said Lattimer, and hurried on to the stage.

'When did *you* come in?' said Coral, sitting down next to him.

'About ten days ago,' said Reginald, glowing all over.

'Good gracious, have you been here all the time?'

'Pretty well.'

'Why so modest?'

'Well, what would a conceited man do?'

'Introduce himself to the company with the words, "Talking of my novel *Bindweed*, now in its one hundred and fiftieth thousand——" They're longing to meet you.'

'That always seems strange to me somehow. In fact, I don't believe it.'

'Well, I can't prove it. But come up after-wards and meet Miss Masters. She'll amuse you.'

'Right. How do you like being back?'

'This is almost as queer to me as it is to you. I wish you could see a musical-comedy rehearsal. I'm a perfect idiot to be doing it really.'

'You'll be wonderful.'

'In the sense that everybody will be full of wonder as to how I had the nerve to take it on, I expect you're right. How's Mrs Wellard?'

'Well and happy.'

'Why don't you bring her along to a rehearsal one day? Or wouldn't it interest her?'

'I feel shy enough about coming myself, and as for—— I'd simply never thought of it.'

'Well, think of it now.' She got up. 'I must just speak to Ned. Goodbye.'

There seemed to be a good deal of coming and going at this rehearsal. Lattimer's 'Just a moment, darling' became more frequent. Nixon had a word to say to everybody; he even sat down next to Mr Venture, and after gesticulating to that immobile man, got up again. The players looked as if they had given up hope of getting on with the play.

'What's happening?' said Reginald, as Nixon came near him for a moment.

'What? Oh, it's you, Wellard. Sorry, didn't see you. The Banks girl has got appendicitis. Or hasn't. I don't know. After yesterday she might have anything.'

'Was she the one—*Diana*—who was——'

'Yes. Lattimer's too fond of that sort of thing. Sarcasm never gets you anywhere. It's much too easy.'

'She's thrown up her part?'

'Or got appendicitis. I suppose a doctor knows the difference, but I'm damned if I do.'

'Who are you going to get?'

'There's a girl up at Golder's Green—we're going to have a look at her tonight. I've just been telephoning for a box. It's the Globe play. You didn't see it, I suppose?'

Reginald hadn't.

'You'd better come along too.'

Reginald was doubtful if he could manage it.

'Coral's coming.'

But as a matter of fact he thought that perhaps he could. In fact he'd love to. Thanks awfully.

He went out and telephoned to Sylvia. Later, as the rehearsal went on and on, it was suggested that they should have such dinner as was possible somewhere together.

'With me,' said Reginald eagerly.

'Nonsense, old man.'

'No, really.'

'Oh, well, we can settle that afterwards,' said Nixon.

Reginald telephoned to Sylvia again.

III

As he let himself into Number 6, Hayward's Grove, that night, he was feeling remorseful. He had nothing to apologize for, but he wanted to apologize. Sylvia had had dinner alone, had spent the evening alone, at the shortest possible notice. No time had been given to ask Margaret, or some other friend, to keep her company. Well, he was sorry, terribly sorry, darling, but it wasn't his fault. You know what things are like in the theatre. At rehearsals. Your time simply isn't your own. You can't just go out in the morning and say 'Back at five', as an ordinary husband can. It may be five in the morning for all you know. Something goes wrong, you know how it is, and you have to see this person, talk to that one, dash off to Golder's Green, or wherever it may be, and then where are you?

Yes. All very well for Nixon to talk like that to his wife (had he a wife? How little one knew about these people), but for Wellard it was absurd. He was a spectator, not a performer; with nothing but his own pleasure to consider. Well, he *had* considered his own pleasure. He couldn't drag Sylvia about with him everywhere—particularly in this new world where wives and husbands were so seldom mentioned, and nobody ever seemed quite certain who, at any given moment, was married to whom. Suppose he had said to Nixon, 'Yes, I should like to come, but I must bring my wife.' It would sound too ghastly, as though he were afraid of her, or she were jealous. Trailing round after him, so that he shouldn't be alone with the pretty actresses. Horrible! Sordid! Like one of those terrible films. No. And if he had said 'Sorry, I'm afraid I'm engaged——'

Well, he had said it. At first. And then when he had heard that Coral Bell——

She's such good company, that's what it is. Stimulating. Clever, and makes the other person feel clever too. I know that if I say anything, she'll see what I mean at once. Same with Lena. And that Miss Voles. Well, it's just—naturally a man likes—I mean it's only natural.

All the same . . .

Well, look here, what about doing what Coral Bell said? Taking her to the theatre tomorrow? And introducing her to Lattimer, and Venture, and perhaps that Miss Masters, and, well, all of them. Jove, she'd knock spots off them! Now they really would see what a lovely woman was like. Yes, that was it. That would make it all right. . . .

He went into the drawing-room, the words on his lips. ('I say, I've got rather an idea.') Nobody there. Sylvia gone to bed, poor darling. Finished her book, and gone to bed. Sandwiches and drinks on the table. Two glasses, both unused. Funny. She must have gone very early. Still, she'd hardly be asleep yet.

He listened outside her bedroom door. No sound. He tapped gently. No answer. He went in on tiptoe. Still no sound. He turned on the light. No Sylvia.

He tried the bathroom; the morning-room, since the drawing-room fire was out, and she might have gone there for the gas-fire. Outside each room he called gently 'Sylvia'—and went in. She was not in the house.

'My God,' he thought in one sudden icy moment of fear, 'supposing she's left me!'

The next moment he remembered that that was the sort of thing which happened on the stage, and would not be likely, therefore, to happen in real life. He laughed as he found himself thinking this, and then thought, but with less fear now, 'All the same, people run away in real life.' He remembered somebody who had . . . but of course that was different. Not like Sylvia and him.

She had gone out, of course. Margaret had rung her up; or she had rung up Margaret and invited herself to dinner. He wandered into the dining-room, and looked round for evidence that she had dined out. Sherlock Holmes would have found something. All that Reginald found was two places laid for breakfast, which told him nothing. . . . Except that if she were running away, she hadn't mentioned it to Alice. That he could think of it lightly, jokingly like this, made him now quite certain that she had not run away. He laughed to think what an idiot he had been ever to think . . .

Supposing she had?

He didn't really suppose she had, because he knew that she hadn't, but he let his mind run on. Supposing she had, how 'impossible' would it seem to him? Was it now entirely inconceivable? He walked up and down, eating sandwiches, and wondering. . . .

Running away with another man meant (horrible!) loving him. Could Sylvia love another man like that? Love is much more personal to a woman, he thought, than to a man, physical love. Any decent man could contemplate spending the night with any decent woman, even a stranger, without alarm or disgust. But most women would have to have some strong feeling for the man first. A man could leave his wife and take a mistress, any mistress, just because he was bored with his home. A woman couldn't. Wouldn't. She might run away, but not to a man. Sylvia loves only me; she couldn't, she *couldn't*, love any one else. . . . Not as she loves me.

But she could be bored with me, and run away from me—where? Well, just somewhere. Anywhere. That is just the one thing which one will never know—whether one is perhaps boring somebody else. How boring is the other man's golf story, how interesting seems one's own. How incapable one is of looking at one's own story with another's intolerance. Perhaps I have been boring Sylvia all these years. Have I? Heavens, how bored she must have been at Westaways. . . . Was she?

He looked at his watch—twelve o'clock. This was really rather too bad of her. I mean, twelve o'clock. She couldn't not be back at *twelve.* Unless, of course, she'd had an accident.

An accident! Why not? People had accidents every day. Every hour. An accident, Sylvia hurt, Sylvia dead.

Sylvia dead. Westaways without Sylvia. Life without Sylvia. On and on, day after day, night after night. Westaways would have to be sold. He couldn't possibly live there without Sylvia, not even if Mrs Hosken and Alice stayed on. . . . As, no doubt, they would. . . . He would sell it, and go abroad, go round the world, explore a bit perhaps. One wouldn't really mind what happened to one; in a way that would be rather an advantage to an explorer, not minding. . . . Like a man in the condemned cell, having a sudden pain in the place where he thought his appendix was, or breaking a tooth, and knowing that he was the only man in England, literally the only man, who needn't feel anxious. Who could feel quite gay about it. . . . Almost a short story there, if he were a writer. Really a writer. . . . Of course the man would get reprieved. . . .

Twelve-fifteen. She *had* had an accident. Nothing else was possible. Oh God, don't let her have had an accident! I don't know who you are, but *if* you are, but whatever you are, oh, God, just this time, let it be all right. I swear I do try to be good. *Is* it goodness you worry about all the time? Only goodness? Is the difference between Shakespeare and Bunn just one of Faith and Religious Observance to you? Do you realize that Leonardo was a greater painter than Hayley, and does it matter to you at all? Sorry; I'll believe anything, but don't let her have an accident.

What should he do? Ring up Margaret? But of course it might not have been Margaret. He could wake up Alice, and ask her if she knew where her mistress had gone. But that would look rather—and Alice mightn't know—and—— People don't have accidents. Not people like Sylvia. Look at all the times Sylvia hadn't had an accident. Suppose they'd all had supper together tonight, as he'd thought of suggesting, only not being dressed— well, if they *had* been dressed, think how late that would have made him, and he wouldn't have been having an accident at all. He'd just have been having supper. . . .

Nearly twelve-thirty. Something *must* have happened. She's dead, she's dead. What shall I do? I can't go on doing nothing. How long do I go on doing nothing? She couldn't not be back by now, wherever she'd been. Oh, Sylvia, Sylvia!

There was a faint noise from below, a scraping, like that of a mouse. He rushed to the door, and out on to the landing. A key in the front door, a door opening and shutting, a rustling of clothes. Sylvia!

'Thank God!' cried Reginald to himself. And then thought angrily because he was so frightened, 'I say, this really *is*!'

He went back to the drawing-room as Sylvia came daintily up the stairs.

IV

'Hooray, darling, you're back,' said Sylvia happily.

It wasn't a very good opening.

'Back!' said Reginald. 'Do you know what the time is?'

'No, darling. I hadn't got my watch. Is it very late?'

'Half-past twelve,' he said coldly. And added 'Just on.'

Sylvia laughed. Adorably, anybody else would have thought, but not, at the moment, Reginald.

'And all the time I was thinking how late *you'd* be because of Golder's Green being such a long way off, and how I'd wait up for you.'

'Golder's Green isn't Manchester, you know.'

'No, darling. I don't think I really know where it is. Oh, I must have a sandwich. How nice of Alice.' She sat on the arm of a chair and began to eat one. 'Have you been in long, darling?'

'An hour,' said Reginald coldly. And added, 'Nearly.'

'Darling, you shouldn't have waited for me.'

'You realize, don't you, that I hadn't the faintest idea where you were?'

'Well, I couldn't tell you, darling, because I didn't quite know where *you* were. I mean, where you were having dinner.'

'You might have left a note.'

'I did think of it, darling, but it was all in rather a hurry, and I was so certain I should be back before you.' She blushed a little (that faint shyness which she kept for Reginald) and said, 'I love leaving you notes, and finding notes from you. We don't seem to have done that so much lately.' She gave a little sigh.

But Reginald still had his grievance; his two grievances. First, that she had robbed him of that lonely evening which he had been imagining for her so remorsefully; secondly, that she had so frightened him.

'Where *have* you been exactly?' he asked, and even as he asked, thought how absurd it was to say 'exactly'.

'The first-night at the Palace, darling,' said Sylvia; happily, proudly, as if waiting for his excited admiration.

It did not come.

'The Palace? What on earth—who—how——'

'Lord Ormsby took me, darling.'

'Ormsby! You don't mean that?' said Reginald sharply. Ormsby! Going to a first-night with Ormsby!

'Well, of course I mean it, darling.'

Absurd to have said, 'You don't mean that?' I'm talking like a man in a book, he thought, and felt annoyed again with Sylvia for not over-looking it when he talked like a man in a book.

'Alone?' he asked.

'I suppose so, darling. I mean we just went, and there were people there I knew, and Lord Ormsby introduced me to lots of others. There was a—I'm afraid I've forgotten his name, darling, he sat on my left, and was awfully keen on your book, and is longing to meet you.'

Going to a first-night with Ormsby—alone! And then supposing that, in the face of that, it mattered whether some fool was keen on his book or not! What else could the poor devil say?

'Look here, Sylvia, I suppose you know just what Ormsby is?'

'How do you mean what he is, darling? He owns all those papers, doesn't he?'

'You know perfectly well I don't mean that. I mean his private character. His reputation—with women.'

The moment he said it he realized that he had said something irrevocable. His love for Sylvia, hers for him, this intimate secret love of theirs with each other, her faithfulness to him, these were things about which no words were ever to be said. They were there, they could never be questioned; if they were questioned, then the world was at end. Not for a moment did he question them now; but he had said something which seemed to bring them suddenly, yet however remotely, into the category of things questionable.

Sylvia's hand, reaching out to the tray, came back slowly. She looked at him; angry, hurt, bewildered? He could not tell. How little he could tell of her. I don't know the least thing about you, he thought, but I love you so at this moment that my heart aches. Oh, why am I saying all the things I don't want to say? Don't look at me like that. Say something. Let's both lose our tempers.

She gave a little sigh.

'Well?' he said doggedly.

'Darling, am I supposed to know the reputation of all the people you introduce to me?'

He burst out indignantly, 'I didn't—I mean it was—— You know quite well that isn't the point.'

'I only asked, darling.'

Even in his anger he saw the cleverness of her question, and felt proud of her; and furious with her for being so clever, and for not losing her temper.

'There's a difference', he explained carefully, as if to a child, 'between going in a crowd to a woman's house and going out alone at night with that woman's husband.'

She said nothing. She put her hand back to the tray, poured herself out a little lemonade, and drank it.

'Darling,' cried Reginald, in sudden terror at the way irrevocable words kept leaving him, 'you *know* I don't—I mean it's nothing—it's not—it would be an insult to you to suggest such a thing. It's just that Ormsby has this reputation with women, and people seeing you and him together at the Palace tonight—that of all places—will say—people who don't know you—they'll say—I mean they'll wonder who you are. It's horrible to think of . . . what they'll think . . . being Ormsby.' His voice trailed away, as he watched her from lowered lids. For the moment she just looked puzzled.

'Why did you say "that of all places"?' she asked.

'Well, you know who Veno is.'

She shook her head. 'Veno? What a funny name.'

'He's the half-caste who put the show on.'

'Oh! But what——'

'Ormsby finances him—on condition that he has first choice.' Reginald laughed contemptuously, and added, 'You might say that he owns the Preference Shares.'

For what seemed a long time nothing more was said. The Dresden shepherdess clock on Mrs Carstairs' mantelpiece ticked—ticked—ticked. Irrevocable moments. Irrevocable words. But every moment is irrevocable, every word is irrevocable, and the world goes on, and nobody is very much changed, and nothing has really happened. Silly to think that all this is going to make any difference. It can't, Sylvia, can it? Tick—tick—tick. . . .

With a long mournful sigh Sylvia stood up.

'I had been so terribly happy,' she said. 'You've spoilt my happiness.'

She moved slowly, mournfully, towards the door.

'Sylvia!'

Slowly, mournfully, she took her loveliness, and all the peace and rest and comfort which went with her, from the room.

Chapter Seventeen

I

Reginald lay awake in his dressing-room, going over it in his mind. He had been perfectly right all through. Ormsby *was* that sort of man; nobody could want his wife to be seen about with that sort of man; nobody could help being annoyed if his wife, without consulting him, had gone out at night with that sort of man. He had been perfectly right all through. (How nice to be perfectly right.)

Just consider a moment. Everybody in London knew Ormsby by sight. Well, not quite everybody, but everybody in the stalls at the first-night of a musical show. Nobody knew Sylvia. To the stalls she would just be an astoundingly beautiful young woman; unknown; not, therefore, in what was called Society; not before seen at a first-night; some new arrival to the stage, presumably then, which absorbed and discharged so many beautiful young women. Presumably then, also, of the musical-comedy stage. With Ormsby! At Veno's first-night! What would they think?

Did it matter what they thought, since, thinking this, they could not possibly know Sylvia? Did he mind what people, strangers, said about him? '*Bindweed?* Oh, that's that fellow Wellard. You've heard about *Wellard,* haven't you?' And then some idiotic lie, or disgusting scandal. How many such lies, such scandals, he had heard at the club about his acquaintances. Did one mind if people who didn't know you thought you were this, that or the other? No. But one's wife. . . .

If it comes to that, thought Reginald suddenly, all that I know about Ormsby is just hearsay. I don't *know* anything. How can I? He went on thinking about this for some time, a little ashamed; and then remembered with relief that five minutes' conversation with Ormsby made it sufficiently certain that he was what he was said to be. How absolutely right, then, I was, he thought, to say what I did to Sylvia. (How nice to be absolutely right.)

So much for Reginald, the man who is always right. Now let us consider the erring Sylvia. He tried to put himself in Sylvia's place.

You are taken by your husband to the house of a friend of his. You meet your host and hostess. Later your hostess asks you to lunch, and you meet your host again. Later still he comes to your house; naturally you are hospitable to him. He calls again, not knowing that your husband is out (how could he know?) and suggests taking you to a theatre. It happens that your husband has unexpectedly left you to your own resources that night, so naturally you accept. All eagerness and joyous anticipation. And then you come home, full of your happy evening, longing to tell your husband all about it, and suddenly, crashingly out of a blue sky, he spoils your happiness.

'You've spoilt my happiness.' . . .

He was forty-one. She was twenty-six. A child. He had spoilt her happiness. How dared he marry her? How dared he, married to her, so take her love for granted? How dared he question her who had condescended to him so royally?

'You've spoilt my happiness.'

If the door would open now, and she would come in! How wonderful of her to come in now and be friends again. Listen! A rustling outside the door. Look! The door is opening. Oh, Sylvia, you darling! . . . No, how could it? It was he who had spoilt her happiness; it was for him to ask to be forgiven.

He went over in his mind all the other quarrels which they had had. Not quarrels, disagreements. Never like this. Never before had they carried a disagreement over into the next day. A quarrel, an apology, friends again, lovers again. That was the way when, as Coral Bell put it, you were still on the higher plane, still in love. Once safely on the lower plane, your quarrels need not be made up. You were cross, you went to bed, you woke up un-cross, and all went on as comfortably as before. But when you were still in love, everything mattered so terribly, for each could still hurt the other with a word, with a look, and every wound, left untended, slowly festered.

He pictured her in the next room, awake, miserable, wondering if he would come to her, wondering if she should, after all, go to him. Suddenly he felt that it would be a very shameful thing if she came in now to say that she was sorry, when the fault was his. No, he would go to her, lying there awake, miserable, and ask her forgiveness. Somehow they must be friends again tonight.

He went to her, gladly, eagerly. Eagerly he opened her door and called 'Sylvia!' He turned up the light by her bed, eagerly. There she lay . . . deeply, beautifully, utterly, asleep.

So it all meant nothing to her! He went back to his room resentfully, slammed the door and lay awake for another hour. Then he too went to sleep.

In the morning he had not forgotten. She was already among the breakfast-cups when he came down, deep in *The Times*. At the opening of the door, she was up and close to him, the paper on the floor. What was he going to say, what was he going to do? He seemed to have no choice; the words came unsought to his mouth, the movement to his hand; a friendly 'Hallo, darling', an affectionate pat on her shoulder, and he had slipped past her to his chair. Thus the happy husbands on the lower plane greeted their wives, blending their casual salute of a club acquaintance with something of the warmer intimacy reserved for a favourite animal. He had achieved it triumphantly.

Yet he did not feel triumphant as he buttered his toast. There's a devil in me, he thought. I wanted to take her in my arms. Why wouldn't he let me?

'The paper, darling?' She passed it across to him.

'Oh, thanks.'

It was open at the theatre page. She had been reading about the first-night. He felt angry again; glad that he had not surrendered to her.

'Sure you've finished with it?' That was how happy husbands talked. He had listened to them in plays.

'It's all right, thank you, darling.' That was how happy wives always answered. He had heard them.

He read, silently. She peeled an apple; silently. . . . Time he said something.

'Seems to have been pretty good last night,' he said, and registered it as the correct line to take. 'Last night' was brought safely to the lower plane and took its place among the incidental ups and downs of a happy marriage. Now they were both happy again.

'Awfully good,' said Sylvia. 'I *wish* you could have come.'

'Well, I wasn't asked.' Excellently said, with just the right shade of friendly irony, the right smile.

'Of course you were asked, darling! We had the two tickets for both of us, and then when I had to give them back because you couldn't come, Lord Ormsby asked if I could come with *him*. It would have been lovely if you'd just been coming home in the ordinary way, and I could have told you about it, and we could have gone together.'

'Oh, that's how it was?' said Reginald.

So that's how it was. If he had not made this unnecessary visit to this unnecessary play, if he had not forced himself on Lattimer and Nixon and Coral Bell, all concerned with business, he with pleasure only, then that unhappy night, this unhappy morning, would never have been. . . .

Her head out of her bedroom door as he comes upstairs.

'Hurry, darling, you've only got twenty minutes.'

'But why—it's only—'

'Guess!'

'We're going out somewhere? Clever of me. How do you do?' He shakes her hand.

'Well, just one.' She comes into his arms. 'But you must hurry, darling. And white waistcoat and everything. They're all put out for you.'

'Righto. Buckingham Palace? What about the knee-breeches?'

'Not Buckingham, darling.'

'I say, we're not going—'

She nods excitedly.

'However——?'

'You *must* hurry, darling. I'll tell you at dinner. Isn't it fun?'

That's how it would have been. And this morning they would have been talking about it happily, saying to each other, 'Didn't you *love* the way he——' and 'Oh, but much the best thing really——' and 'Funny how the critics never seem to notice the things which everybody else notices'. And then suddenly from him, 'I've got rather an idea. Why don't you come along to a rehearsal with me now? . . . Of *course* they wouldn't mind. And they'd all simply love to see you. We'd collect somebody for lunch, if you liked.'

Well, he could say all this now. It was easy . . . Now!

He found that he couldn't. How was he to begin? Last night was over, forgotten, it would be silly to drag it up again; and yet he knew that they could not go happily off together with the faint spectre of that night still between them, unexorcized. At least, he could not. After the way she slept last night, it could not be supposed to matter much to her. So how could he refer to it again? She would hardly, he thought bitterly, know what I was talking about.

'More coffee, darling?'

'Thanks.'

The moment had passed. If his apology had not come, now it was not coming. I'm being a sulky child, he thought, I can feel myself being one, I can stand outside myself and watch myself contemptuously, but I can't do anything. Anyway, there's nothing to do. If I did apologize, she'd say, 'Oh, but I'd forgotten all about that!'

'Going to the theatre, darling?'

Silly question. She knew quite well he was going. She only said it to make it look as if he were wasting his time going to the theatre; to let him know that she knew quite well how unnecessary this theatre-going was; to make him feel awkward if he spoke to another woman there.

What was the answer? He thought:

If one hated one's wife, one would say, 'Well, naturally,' in the coldest voice possible.

If one loved one's wife, one would say eagerly, 'Yes, if you'll come with me. Do!'

Going to the theatre, darling?

'Well, naturally,' said Reginald in the coldest voice possible.

II

Reginald out of the house, Sylvia went about her business. First, a few letters to write, a few bills to pay. Then to Mrs Stoker and her slate.

Mrs Stoker liked Mrs Wellard; thought her the most lovely thing which had ever come into her kitchen. One of the Good Ones too, not going where some of the others were going, with their paint and their fastness and their loose talk. They smiled at each other and discussed the day's meals, Sylvia leaning against the kitchen table, Mrs Stoker standing opposite to her, slate propped against her waist. They were agreed on the necessity of feeding Mr Wellard up, but differed as to Mrs Wellard's need.

'You can't hardly call that a luncheon,' said Mrs Stoker gloomily. 'What I say is good food never did anybody any harm.'

'I never want a very big lunch,' said Sylvia.

'You don't eat more breakfast than a sparrow,' said Mrs Stoker. 'A good-sized sparrow. Still, I will say you look well on it.'

Sylvia began to tell her about 'last night'. Mrs Stoker had never been inside a theatre. Her father ceased to hold with the theatre from the night when he came home slightly drunk, and found, to his relief, that his wife had just left him for the impresario of a Performing Elephant Act at the local music-hall. His manhood demanded its customary assertion. An elopement in the company of three elephants being easily traced, Mr Bagsworthy followed it successfully, but was less successful than he had hoped in knocking the other fellow's head off. He returned home with a prejudice against all forms of public entertainment, which expressed itself bitterly in the word 'Mummers!' For some reason this word gave him a satisfaction which no arrangement of expletives could have brought. 'Mummers,' he muttered through the sponge, as he bathed his eye, 'that's what they are. Mummers!' From that day the dangers of mumming, and of any association with mummers, were kept in front of his daughter. 'All mummers,' Mr Bagsworthy would say mournfully, as he led her past some brightly lit building, 'all the whole lot of 'em, elephants and all. Just mummers.' And Mr Stoker, when his turn came to listen to the Bagsworthy creed, proved to be equally orthodox. 'That's all right, my girl,' he said. 'We'll have no money to waste on fripperies of that sort. Look at Rome. *Panem et circenses* and all that, if you see what I'm referring to. Eh, Bags?' Mr Bagsworthy, who strongly objected to being called 'Bags' by his future son-in-law, even if he had picked up a bit of Greek, said 'Ah!' with the air of one adding a scholarly footnote.

But Mrs Stoker's views had broadened with her widowhood. She still felt that a personal appearance in ballet-skirts before a lot of strangers would be sinful, but as long as her mistresses did not ask her to do that, she was prepared to acquiesce in their play-going, and to admit that even the current parlourmaid, though better without it, might balance her account by good work in other directions. Sometimes she regretted her increased breadth of view; as when asked by an argumentative house-painter to 'look at Shakespeare' . . . and she had looked at Shakespeare. But she still found a fascination in the gossip about the theatre (that fountainhead of gossip) which was now beginning to come her way.

'You must have enjoyed yourself, madam,' she said to Sylvia. 'Now I wonder if Sir Edgar Baines was there. Sure to be, I should think.'

'I shouldn't have known him, anyhow,' said Sylvia. 'Who is he?'

'Sir Edgar Baines, Baronet? Oh, he's very well known, madam. A great friend of Mrs Carstairs. Many a time he's been to luncheon here. And dinner. He'd be sure to be there.'

'Perhaps Lord Ormsby did point him out to me. There were so many I simply couldn't remember them all.'

'Ah well, he'd be there, and his lordship would know him, I've no doubt.'

'Lord Ormsby did say he'd met Mrs Carstairs. Did he ever come to dinner here?'

'His lordship? No, madam.' Mrs Stoker's lips were compressed ever so slightly.

'Oh?' said Sylvia, and was for going on to other matters, when the telephone-bell rang.

'Excuse me, madam.' And then, 'A Mr Bellamy, least it sounded like,' said Mrs Stoker, putting down the receiver. 'I expect you'd like to speak to him upstairs comfortably.'

'I don't think I know—— Are you sure it's for me?'

'He said Mrs Wellard, madam.'

Sylvia went to her bedroom, took off the receiver and settled down comfortably.

'Hallo!'

'Is that Mrs Wellard?'

'Yes?'

'This is Mr Fondeveril. I don't know if you remember me. We met——'

'Oh! Of course I do! They said Bellamy!'

'Perhaps I should have given my full name. John Fondeveril. They used to say in the clubs, you know, I dare say you've heard—Always the same, always game, John Fondeveril.' He laughed it off carelessly, and there was an answering laugh from the other end of the telephone. 'Mrs Wellard, I wondered if you would give me the great pleasure of your company at lunch today.'

There was a momentary hesitation at Mrs Wellard's end. Was Sylvia perhaps wondering what *his* reputation with women was like? What husbands said when their wives went about with him?

'I should love to.'

'That is most kind of you. Would the Ivy suit you? They give you a very good *Sole Veronique* there. Or is there anywhere else——'

'No, that would be lovely, thank you.'

'Then shall we say one-fifteen?' There was a click, as it might be of a gold inscribed hunter being brought into consultation. Undoubtedly one-fifteen was an authentic moment.

'One-fifteen. That will be lovely.'

'Till one-fifteen then, at the Ivy. *Au revoir.*'

'Goodbye.'

For Mr Fondeveril also had been at the Palace; and, seeing his son-in-law and the lovely Mrs Wellard together, he had remembered what his daughter had said to him all those weeks ago. If she was anxious about Bob then, how much more anxious must she be now. He decided that he must Do Something. Something diplomatic, delicate. A word to Wellard? Then his son-in-law's character would be in the open, and it would be possible no longer for him to pretend ignorance of it. Something tactful, then, to Mrs Wellard; asserting nothing, excusing nothing, condemning nothing, but just talking in a large general way of Care and A Woman's Good Name and Jewels, in the detached manner of an Elder Statesman. At lunch, say; over a glass of good wine.

He was there, waiting for her. He bowed over her hand, as, he hoped she would feel, he (or was it somebody else?) had bowed over the dear Queen's hand in the days when even the young men had leisure for courtesy. He led her to a seat, as he had so nearly led Lady Randolph Churchill on a Melba night at Covent Garden. They sat down side by side.

'I have ordered a few oysters bearded in their shells,' he said. 'Then with your permission I suggest the *Sole Veronique.* After that, Mrs Wellard——?'

'Oh, I think that will be enough for me.'

'A bird of some kind?'

'Oh no, please.'

'An *omelette aux fines herbes,* perhaps? Or just a sweet?'

'Yes, I think a sweet. That will be lovely.'

'A *pêche Melba.* You never knew Melba, Mrs Wellard?'

'No. No, I'm afraid I didn't.'

'Ah!' There was a full-length novel in his sigh, of the Great Singer who had sacrificed Love to Art, mainly at Mr Fondeveril's expense.

'She must have been lovely.'

'We don't breed those women now.' He picked up the wine-list. 'You will join me in a glass of wine?'

'Well, I——'

'A light hock? A Johannisberger '21? A dry year.'

'Yes, that would be lovely.'

He took out his watch. 'You have that enviable gift of punctuality, Mrs Wellard. So rare in women. Ah, you were—— This? Yes.' He put it back in his pocket. 'It was presented to me by a well-known City firm. I had been called into consultation financially, and managed to straighten up their affairs, and they—' he made a gesture—'insisted—well—' he made another gesture—'what could I say? You have lemon? That's right. Well, how did you enjoy last night?'

'Were you there?' said Sylvia eagerly. 'Didn't you love it?'

'I gather that *you* did, Mrs Wellard.'

'Oh, but didn't *you?*' said Sylvia, her happiness dying out of her eyes.

'Well, yes, but in a more critical way, naturally. One forms the habit in the Studios of seeing things in Relation to Background. One looks for Composed Masses rather than for Flat Surfaces, if you see what I mean.'

Sylvia tried to look as if she did.

'You mean that a scene might be good in itself without fitting in with the rest of the show?'

'You have caught my meaning exactly,' said Mr Fondeveril gratefully.

'Well, I enjoyed every minute of it,' she smiled.

'You are so young,' he said indulgently. 'You remember what Wordsworth said, Mrs Wellard?'

Sylvia, not having made use of the quotation that morning as a clue for 17 across, shook her head.

' "To be young is very heaven." My dear wife would have agreed with him. She had that *joie-de-vivre* which so few have nowadays. In the hunting-field, in the *salon,* on the moors, wherever she might be.' He drank a glass of hock to her memory.

'You must have been very lonely without her,' said Sylvia gently.

'I had my Maggie. Lady Ormsby. She was a great companion.'

'Oh, I should *think* so! I think she's a darling.'

'We went about everywhere together. Inseparables. We might be on Hampstead Heath one day, at the Zoological Gardens another, wherever we were, Maggie would tell me what she would do if she were this or that, the Head Keeper or whatever it might be, and always, Mrs Wellard, she would put her finger on just the One Essential Point. A great gift that. Organizing Power.'

'She must be a wonderful organizer. You can see that from her house.'

'Yes.' He was thoughtful, wondering how to Get to Grips with his problem. He looked up absently, and bowed absently to a stockbroker who had just gone past their table. 'One of our proconsuls,' he said absently. Miss Prentice made an entrance and waited for hands. Catching Sylvia's expectant eye she executed her mechanical smile, and Sylvia smiled happily back, feeling that she knew all London.

'In many respects', said Mr Fondeveril, 'she has had a hard life.'

'Miss Prentice?'

'My daughter, Maggie. Lady Ormsby.'

'Oh! Yes—— I suppose——'

'To be bereft of a mother at her tender age—and such a mother! I tried to take her place, but naturally I could not always be with her. One was sent here and there'—he indicated the Bahamas and Nova Zembla with a couple of gestures— 'they would tell you at the Service Clubs how it is, a telegram, a few hasty moments to pack a suit-case—it was an odd upbringing for the child. A Bohemian existence. She had friends in the Latin Quarter, naturally,' said Mr Fondeveril, carried into a side current by the promising implications of the word 'Bohemian', 'de Musset, of course, was before her time, but Renoir was still quite a young man. However——' He emphasized with a shrug the difference between Renoir and a real mother. 'And then suddenly to be plunged into the vortex of Social Life; Peeress of the Realm, *persona grata* at Court, mistress of millions. But through it all, Mrs Wellard, she has kept her good name. That highest jewel in a woman, far above rubies. No breath of scandal', said Mr Fondeveril, 'has ever—has ever', said Mr Fondeveril, 'breathed upon her. Scandal', said Mr Fondeveril, going out to meet the Johannisberger '21 half-way, 'spreads her wings in the most unlikely places, and her shadow falls alike upon the spotless as upon the—' he rejected 'spotted' just in time, and ended 'as upon the transgressor'.

'I think it's horrid the way people talk,' said Sylvia.

'It is natural that we should feel it more deeply than most,' said Mr Fondeveril. 'A collateral of her mother's', he added in a lowered voice, 'was mixed up in the Tranby Croft Affair.'

'Really?'

'In perfect innocence, of course, but her name was—mentioned.'

'But that was cards, wasn't it? How could she——'

'One thing leads to another, Mrs Wellard. There was Talk. In the old days one would have called the fellow out,' said Mr Fondeveril, putting his hand lightly to where his sword-hilt would have been, 'but now—— You are from the country, my dear Mrs Wellard. It must be difficult for you to realize what a—a *camorra* of gossip and scandal London has become.' He stopped short at Mrs Wellard's sudden look of surprise. *Camorra*, that *was* the word, surely? The cheese was *camembert*. Reassured, he said again, 'An absolute *camorra*.' But Sylvia was only surprised because she had just seen her husband.

III

There was a taste of warmth in the air. The crocuses would be dying now at Westaways, their task fulfilled, their fading purple and gold dipped in a last salute to the sun. Bravely they had seen the winter out, and, dying, had handed on the torch to the waiting daffodils. Green spires on Emperor and Golden Spur were touched with a first faint yellow, now day by day, almost hour by hour, a new candle would be lit to the glory of spring.

Spring at Westaways. The daffodils in the orchard, beneath the black and white of pear and plum. The high green banks under the hedges, starred with pale primroses round which periwinkle and wild strawberry ran. The grey walls of Westaways down whose sides mauve and purple aubrietia poured, and pink phlox, catching up blue forget-me-nots in their stream; golden showers of burbaris waiting to break; brooms forming into a pale yellow cloud; clumps of polyanthus in a bewildering medley of colour; and then the deep oranges and reds and umbers of careless wallflower and prim tulip.

'We've missed the crocuses,' thought Reginald gloomily on his omnibus. 'Are we going to miss the daffodils?'

He felt homesick suddenly. London was a good place to visit, but not a good place to live in. You always had to be doing something in London; in the country you could do nothing. 'Doing nothing'—which meant doing everything: thinking, seeing, listening, feeling, living. He was going to waste a morning now, the first morning of spring; whatever he did he would be wasting it. A little honest work? Funny expression, that. Why was 'work' honest? It was the primal curse on man. By the sweat of thy brow shalt thou eat bread. It seemed that man was intended for better things; should strive, then, for better things; should strive to avoid work. 'Work' was a punishment, to escape or to get through quickly. Not man's final goal.

Still there's this to be said for work, he reflected gloomily. It takes you away from your thoughts. . . .

However, it appeared that there was something other than work which could take him away from his thoughts about Sylvia. At the theatre there was a letter for him from Mr Pump. Mr Pump had never managed to assimilate Reginald's London address. However urgently Reginald might have written from Hayward's Grove, the answer would have come by way of Westaways. Luckily he didn't want to write to Mr Pump nor minded how greatly Mr Pump's letters were delayed. For Mr Pump was not pleased with him. Caressing his long white beard with one hand, and holding the lapel of his frock-coat with the other, Mr Pump had told him the Duty which he owed to (1) Mr Pump, (2) England, (3) Himself: the duty of delivering a second novel in time for autumn publication. At Reginald's reply that Mr Pump had done quite well out of the first book, and England would doubtless do quite well without the second, and that, as for himself, he was prepared to take a lenient view of his own default, Mr Pump had abandoned the national claim, and concentrated on his own, reinforcing it with much talk of Overhead Charges, Outlay and the Building Up of a Public. As Reginald was lunching with Mr Pump at the time, thus increasing Outlay by several shillings, he felt uncomfortable but stubborn, and Mr Pump, after paying the bill, had called for a taxi ('Overhead Charges') and removed himself frostily to his office. Now he was Pumps Limited; getting smartly into touch with Mr Wellard by way of the theatre.

Pumps Limited had had their attention called to the production of a play which, they understood, was, in fact, a dramatized version of a novel published by them under the title *Bindweed*, and wished to remind the author that by the terms of their agreement with him all moneys derived from dramatic and cinematographic versions of this book were to be divided equally between author and publisher.

'Good lord,' said Reginald, 'I'd absolutely forgotten! And I've had a hundred pounds already. No, I haven't, I've had ninety; Nixon's agent had the other ten. Does Mr Pump think he's going to get fifty of that—or forty-five? I'm damned if he gets fifty. And what about all the other royalties? And film-rights? If we sell those, as Nixon seems certain we shall, and Venture gets half, and Nixon gets half, and Pump gets half, what do *I* get? Looks like *minus* a half. In fact, the more we sell for, the more I pay. That's cheery.'

He tried to remember the exact terms of his agreement, but realized that he had nothing on which to stimulate his memory. The agreement had never meant anything to him. What had Raglan called Pump on that first day? 'A swindler and a bloodsucker.' A bloodsucker certainly. The blasted unhygienic Pump, as Ormsby had so well put it. And now he was tied to him for six books (or was it twelve?)—yes he did remember that part of the agreement, remembered liking it at the time!—and every single one would be messed up in this way, and every single one would be a constant maddening irritation to him. Not the irritation of making less money than he had expected, for he lived happily within his income, but the irritation of being, as he felt, cheated, the irritation of wrangling about this wretched agent's-commission, of continuous wrangles, week after week. Always being reminded of it! Writing a cheque for Pump every week! How could anybody possibly tolerate writing a cheque for Pump every week? And then a weekly letter back from Pump, protesting against the deduction of commission, and another wrangle!

'I hope the play's a failure,' he thought viciously. 'Serve him dashed well right if it is. Well, that settles it. I'll never write another book. Not for Pump to get his messy paws on. Why did I ever get mixed up in all this?'

He lay back in his stall, brooding over his troubles. The rehearsal went on, but at first he hardly noticed it. Should he talk to Nixon about this? But Nixon was a professional, he an amateur; Nixon would despise him for his ignorance, his amateurishness. Fancy getting mixed up with Pump! What about this fellow playing the love-scene now—Toddy, as they all called him. Reginald had been introduced to Toddy, and liked him because he knew the initials of every first-class cricketer who had ever played. One couldn't help liking an actor who knew that; just as one couldn't help liking a first-class cricketer who knew all about the stage. He would ask Toddy to have lunch with him. Better than going to the club, and sitting next to somebody one hated. And brooding.

Or Coral Bell? But somehow (what was it?) he felt a little 'off' Coral Bell. That party last night: was it the feeling of being the one amateur among three professionals; the fact that (naturally) she had been talking to Nixon and Lattimer most of the time; the absence of any sort of intellectual intimacy between them— what was it which had left him with the impression of having been ever so slightly snubbed? Or was it just that he realized now that they belonged to different worlds; that she only came into his as a Jack-o'-lantern with whom he could never catch up? Or was it—Sylvia?

But Toddy was different. One didn't want to make contact with Toddy. One only wanted to discuss cricket with him. One could talk cricket with Toddy for ever.

Apparently not today, though.

'I'm terribly sorry, old man, but I'm just going to give Coral a couple of oysters at Drivers. We want to get back early, and run through that scene again.'

'Oh, well, another day, perhaps.'

'Rather!'

The keenness of this maligned profession! It played golf, it went into Society. Well, what on earth was it supposed to do, when it wasn't rehearsing? You couldn't stay at home and act all by yourself. What was it to do? Read improving text-books by men who knew nothing about acting? Or study Shakespeare?

Miss Masters was in a corner, putting on her hat.

'Good morning,' said Reginald with a smile, on his way to the door.

'Hallo, have you been here? I'm glad I didn't know. I should have passed out, I should have thrown up altogether.'

Reginald fell for the old compliment, and wondered, not without exhilaration, that anybody could be frightened of him.

'Are you lunching anywhere particular?' he asked suddenly. 'Why not come round to the Ivy with me, and see how terrifying I really am?'

'Sposh,' said Miss Masters. 'I should adore to.'

IV

Miss Masters might have been described as a woman of her word, though, in the opinion of her friends, she was almost too faithful to it. There was a time when she was always 'passing out';

a time when everything was 'dim' for her, as once it had been 'grim'; days when the world was 'definitely' this, that and the other or most of its incidents 'shame-making'. To these milestones of the past Life was now adding 'sposh' and 'mottled', and when it became definitely mottled, there was really nothing for a girl to do but to 'throw up'.

'Well, how do you like your part?' said Reginald, when she had decided on the smoked salmon.

'Absolutely "sposh",' said Miss Masters with conviction.

'Really? I'm so glad.'

'Isn't it a bit extra listening to somebody rewriting your book for you? I mean I should have thought it was a bit too mottled. I mean definitely. Of course I don't know what Phil's done, but I mean it must be a bit extra having another man re-writing your sposh scene, and leaving out the Night in the Harem altogether. I mean I should throw up definitely, I should pass out altogether, if I wrote a book, and Phil or somebody came along and made the Vicar do the girl wrong when I mean it wasn't that sort of book. You know what I mean. Too mottled altogether.'

'It is rather disconcerting,' admitted Reginald. 'I try not to think of it as my book any longer, and then when I do recognize a line I've written, I feel rather proud.'

'Of course I haven't read the book,' said Miss Masters. 'I mean I thought I oughtn't to. I mean it would be disconcerting, wouldn't it?'

'Definitely,' said Reginald, smilingly exchanging words with her.

'I mean you *can* only call it mottled when the book says a girl has black hair, and Phil makes it golden, and Ned Lattimer says play it as if it were mouse-coloured, and a girl's own hair is chestnut. Well, I mean you either pass out or you don't.'

'Where did you first meet Lattimer?'

'Ned? At Wolverhampton. Have you ever been there?'

'Never. I don't think I want to.'

'It *is* a bit dim. I was playing *Rachel* in *The Night Light.* Ned was in front—waiting for a train, I should think. He came behind specially to see me, well, I mean I nearly passed out when I heard it was the great Mr Lattimer, I nearly threw up altogether. He asked me why I had gone on the stage. Well, I mean, when you're nearly passing out, you can't say straight off because you admired Mrs Siddons and had read all Shakespeare when you were ten. It was all I could do to utter at all, and I just gulped out because I had seven sisters at home and my stepmother beat me. I mean it was the only thing I could think of. Ned Lattimer said, "Ah, that explains it. I was wondering," in rather a bleak manner. Then he asked me which of Shakespeare's heroines I wanted to play. Well, really, I wasn't quite compass by this time, I mean I was sort of hesitating between *Perdita* in *A Tale of Two Cities* and *Little Nell* in *The Dolls House,* when Alec, our manager, I could have kissed him, said "She'd make a good *Viola,* don't you think?" Well, I mean anything looking less like a producer who thought I'd make a good *Viola* than Ned, I mean, if you'd seen his face, so I pulled myself together, and said I'd murdered Viola once at school, and once at the Academy, and it would look as if I had something against the poor girl if I did it again. Ned liked that, and told me to come and see him in London. So I did.'

'Accompanied by stepmother?'

Miss Masters flashed a smile at him and said No. It was rather dim for the stepmother, but she'd had to pass out at Wolverhampton.

The luncheon went on. Miss Masters, thought Reginald, was good fun for a lunch; well, a quick lunch; well, the smoked-salmon course, anyway. But think of being married to her! Sposh for five minutes perhaps, but after that dim and grim and mottled and more than a bit extra. He would throw up, he would pass out altogether. Definitely.

Married to her! How impossible every other woman was when you thought of her as a wife. (And how much more impossible every other man must seem to a woman.) Reginald remembered suddenly the report of a divorce case in which Counsel in his opening speech gave details of the marriage, and went on, 'For three months they were fairly happy together, and then differences between the parties began to arise.' That had always stuck in his memory. The modest view of marriage which 'the parties' had taken! So long as they were 'fairly happy' the marriage was a success; but three months, of course, was a little below the average. Poor dears, they hadn't expected much, and they should have been more greatly rewarded. ('And what will you have now, Miss Masters?')

'Differences began to arise.' Now, after six unbelievably happy years, had a difference begun to arise between Sylvia and him? Absurd. For how could one be married to anybody but Sylvia? ('Really? Just cold beef?' 'That's all, really. I throw up entirely if I have anything hot in the middle of the day.') So if he had married Miss Masters, he would have had cold beef for lunch every day. There you are. Oh, let's get back to Westaways, and away from swindlers and bloodsuckers, and satyrs like Ormsby. Spring was here, summer was coming. Spring and early summer at Westaways with Sylvia. Going up to London for the day with her, going up without her and being met by her, coming back to Sylvia . . . and to the flowers in the garden, and the pink and white blossom drifting from the trees.

'Really?' said Reginald. 'Whatever did you do?'

His eyes wandered away from her, and suddenly he saw Sylvia. Sylvia! Lunching with somebody, somebody hidden by the projecting wall from him, and talking eagerly, smiling at that unknown man.

Ormsby! Of course! And in an instant he felt a passion of hatred against Ormsby, and for one terrifying instant a complete hatred of Sylvia. After last night—this! Then her companion leant forward, and he saw that it was just Mr Fondeveril.

Gratitude and remorse, and love for Sylvia, so flooded him with happiness that he could hardly breathe. He wanted to get up and wave his arms. He wanted to rush over to Sylvia, and, kneeling at her feet, ask her to forgive him. He wanted to kiss Miss Masters. Well, he would on the first-night, you see if he didn't, and Coral Bell, and everybody. (Except Mr Venture.) Oh, Sylvia, thank you, thank you!

'I say, I'm terribly sorry,' said Reginald, turning back to Miss Masters with a sudden realization, which did not, however, impede his happy smile, that he was being rude to her. 'But I've just seen——'

He was saved from anything so mottled, so dim, so utterly bleak as 'my wife'. I mean, to ask a girl to lunch and then to have a complete absence, to be hardly composs, because you've just seen you dear little wyfikins round the corner—well, I mean! He was saved, because at that moment Miss Masters had herself caught sight of Sylvia.

'Helena Rubinstein!' said Miss Masters. 'Pond and all his Angels! Shades of Elizabeth Arden! And to think that——'

'What's the matter?'

'No, don't look. Look at *me*.'

Reginald looked.

'Would you say I was pretty?'

'Rather! Lovely!'

'My poor, poor man, we're wrong. Both of us. If you want to see what it's really like, look over there. Where the fork's pointing. Well?'

'Yes,' said Reginald.

'Did you ever in your life——'

'Never,' said Reginald.

'Whoever is she?'

'That?' said Reginald carelessly. 'Oh, that's my wife. I'll introduce you tomorrow. She's coming to rehearsal with me.'

Chapter Eighteen

I

In the spring they went back to Westaways, leaving Pumps Limited to the attention and necessary action of Nixon's agent.

'Of course he'll take his ten per cent on the book and everything, but you'll find it's worth it,' said Nixon. 'Though perhaps Mrs Wellard won't think so. I've got a wife and a mother and an unmarried sister, and the only thing they ever agree about is the iniquity of that ten per cent.'

'What I want to avoid is the exasperation of reminding myself every week that I've been a fool.'

'Oh, well, he'll do that for you.'

Reginald went off with a letter of introduction, his mind absurdly full of that unmarried sister. For some reason he was convinced that she had had a great influence on Nixon's life. Older than he, strict with him when he was a child, disapproving of him when he was grown up; suspicious of the loose world into which he was now thrown. 'It is she who has prevented him from being a "good fellow". That's his trouble, that's why he looks wistful sometimes. He knows everybody, everybody calls him Phil, but he has never really been at ease. I'm not a good fellow, but then I've never wanted to be; at least, never thought I could be. He did want to be and he can't, and it's all her fault.'

Funny, he thought, this sudden glimpse into Nixon's family life; and all because of Pump.

He had a more revealing glimpse on the first-night, when

Sylvia and he, having gone into Nixon's box after the Second Act, were introduced to Mother and Sister.

'We always come up on Arthur's first-nights,' said Sister. 'We have a tiny house at Bournemouth. Do you know Bournemouth, Mr Wellard?'

So 'dear old Phil' was really Arthur. Yes, he would be, of course.

'It isn't what it was,' said Sister, still talking of Bournemouth. 'I often wish—but of course—' She shrugged, and then went on quickly, 'I do think, though, *of* those places—I mean when you think of *Eastbourne*—and of course many people *have* to live there because of the pines. It suits Mother. That's really why—unless we lived abroad.'

'I quite agree,' said Reginald, not quite knowing what he agreed to, but understanding Miss Nixon's difficulty in maintaining a spirited defence of Bournemouth which did not disestablish her grievance against Arthur for keeping them there.

Sister left Bournemouth for a moment, and explained that Arthur's wife never came to first-nights, because they made her so nervous, and she was afraid that her nervousness would make Arthur still more nervous. 'Don't you think it's funny, Mr Wellard? I should have thought it was her place to be by her husband's side. I know I shall want *my* husband with me, if ever I had to do anything like opening a bazaar, or giving away prizes, after I was married.'

Poor dear, thought Reginald. Aloud he said, 'I expect they've found out by this time what they like best. Let's see, *how* many plays has your brother written?'

Miss Nixon tried to work out how many times she and her mother had made the journey from Bournemouth. 'Because that's what it really comes to, doesn't it, Mr Wellard? I often wish we had a little flat in London. I think this is the sixteenth time, I mean coming up like this. We always stay at the De Vere Hotel. I think that's one of the nicest, if you don't stay at the Carlton. It's nice and quiet, and of course they know us now. They all come to our table and wish us luck. Mother may be going to see a specialist tomorrow, so then we shall go down by the afternoon train. We generally go by the twelve-thirty.'

Mother, in contrast to her angular daughter, was stout and contented. She was genuinely glad to meet Mr Wellard, genuinely enthusiastic about his book, and genuinely unafraid and unashamed of her rather complicated internal troubles. 'What I say, Mr Wellard, is that at my age my inside is my own, and I don't want other people cutting it open just to satisfy their curiosity. Whatever I've got, I expect I've got it by this time. Arthur and Milly are always wanting me to consult a specialist, but if you consult a specialist, it means that you have the operation he's a specialist in, because that's what he's for. Can you imagine a manager consulting Arthur as to whether he ought to produce one of Arthur's plays at his theatre, and Arthur saying No? This play's going well, isn't it? Arthur's plays always go well on a first-night, and then the critics tell you why you didn't really enjoy it as much as you thought you did, and how much nicer it would have been if somebody else had written quite a different one. But whatever they say, I always think he looks the handsomest man in the theatre. Do you know Bournemouth at all?'

After the play was over, Reginald and Sylvia went behind. Here Sylvia became surprisingly involved with an old schoolfellow, and Reginald, his introduction parenthetically acknowledged, left them to the dormitory which they had once shared, and to which, husbandless, they were now again in secret flight. For them suddenly the chill passages, the clattering stairs, were other passages, other stairs, no less chill, no less resounding; the press of people was translated into another throng no less intent; and the voices which they heard were shrill and unformed and eager as their own. Behind these doors were bosom friends and deadly enemies; such friends once, such enemies—that girl, what *was* her name, do you remember, Sylvia? And Sylvia remembered perfectly—or was she thinking of that *other* girl? No matter.

Tonight is tonight. Tomorrow, remembering their sacred promises to ring each other up 'and arrange something', they will have forgotten the other's style, address and telephone number, and realize the impossibility of arranging anything with a Christian name and the complete particulars of a frock. But again, no matter. Yesterday is yesterday.

Reginald, a bachelor again, edged into Coral Bell's dressing-room. This was almost goodbye. He imagined himself saying goodbye to her in a scene on the stage.

'This is—goodbye, Lady Edgemoor.'

'You're not—*going?*' Hand at her breast, fear dawning in her lovely eyes.

He nods. If he spoke, he might forget that he was an Englishman.

'Where?'

'Westaways. I mean West Africa. Or is it East Africa? Or one of those expeditions which people join? Anyhow, I'm—going.'

'But—why?'

'I think you—know, Lady Edgemoor.' He looks her straight in the eyes. She knows.

'Because of—me?' she breathes.

Now to be a perfect gentleman.

'Let us say because of the Income Tax.' No, that will get a laugh. 'Let us say because of the weather.' So will that. Then let us say nothing. Just raise the arms and drop them.

'You're not—in love with me?' she whispers.

Well, as a matter of fact, that's the whole point. Of course I'm not really—damn this crowd—but you did rather get me tonight. I do like intelligence in a woman, provided she's got a certain amount of looks. Of course I know the things you said tonight weren't your own—some of them, in fact, were mine—but you do say things like that pretty often, and you *are* that sort of woman, and—good, we're getting a move on. Who *are* all these people?

'Darling, you were too marvellous!'

'Did you like it? It *is* a good play, isn't it? I'm so glad for Phil's sake.'

'Congratulations. You really were too———'

'Thank you. *And* for the lovely flowers, it *was* sweet of you.'

'Coral, darling, you were too lovely.'

'Isn't it nice how everybody likes it? I'm *so* glad.'

'Congratulations. I———'

'Oh, Mr Wellard, it *was* nice of you and Mrs Wellard to send me those lovely flowers. Is she here? You will thank her for me, won't you?'

'You really were—I don't think I ever———'

'*Isn't* it nice? Pearl, darling, this is Mr Wellard. He wrote the *book,* you know. Oh, Dick, you darling, I loved your telegram. *And* the flowers. You angel!' She kisses the angel.

Reginald talks to Pearl. He feels humiliated, and angry with himself for feeling so. He feels ugly and uncomfortable. His mouth is stiff. When he talks he can feel his mouth talking. He hears every word that he says, and no word that Pearl says. The dressing-room is hot and crowded. He is jammed against the wall. He had never thought of himself as a gesticulatory talker, but the fact that he cannot move a hand seems to tie his tongue. Everything that he says is futile, and he can hear himself saying it.

So that's goodbye to Coral Bell. Well, I'm glad. These actresses are all alike. Let's get home, nobody wants us. Oh, well, I suppose we ought just to see Miss Masters. Where's Sylvia?

He edged his way out, found Sylvia, and withdrew her from her school.

'Come on,' he said, suddenly abandoning Miss Masters. 'Let's go home.'

'Tired, darling?'

'Horribly,' said Reginald. 'At least, tired of London.'

Chapter Nineteen

I

Grandmamma, looking smaller and more anxious than ever, came into the hall. 'Oh, there you are,' said Marmalade from the radiator. 'I finished the cod's head. All the same, if you *are* going into the kitchen, you might tell that woman that these pipes are cold again. What *is* the good of——'

'Come on,' said Grandmamma, and went out of the front door.

'Come where? I was talking about these pipes. If they're not meant to be hot, what *are* they meant to be? A cat——'

John Wesley, looking more like a long black leopard than ever, came into the hall.

'Oh, there you are,' said Marmalade. 'I finished the cod's head. All the same, if you *are* going into the kitchen, you might tell that woman that she's getting careless. These pipes are cold again. A cat doesn't take the trouble to settle down on cold pipes just because he likes the shape of them. I always understood——'

'Come on,' said John Wesley, turning out of the front door. 'You'll be late.'

'Late for what? I finished the cod's head. And I was just looking forward to a——'

'They'll be here in a moment. They're coming back.'

'Ah! They've heard about these pipes, I expect. Well, thank goodness there'll be somebody in the house now who knows what a cat wants. All right, I'm coming. If anything's said about that green thing in the dining-room, I want to be there. However careful a cat is, if people put things on the very edge of things, and then blame a cat because—— All right, I'm coming.'

So there they were, all three of them. 'Oh look, darling!' cried Sylvia, as Reginald stopped in gear outside the gates. 'Waiting for us.'

She jumped out; and in a moment Grandmamma was in one arm and Marmalade in the other. John Wesley waited for Reginald, and as soon as he was available did figures of eight between his ankles.

'Well, John, how's everything?'

John Wesley continued to indicate that everything was very much all right.

'Hallo, Marmalade, glad to see me?'

Marmalade nodded casually.

'Shall I put the car away for you, darling?'

'No, let's leave it. I can't wait. Come on, I want to see everything. Oh, Sylvia, *look* at the daffodils! Oh, gosh! Come on.'

Followed by the three cats, they climbed the stile and came into the orchard, hand in hand.

'That bank's better than ever, did you ever see so many primroses? Look, there's a bluebell, and there's another. Oh, lots. I didn't think they'd be out till next week. Oh, hundreds. I say, *aren't* the daffodils lovely? Good, the cherries aren't quite out, that'll give us an extra day or two. I was afraid—There's a plum right out. And a pear nearly. It's going to be quite all right, we shall get all the blossom, and practically all the daffodils—perhaps a week earlier would have been better. Anyway, thank God we came today. I say, let's—— Oh, bother, no, that's no good. Never mind. Are you enjoying it as much as I am, sweetheart?'

'I expect so, darling. What were you going to say?'

'About what?'

'Being no good.'

'Oh! Just a wild idea that we'd pick flowers together this afternoon for the house. But of course they'll have done all that.

It is such fun picking flowers with you. I mean watching you do it, and helping, and knowing you won't mind if I don't do it *all* the time, and then doing a bit more, and knowing that nothing matters but just Sylvia and the flowers.'

'Do you love it so, darling?'

'Terribly.'

'So do I, darling.'

'It makes London look so silly, doesn't it? I mean, what's it *for?*'

They went into the house for a minute.

'Must we?' asked Reginald. 'You'll get caught up by Mrs Hosken, and talk and talk and talk, and I shall never see you again. I can't wait for you. I want to look at every flower and every bud, and see what's dead, and what isn't, and I want you there so as I can say, Look, all the time. But I can't wait.'

'I promise I won't talk to her, darling. Except just to say Here we are, and How are you, and we'll have a long talk later. I'll only be a minute.'

'Oh, well, if you promise.'

She kept her promise. Reginald spent the minute wandering through his house and wondering what was wrong with it. Complete absence of Wellards, he supposed. It would take a day or two for Westaways to realize that they were back, and settle down to its old self. Meanwhile it belonged to nobody.

'Doesn't it look funny without flowers?' said Sylvia, as she joined him. 'So empty.'

'Of course! I knew there was something. I say, what luck! Now this afternoon we really *can*——' He broke off suddenly. Sylvia was looking shy and secret.

'Come on, darling.'

'Sylvia! You wrote to Mrs Hosken and told her not to?'

Sylvia nodded.

'So as you and I——?'

She nodded again, shyly, her eyes in his.

'You angel.'

So that was Sylvia Wellard. Reginald Wellard, the famous writer, the lover of beauty, the man of imagination, the fellow of most excellent fancy, had managed to think of it all two days later. Good. No wonder he looked down on his wife.

It was one of those April days which hold their own for ever in the memory against all the bleak statistics of April, so that 'April' means just a day like this, and for the hope of a day like this one can suffer much from April with out disfavouring her. At first, as Reginald and Sylvia hurried here and there in the garden, they talked eagerly, exclaiming at each new discovery, pointing out to each other the promise of this, the fulfilment of that, lamenting here a casualty, welcoming there a revival; but gradually the content of the morning took possession of them, and they found themselves silent in a world suddenly alive with happy sound: a thrush urgent in the pear-tree, bees visiting in the aubrietia, the first cuckoo echoing from a distant wood. As they sat there, Reginald felt rather than thought, This is Westaways, I am one with it again, and his mind registered no beauty, analysed no impression of beauty, but brought only that happy acceptance which it brings to a beautiful dream.

II

The dream went on through the magical afternoon, as they picked their flowers together, but at tea-time the world broke in on them again, for with tea came the Hildershams.

'Sylvia! Say you don't mind our bursting in on you like this, your first day back, but we heard you were coming, and it seems such ages since we saw you.'

'Grace, of course! It's lovely of you to have come.'

Even Reginald was glad to see them. They were part of it, they belonged to the country. Ages since we have seen them. How absurd of us never to have come down for the weekend. Why didn't we? Just didn't, I suppose. After all, we're not week-enders.

We belong to the country too. I'm glad we didn't now. It makes it more like coming home.

'Well, you've had a great success,' said Hildersham, a little as if he were responsible for it, or, at the least, had maintained its probability against the rest of the world.

'Well—I hope so,' said Reginald.

'*The Times* said so,' said Hildersham, opening his blue eyes at the doubter. 'I read it this morning.' And lest this should not settle the matter, he added that he had also specially bought the *Post*, the *Mail*, the *Telegraph* and the *News* in the village, and they *all* said so.

'Good,' said Reginald. 'I haven't really seen the papers yet.'

'Oh, they did,' put in Grace. 'Fairlie brought them back, all except the *News*, and I read them.'

Hildersham, avoiding Reginald's admiring eye, uttered something about the impossibility of being too careful in These Days. When Bolshevism was Rampant. 'Actually', he said, 'it was Mrs Coleman's carelessness. I distinctly asked for the *Express*.'

They talked a little of London, Grace wanting to know if skirts really were longer, 'I don't mean for evening, of course, but the afternoon. Is it just a few fashionable people, or is it *General*? Of course in the country, well, we simply couldn't do it'; Fairlie wanting, to know what they said in London about the chances of an election in the autumn. The Wellards spoke for London in these matters as well as they were able. But as soon as the tea things were settled, and there was no further anxiety to be felt about Alice, Fairlie and Grace looked at each other, and Grace seemed to be imploring 'Do let *me* tell them, Fairlie! After all, *I* told *you*,' and Fairlie's answering look said, 'I think you had better leave this to *me*, my dear. This is no longer just a piece of idle gossip. You shall have your turn later.' And then he put down his cup, wiped his moustache, and said gravely, 'You haven't heard *our* news, I suppose?'

For one ridiculous moment Reginald supposed that Mrs Hildersham was going to have another, and struggled with a compelling impulse to look at her. I suppose Sylvia knew at once, he thought. Possibly Hildersham read his thought, for he went on quickly, 'About the Baxters?'

'No. What?'

'Mrs Baxter is divorcing him.'

'Good lord! Who?—or just——'

'I'm afraid so. Quite definitely. A Miss—— Voles, is it?' He looked at his wife for confirmation.

'Miss Voles,' said Grace eagerly. 'He knew her years ago, and then they met again suddenly. Isn't it dreadful?'

'It isn't Right,' said Hildersham, shaking his head. 'It's—— In These Times. We can't Afford—— I mean Anything Like That—— —— Of course they never really belonged. Still, there they were. One can't just Please Oneself. One has to Consider.'

Reginald and Sylvia found themselves looking at each other; considering.

'Oh, did you meet her?' cried Grace.

'Yes.'

'Oh, *what's* she like? How old is she? Quite young, I suppose. Would you call her pretty, Sylvia?'

'She must be as old as Betty. Older.'

'Not exactly pretty, Grace.'

'Attractive? Well, I suppose she must be.'

'Very,' said Reginald slowly. 'Oh, yes . . . Very.'

'Poor Betty! How awful for her,' said Grace. 'Just *think* what it would be like, Sylvia! What *should* I do if Fairlie ran off with some other woman?'

Flattered and self-conscious at this indirect tribute to his virility, Fairlie looked down his nose, with the air of a man who had broken many a heart by his insistent faithfulness to his wife.

'Of course,' said Grace, developing the theme, 'it would be worse for me because of the children.'

Fairlie's conduct now became almost heroic. One seemed to see the Beauty Chorus offering itself to him one by one. In vain.

'Well,' said Fairlie modestly, 'I don't think—— But in any case this isn't just a personal matter. Not as I see it. *Noblesse oblige;* though I believe Baxter's father—— Still, there he was, at Seven Streams; and now every Tom, Dick and Harry talks of it. That sort of thing Does No Good.'

'*Noblesse* so often doesn't *oblige,*' murmured Reginald.

'There are blacklegs in every camp, of course, but the principle is the same.' He helped himself to a potted meat sandwich, and thought: 'If it comes to that, our host and hostess are hardly doing their duty to their country. Let's see, *how* long have they been married?' Grace was thinking: 'Really, I wonder sometimes he doesn't. He's just as young as ever, and they *are* so attractive nowadays. I couldn't stay here possibly, but I suppose I'd soon get used to it somewhere else. Is it half the income you get or a third? And of course I should have the children.' Reginald was thinking: 'Can you have a "blackleg" in a "camp"? Oh, well, never mind. Baxter! The turmoil that must have been going on inside that sleek head!' And in Sylvia's transfigured face you could read the thought: 'All those years!'

'Did you guess anything, Sylvia?' asked Grace.

She was almost married again by this time, and hardly liked to trust herself any longer with her thoughts. Sylvia looked at her, as if puzzled how to answer.

'It was——he had only just found her again. That evening.'

'Still, you must have seen.'

Hildersham produced a cough which deceived nobody. Grace brought it into the open by saying, 'Oh, Fairlie, but we're all friends here,' and explained, 'Fairlie hates gossip.'

Hildersham looked across at Reginald and said, 'It's no good expecting a woman to understand.'

'Understand what?' asked Grace.

'Exactly.'

'We only just met her that once,' explained Sylvia, 'and there were a lot of other people there.'

Grace nodded, as if in the secret, and said, 'Oh, well, wait till I get you alone.'

Women have no reserves but the one, thought Reginald; the reserve of their body from the marauding male. In all but this how much more shy, more modest, more sensitive, are men. Or is it that we are just the greater hypocrites?

'You women!' said Hildersham, shaking his head genially at Sylvia. 'Come on, dear, they must have a hundred things to do.'

Grace got up, and said to Sylvia, 'Don't you hate the way men always talk about women, just as though we were all alike?'

Sylvia looked at Reginald as if for the answer.

'One can generalize about land and water,' he smiled, 'and, you know, they *are* different. But that doesn't mean that one thinks the Regent's Park Canal is the same as the Pacific.'

'Good,' said Hildersham. 'That's how it is, dear. Come on, Grace.'

On their way home he found himself thinking that it would be rather exciting to have an entirely new wife. Like Baxter. For the honey moon, anyway. Decency had its disadvantages. Perhaps in the next world one would get rewarded for it. A succession of Sylvia Wellards, for instance. . . .

'Didn't she look lovely today, Fairlie? London's done her good.'

''m.'

Oh, well, there were plenty of other things in life.

III

They were alone in the garden again, with this astonishing news; between them.

'Baxter!' said Reginald.

'Are you surprised, darling?'

'Staggered. People divorce each other every day, and one thinks nothing of it, and then it happens to somebody one knows, and it seems unbelievable. Doesn't it to you?'

'I saw them together in London. One afternoon.'

'You never told me,' said Reginald, and immediately thought of all the things which he hadn't told Sylvia.

'There wasn't much to tell, darling. I didn't speak to them.'

'Did you think then——'

'They were so utterly happy, and away from everybody else.'

'What were they doing?'

'Nothing. Looking at a shop-window. Just being together. It was lovely just to see them being together.'

'Yes, but——' Dash it, thought Reginald, there's more to it than that.

'Are you sorry about it, darling? I'm not. I'm glad.'

'No, not sorry exactly——'

'You never liked Betty, did you?'

How personal women always were!

'I'm not worrying about Betty.'

'She'll marry again, don't you think? She's attractive to men. I mean most men.'

'I suppose so.'

'What is it, darling?'

'Nothing. But I always wonder a little about the—the morality of it. I mean of that sort of thing generally.'

'Morality?' said Sylvia, looking puzzled. 'Like Mr Hildersham?'

'Well, no,' smiled Reginald, 'not quite like that, but I suppose there *is* a moral question involved. I mean, if you swear eternal things to a woman, there *is* a case for keeping to them. Of course there is also a case for saying that real love is so much the most beautiful thing in the world that it must be found at whatever cost. Which is right?'

Sylvia was silent; and then, pointing with her foot at a saxifrage in the wall, said, 'Isn't that pretty?'

'Yes. I wish they didn't lose their colour. They all do.'

'If I'd been married when we first met, wouldn't you have asked me to come away with you?'

Reginald looked at her for a long time, and then he shook his head.

'Why not?'

'It simply wouldn't have occurred to me, Sylvia.'

'I would have come.'

'Would you leave me now, if you loved some body else?'

'I couldn't love anybody else—*new*, darling. How could I?'

Reginald laughed at her lovingly and said, 'Sweetheart, you make it all very difficult. I never know how you managed to love *me*, and I never know why you don't get tired of me. You were like something out of a fairy-story to me when I first saw you. You are still. I hardly dared to ask you even as it was. If you had been married, I should have known that your husband adored you, and I should have supposed that in some magic way you loved him. How could I have dared to push myself in between you?'

Sylvia put her hand in his and said, 'I'm glad I wasn't married. I'm glad I didn't make a mistake before I saw you.'

'That's the trouble, you see. What is one to do about the people who make mistakes? And if they make it the first time, mightn't they make it the second time? That's really the case for tying you up so tightly in marriage, so that you don't easily give way to every new fancy which comes into your head.'

'Mr Baxter's wasn't a new one, it was a very, very old one.'

'Yes, well, let's hope that he hasn't made a mistake about it this time—as he evidently did when he married Betty.'

'Darling,' said Sylvia anxiously, 'you aren't——? Grace said something about Fairlie not wanting her to know Miss Voles, if they——You aren't——?'

'Good Heavens, no. I'm longing to see them both. Well, of course! I only—I say, this is frightful. You didn't think—— I mean *Hildersham*——!'

'They were so happy that day. Sort of peaceful and entranced.'

'There you are, that's good enough. It's really pretty difficult to be bad and happy at the same time. Peacefully happy. I'm sure Baxter couldn't manage it. But I do just feel, you know, that deserting a wife isn't necessarily a noble thing in itself, and worthy of admiration. That's all. My one point of contact with Hildersham.'

'Of course it isn't, darling.'

'A good many people talk as if it were.'

'What I think', said Sylvia earnestly, 'is that marriage without love is much worse than love without marriage.'

'You're perfectly right, sweetheart,' said Reginald, surprised that she had put it so well. (Did I really think once, he wondered, that I couldn't talk to Sylvia?) She was right. It was love which made marriage holy, not marriage which sanctified love.

'You see,' he said, following his thoughts, 'at the back of all the argument about marriage and divorce is this horrible religious idea that love is a wicked thing in itself, and only allowable because it produces children. So they say, reluctantly, "Well, you *may* love, if you'll take a frightful oath that you'll only do it with one person as a sort of religious ceremony, and with the sole idea of bringing a child into the world." That's why they always——'

'Who's "they", darling?'

'They?' Reginald laughed. 'I don't know who They is exactly, but he's the fellow who runs most things in this world. I never liked They.' He thought for a moment and said, 'If you can imagine a policeman in holy orders, with the blood-lust of a tribal god, and the appearance and manner of an Oxford don rather high up in the Civil Service—no, I never liked him.'

Sylvia said, holding on to his arm, 'Do *you* think it's wrong, loving and not having children?'

Reginald looked at her in astonishment.

'Sweetheart! How *could*——' He was silent, his hand on hers, and then said gently, 'What made you—suddenly——'

'I was so happy, darling. I wondered if you were.'

'You know I am.'

'Would it make you happier if you had a child?'

'If one bought them at the Stores, perhaps I might ask you some day if you'd like a nice one. Because if so——'

'A very small one, just like you, darling, might be rather lovely.'

'They *are* very small at the start, I believe,' said Reginald, smiling at her.

Sylvia gave him her smile in reply, and then said, almost in apology, 'I expect you can't be a wife *and* a mother. I expect after I've been a wife, there isn't much left of me, darling. I do love you so dreadfully.'

'My lovely one, I'm more than content.'

'But if——'

'Sweetheart, I'm utterly happy with you. I can't bear to think of your being frightened and ill and so terribly hurt. I should be terrified.'

'I *am* frightened, but I don't think I ought to be. That's why I've been wondering if you'd like it.'

'No, no, no!'

'But if it ever did happen, you'd forgive me, darling?'

'Oh, my sweetheart!' cried Reginald, in sudden shame of himself, of his sex, of all that women have suffered from men.

Sylvia nodded to herself and said: 'I just wanted to know.'

IV

Sylvia had gone into the kitchen to tell Mrs Hosken all about London. Probably Mrs Hosken was hoping to tell Mrs Wellard all about the country; which meant now all about the Baxters. Not only every Tom, Dick and Harry, but every Harriet was talking of it. It's odd, thought Reginald, walking amongst his azaleas (full of bud; this was going to be their best year)—it's odd that I should be revolted at the idea of discussing the Baxters with Edwards, and that Sylvia should think it quite natural to discuss them with

Mrs Hosken. Why was there this strange freemasonry among women? The Colonel's lady and Judy O'Grady. A sort of defensive alliance, I suppose, against the masterfulness of men, heritage of the days when women were really slaves. If Woman lacks that sense of honour, of good form, of sportsmanship, on which Man so prides himself, it is be cause subconsciously she is always at war, and in war there are no such things as honour, good form, and sportsmanship. All is fair in love and war, says Man, and then blames Woman for living up to it.

This silly generalization about Man and Woman! And yet not so silly. Silly to say that if you toss a penny six times, you will get three heads and three tails, but true to say that the more you toss it, the more you notice a tendency toward that distribution.

His eye was suddenly caught by the ceanothus (*gloire de Versailles*) whose barren stalks, as usual, showed no sign of the blue loveliness to come. He wondered again if it justified its preservation. Nature oughtn't to do this sort of thing. A tree in winter showed a different beauty; a delphinium in winter at least showed nothing; it simply wasn't there, until its first delicate pale green excited your imagination; but this was an offence to the eye until it became a pleasure, and one ought to weigh the one against the other before deciding Damn! There was that bindweed again . . .

Yes, it was just here, nearly two years ago, that he had begun his book. Would he ever write another? No. . . . Oh, anyhow No, be cause of Mr Pump. And yet—could you just go on doing nothing? It hadn't seemed like nothing two years ago. He had thought himself very busy. Could he settle down to that sort of business again? Just thinking and digging up weeds? Damn Pump! Well, he could write, even if he didn't publish. Or— why not? Write a play.

A play! He stared at the ceanothus, hoping for inspiration. None came.

Somebody had said that every man ought to plant a tree, write a book and beget a child. How like Somebody! You can plant a tree by yourself, write a book by yourself; but to beget a child needs the co-operation of somebody else. Fortunately only a woman, so we need not worry about her. The decision is in our hands.

Well, he had planted his tree, written his book. He could hardly hope that the book would survive, but a hundred years from now his trees would still be standing. Did he mind if he left no child? I have no illusions about children, he thought; no sentiment about the name of Wellard. I'd far sooner that Westaways came to somebody who loved it than to a son of mine who only liked it. I think that fatherhood is a ridiculous profession; that it is as impossible to take oneself seriously as a Father as to take oneself seriously as a Bishop or a Judge. No, it's the other way round. A Father, Bishop or Judge must take himself with a portentous and revolting seriousness if he is to make any sort of job of it. I should be hopeless. If I had a child, I would sooner have a daughter and leave it to Sylvia whose child it would be, and If I want a child, it is just selfishly, so that I can enjoy a new experience.

All the same, I wonder why Sylvia . . .

He felt absurdly happy suddenly. Happy in this new realization of Sylvia; happy to have the whole pageant of summer before him; happy in this ridiculous idea of a play, which he needn't write, probably couldn't write, almost certainly wouldn't write. Happy, somehow, in that brief contact with a child whom he didn't want, wouldn't have, yet could have; the child who had been for a moment alive in thought between them; happy in the knowledge of a fatherhood and motherhood within their reach if ever they came to need it.

Meanwhile if he had to create something, he could write a play. He looked at the ceanothus thoughtfully. A play. Yes. He went back to the house, came out again with a trowel, and began to dig up the bindweed.

Chapter Twenty

O nce more the candles had been blown out; once more the moonlight came through the open windows of Sylvia's bedroom. There was a gentle rustle of starlings under the eaves. An owl called plaintively, first from one side of the house, and then suddenly from the other, and from a distant fold of the hills a watch-dog barked in faint answer to some romantic challenge. The little noises of the night made the country seem more still than silence, and Reginald and Sylvia more withdrawn from the world.

Sylvia whispered:

'Happy, darling?'

'Yes, Sylvia.'

'We're so alone here. I never felt like that in London.'

'Alone with Sylvia and Westaways.'

'That *is* all you want, darling?'

'Yes. Except for a few people to look at you. If ever I were in *Who's Who,* my Recreation would be "Watching people's faces when they first catch sight of Sylvia". '

'I expect you *will* be in *Who's Who* now. You ought to be.'

'Watching people's faces when they first catch sight of Sylvia. That was what I said.'

'I heard you, darling. Do you really like it so?'

'Love it. Do you?'

'Yes . . . Oh, *yes.*'

'I often wonder what it must be like.'

'Would you like to be one, darling?'

'Just to try. There was once a man who was allowed to be whatever he liked. And he chose to be a marvellous athlete from fifteen to twenty-five, a beautiful woman from twenty-five to thirty-five, a great writer from thirty-five to forty-five, a successful general from forty-five to fifty-five, a world-famous statesman from fifty-five to sixty-five, and a gardener from sixty-five to seventy-five. Then he went to Heaven.'

'Is that true, darling?'

'No, not true that he was all those things, but true that somebody wanted to be something like that. I forget who he was, and I forget some of the things, but it would have been a good life. What would you have chosen, Sylvia?'

'To have married you when you were thirty-five.'

'And you did. It's funny; I said it all without thinking, and it would have been just right. Do you like being beautiful, Sylvia?'

'Oh, I love it, I love it!'

'You're the only person who has never really seen how beautiful you are.'

'You're the only person who has,' whispered Sylvia.

The little clock on Sylvia's mantelpiece ticked—ticked—ticked. Heaven might be just the endless contemplation of beauty. Then the old-fashioned idea of it as eternal adoration and hymn-singing would be right. To see beauty, to adore, to give expression to one's adoration, is there ecstasy to compare with it? If Heaven is all a garden and Sylvia, thought Reginald, how I shall give praise. . . .

A garden in which all the flowers, just for once, come out at the same time, while the blossom is still upon the trees. . . .

'What is it, darling?'

'Nothing, Sylvia.'

'I thought you weren't comfortable.'

'Utterly comfortable.'

'I love talking to you in bed like this. It's so alone.'

'My head on your lovely breast, Sylvia.'

'Talking is ordinary, and this is so special. I like doing ordinary things, when—when they're not ordinary.'

'Nothing you say or do could ever be ordinary.'

'You think that now.'

'Yes, I think that now. But now is all that matters.'

'What will you do when I'm old, darling?'

'I don't know, Sylvia. Will you ever grow old?'

'I'll try not to, darling. I'll put it off as long as I can. You won't mind, will you, if I'm not very clever sometimes. Because all the time I shall be trying to put it off for you.'

'You're better than clever. You're wise.'

'Am I? I don't think I know about myself very much.'

'I'm always thinking about myself.'

'I expect that's the difference between us.'

'I know so little about *you*, Sylvia. I know nothing about you. I'm not sure that I want to know. It's part of your beauty that you're so unknown to me.'

'Then I shall keep my secret.'

'Yes . . . keep it, Sylvia.'

'Do you want to go to sleep, my darling?'

'I don't want to, I don't want not to. I'm just happy. And sleepy.'

'Go to sleep, my darling.'

'May I stay like this? You're so beautiful.'

'Stay like this, my darling.'

'Stay beautiful, my sweet Sylvia.'

'I'll try, my darling. I expect it's what I'm for.'

The Voyage

Charles Morgan. Introduced by Valentine Cunningham

First published in 1940, *The Voyage* is a story warm with Morgan's love of France. Set in the Charente country and the Paris music-halls.

"As one reads one forgets everything, enchanted by the beauty of the setting, fascinated by the subtlety of the spiritual reasoning, the provisional speculations, the ethereal love-story." – *Daily Telegraph*

The Green Hat

Michael Arlen. Introduced by Kirsty Gunn

The Green Hat perfectly reflects the atmosphere of the 1920s – the post-war fashion for verbal smartness, youthful cynicism and the spirit of rebellion of the "bright young things" of Mayfair.

Love in a Wych Elm

HE Bates. Introduced by Peter Conradi

Kent, the "Garden of England", provides the rustic setting for these poignant stories from the creator of *The Darling Buds of May*. Graham Greene liked to compare HE Bates with Chekhov, greatest of short story writers, considering Bates the best writer of short stories of his generation and time. This new selection by Bates' grandson, Tim Bates, shows why.

An Error of Judgement

Pamela Hansford Johnson. Introduced by Ann Widdecombe

An Error of Judgement is a subtle study of human weakness and conflict. Partly a wry social comedy and partly a study in good and evil, it is brilliantly written and observed, assured and skilful, a truly modern work by one of the most underrated novelists of the last century.

"One of the best novels in English since 1939." – Anthony Burgess